CIPHERS

THE KING & SLATER SERIES BOOK THREE

MATT ROGERS

Cover design by Onur Aksoy.
www.onegraphica.com

Join the Reader's Group and get a free 200-page book by Matt Rogers!

Sign up for a free copy of '**HARD IMPACT**'.

Experience King's most dangerous mission — action-packed insanity in the heart of the Amazon Rainforest.

No spam guaranteed.

Just click here.

Follow me on Facebook!
https://www.facebook.com/mattrogersbooks

Expect regular updates, cover reveals, giveaways, and more. I love interacting with fans. Feel free to send me a private message with any questions or comments. Looking forward to having you!

BOOKS BY MATT ROGERS

THE JASON KING SERIES

Isolated (Book 1)

Imprisoned (Book 2)

Reloaded (Book 3)

Betrayed (Book 4)

Corrupted (Book 5)

Hunted (Book 6)

THE JASON KING FILES

Cartel (Book 1)

Warrior (Book 2)

Savages (Book 3)

THE WILL SLATER SERIES

Wolf (Book 1)

Lion (Book 2)

Bear (Book 3)

Lynx (Book 4)

Bull (Book 5)

Hawk (Book 6)

THE KING & SLATER SERIES

Weapons (Book 1)

Contracts (Book 2)

Ciphers (Book 3)

BLACK FORCE SHORTS

The Victor (Book 1)

The Chimera (Book 2)

The Tribe (Book 3)

The Hidden (Book 4)

The Coast (Book 5)

The Storm (Book 6)

The Wicked (Book 7)

The King (Book 8)

The Joker (Book 9)

The Ruins (Book 10)

1

The man had known nothing but pain for the last six months, but alcohol has the universal ability to dull even the most harrowed minds.

He was well and truly drunk.

Self-medication, in his eyes.

He wasn't sure where he was, or where he was headed. He had a general idea, but specifics eluded him. New York City, like most places, becomes a blur at a certain level of inebriation. All he could see were buildings and lights and sidewalks and traffic and rain and the steady incessant flow of pedestrians heading home, or out to their favourite bars and restaurants. He blended into the stream, getting washed downriver along with the rest of the population. He gazed up at the structures on either side of the street — skyscrapers spearing into the heavens.

As he upturned his face he felt the cool sensation of droplets splashing over his lips and cheeks and forehead.

He smiled.

This was the life.

In the grip of the buzz.

When he was sober he had to think, and there were few pleasant memories to dwell on. Not for the last half-year, anyway. Particularly not for the last month. He gazed down at his attire and the smile turned sad. Truth was, if he could wipe his memory, he might be happy. He was dressed in a tailored Armani suit and an expensive overcoat. There was a Hermés cap on his head. He was in decent shape, although that was rapidly eroding under the bombardment of booze. He had some acceptable material possessions and a good head on his shoulders and a reasonable level of intelligence. He could dress up and take himself seriously and get a job. The market was tough, more competitive than ever, but he didn't doubt he could snatch some low-hanging fruit and work his way up from there.

But what's the point of that?

You're only happy if you're progressing. Thirty years on this planet and he'd figured out that much. There was nothing satisfying about staying in one place for very long. Maybe if you became a hippie and sold all your possessions and moved to a shack in the middle of nowhere and took psychedelics all day long and meditated until your eyes became permanently fixed in the wrong direction... maybe that would give you enough peace of mind to live out the rest of your days doing absolutely nothing.

But he'd never been partial to any of that shit.

No, he liked thrills. He liked money. He liked power.

The more, the better.

And now he had none of those things.

You can't stop the spiral until it's too late. He hadn't even realised he'd been aiming downward until it all smacked him in the face when it came crashing down around him. He'd had it all. And now he didn't. That was reason enough to drink.

He'd lost everything.

His position.

His lifestyle.

His family.

Didn't take long for him to find the ability to suppress it in the bottom of a bottle.

There were businessmen and businesswomen all around him, dressed just as nicely as he was, but they were doing okay. They had places to go. They had things to do. They had people to see.

He had nothing.

Not even a destination.

So he kept walking. Somewhat aimlessly, but he figured he was subconsciously heading for the less desirable parts of the city. Away from the hustle and bustle. Under a darkening sky he aimed for the shadows and the housing commissions and the decrepit side of life. He didn't know why. He'd been walking for at least an hour, but the drink still had him in its soothing grip. There was sweat beading on his forehead despite the chill. He crossed Third Avenue Bridge and stared down into the rippling water.

Then he was in the Bronx.

As if he'd teleported.

Passersby eyed his coat. They absorbed the scent of money. He didn't have much of it anymore, but the past clung to him like a mocking shadow. Reminding him, *Remember what you* used *to be.*

He stumbled through Mott Haven, passing an endless series of public housing projects. Residents clad in drab dollar-store clothes sucked on cigarettes and stared him down. But no one made the move. He almost wished they did, yet not for the reasons one might assume. He wasn't Batman. He couldn't beat criminals to a pulp with one hand tied behind his back. In the past there'd been a never-ending stream of hangers-on willing to do anything for the right price, and he'd always paid handsomely for *them* to take care of his problems. They weren't around anymore. The resources and access to henchmen had vanished along with the money.

No, his desire was a little different.

He wanted to be hit, to be slapped or punched in the face or cut or beaten, just to *feel* something. Something visceral. Something real. He didn't have the balls to approach any of the gangbangers himself, so he continued up through the Bronx in this state of limbo, wondering who might be the first to try to steal his twenty-thousand dollar coat.

Then, in the drink-addled haze, he spotted a familiar face.

He pulled to a halt. He was beside Patterson Houses, a collection of fifteen public housing buildings home to a couple thousand apartments. The maze of russet structures dwarfed him, and he remembered how many of the men that had worked for him in the past had come from this development. Of course, he'd never ventured into these parts before. He used to live on the Upper East Side — a notably nicer environment. They always came to him.

Because they were desperate, and because he had what they needed.

Not anymore.

Now he was staring across the street, watching a man in a cheap canvas jacket hustle north under the weak glow of the streetlights. The yellow hue didn't provide the best illumination, but the man in the expensive coat knew exactly who he was looking at.

He'd always remember the shaved head, the wide eyes, the hollow cheekbones, the pale clammy complexion.

Built like a walking skeleton.

He waited a few seconds until the guy hurried out of sight, then followed him into the shadows.

He kept his distance, trying to avoid being seen until it was absolutely necessary. He knew the kid, knew he was a loose cannon. He wasn't about to approach until he knew he could be easily identified. It would be just his luck to startle the kid and get killed for his troubles.

They headed further north up Third Avenue, leaving Patterson Houses behind. Then they turned right on East 146th Street, and a moment later the skeleton ducked into a narrow alleyway behind a disused warehouse with dirty brick walls. He stopped at a big metal side door without a handle and eased it open. As soon as he disappeared inside, the man in the expensive coat strode fast into the alley and caught the door at the end of its trajectory. He followed the guy inside, and gently eased the door closed.

When he turned around, there was a gun in his face.

It hadn't felt real, until it was. He'd followed in a drunken stupor, barely registering what was happening until it all unfolded. He knew how unstable the kid was. That had always been at the forefront of his mind. He just hadn't understood the consequences until they were staring him in the face.

He said, 'Hey, Samuel.'

'Hey,' the kid said.

'What are you doing around here?'

Samuel's wide eyes stared back, unblinking. 'Not much.'

'Didn't think you'd still be around.'

'I didn't run away like the rest of them.'

'What is this place?'

Samuel looked over one shoulder. The man in the coat followed his gaze. The warehouse had been split in two by a plasterboard partition, leaving this cavernous space up the back disused. There was a thick layer of dust on the floor, and a couple of broken pieces of machinery tucked into the corner, and an old rusting forklift in the centre of the room.

Samuel said, 'I'm here to kill them.'

'Who?'

Samuel pointed.

Then the man in the coat saw them. They were tied up, a man and a woman, gagged with packing tape and bound at the wrists and ankles with nylon rope. The bindings were chained to the forklift. A single weak bulb shone far over all their heads, barely illuminating the space. It flickered every couple of seconds. The prisoners fell in and out of shadow.

The man said, 'Who are they?'

Samuel said, 'I picked them off the street.'

'Why?'

'For the thrill.'

'Oh.'

'Are you here to stop me?'

The man looked at the handgun pointed squarely at his own face.

He said, 'No, Samuel. I'm not.'

'Good.'

Samuel put the gun down. Walked over to a folding table along the nearest wall and unsheathed a knife. It was a thing of beauty. About eleven inches long, with a serrated steel blade. He tested its weight, then shot an enquiring look at the newcomer.

The man in the coat took a step backward.

Showing he had no intention of interfering.

The prisoners were awake, and crying. Muffled grunts

resonated from between their gagged lips. The woman was blonde, maybe thirty, with a paunchy build and a plain acne-ridden face. The guy was skinny, wearing a hooded sweatshirt and oversized pants and sneakers. He had male pattern baldness and bloodshot eyes. They were both sweaty and rancid and terrified.

Both junkies.

Especially if they were snatched off the street around these parts.

Samuel walked up to them robotically. There was no emotion in his eyes. The blade in his hand was impossibly sharp, and he proved it by taking it in a tight grip and shoving it through the top of the guy's skull, right up to the hilt. The man's eyes rolled back and his legs spasmed and he went limp. Then Samuel wrenched the blade out and repeated the gesture with the woman.

There was only a few seconds between the two actions. Only a few seconds for the girl to process the death of her boyfriend, and what was about to happen to her.

That was a small mercy, at least.

Samuel left the knife embedded in the top of her head. He used the guy's hoodie to wipe the blood off his hands, then turned and gave a satisfied sigh.

The man in the coat watched, unfazed.

Samuel said, 'Thank you. I'd been waiting all day for that. Now, why are you here?'

'I saw you. On the street.'

'So?'

'I want to talk to you.'

'About what?'

'Everyone left town. Bailed on us.'

'What do you want to do?'

'Why don't we rally up who's still around? Put the old crew back together.'

Samuel smiled.

Under the weak light in the warehouse, his face seemed more gaunt than ever. Skin stretched tight over a skull, revealing every bone.

The man in the expensive coat smiled, too.

To the future, he thought.

2

Six weeks later...

Jason King said, 'Hold on. I need to puke.'

He doubled over and perspiration showered off his face and neck, dotting the white towels laid neatly on the floor of his penthouse.

He was in the living room, beside an unrivalled view of Central Park. Manhattan swept out before him in all its regality. New York was a city of potential, a collection of men and women striving to *climb.* Maybe that's what had brought him here for good. He'd spent most of his life on the road, and a permanent dwelling was a fresh concept, just as much for himself as it was for Will Slater. But now they were side-by-side in a pair of penthouses that cost more than a big-shot CEO hoped to make over his entire working career, and he found himself strangely reluctant to pack up and leave.

That bug had plagued him for decades, but New York had quashed it. He appreciated that it was a city of harsh truths — make it, or go home.

He and Slater had made it a thousand times over, but they would never abandon the climb.

It wasn't about the money.

It was about the pursuit of betterment.

A man stood across from him, practically the same size, the same build. Like looking in a mirror. They were both six-foot-three and two hundred and twenty pounds, give or take, but Rory Barker was at least twenty years older. Which made it all the more impressive that he'd maintained such a fearsome physique so far into his retirement. He was the premier mixed-martial-arts trainer in the country, able to blend the most effective disciplines into a ferocious skillset. A former K-1 kickboxing champion with a professional record for the ages, Rory regularly charged thousands of dollars for mere hours of his time. He was brought into the training camps of professional MMA fighters at pivotal moments, whereupon he would dissect the competition and tell the coaches exactly what they needed to do to lay down a surgical beating on their fighter's opponent. And then he was gone, off to another gym to provide the same service.

His time was exclusive and precious.

And Jason King had unlimited access to it.

The U.S. government always footed the bill.

Now, Rory said, 'What's the hold-up?'

King had his hands on his knees and his panting chest facing the floor. He said, 'I just told you.'

'If you need to vomit, then vomit. Otherwise we have more rounds to take care of.'

King stumbled to the sink and bent over the stainless steel. He retched once, then twice, then sighed.

He looked up. 'Looks like nothing's coming up.'

Rory wielded two leather Muay Thai pads, running the length of both his forearms, and now he slapped them together as he stressed the urgency of wasted time. Sweat sprayed off the pads.

'Then let's go,' he said.

King battled down all the food he'd consumed at lunch and returned to the towels. His chest rose and fell, but he could feel his heart rate settling, inching down from its max. That wouldn't last long.

'Teep, left jab, right hook, left elbow, right side kick,' Rory said.

'Okay.'

King fired the combination off like gunshots — sometimes he wondered if the neighbours suspected foul play. Then again, he and Slater had waged war against a horde of mercenaries in this very building half a year ago, and nothing had come of it. An apartment with a fifteen million dollar price tag came with unrivalled insulation and soundproofing. Those who paid their way deserved discretion, after all.

So he smashed a stabbing teep kick into the pads, then darted in and flicked a precise left jab to freeze the imaginary enemy in place, then pivoted at the hips and put his whole enormous frame into a right hook that rattled Rory to the core, then lurched back in the opposite direction and threw a cocked elbow like his life depended on it, and finally switched direction once more and opened up his hips and put all his weight and momentum into a turning side kick.

His shin hit the pads like a cannonball and Rory staggered, knocked off-balance by the sheer blunt force. The trainer tried to correct himself, but a couple of steps to the left and he committed to the fall. He went down on his rear and landed on the sweaty towels.

He stayed there.

Slightly rattled.

King didn't say anything. Just put his hands on his hips and caught his breath again.

Savouring the opportunity.

Rory looked up from the floor and said, 'Remember our conversation from a few months ago?'

'Which one?'

'The only one we've ever had.'

King raised an eyebrow. 'Are you suggesting I'm bad at small talk?'

'I'm suggesting your business is confidential. An anonymous shell corporation is paying me huge sums of money to train you, so whatever you're involved in is deadly serious. But we both already knew that. So why don't we cut to the chase?'

'I remember the conversation,' King said. 'And I remember emphasising how confidential my business really is.'

'You also said you might be open to discussing it over a beer.'

'I said "maybe."'

'Well?' Rory said. 'What are you doing after this?'

King could have come up with a thousand excuses.

Although he didn't need to come up with an excuse at all.

Rory had only accepted the job as King's head trainer with the understanding that he would get shut down if he ever tried to pry too deep. All King had to do was show the man the door.

But he didn't.

So much had happened since their last talk — most notably, an attempt to destabilise the U.S. economy and shatter the country's global reputation. King and Slater had narrowly prevented the crisis, but they hadn't been able to prevent the collapse of the stock market. The past six months had seen a financial downturn like nothing that had come before it, but the upswing was on the horizon. Jobs vanished, budgets tightened, portfolios were torn to shreds, but the people endured. Just as they always had. The economy was almost out of the woods.

King and Slater had sat around for months, practically tearing their hair out as they watched the economy reduced to ruin because of their own shortcomings and failures. They'd been desperate for a gig. Then Nepal happened. They'd been sent on a mad journey to the peak of Gokyo Ri, and it had almost taken their lives. Now, a couple of months after that, they were back in the same monotonous funk, with no contracted employment in sight.

Times were changing.

And so were the rules.

So King said, 'Nothing. I'm free.'

Rory said, 'You know a good bar around here?'

'Slater does.'

Rory seemed to sense King's hesitancy. 'If you don't want to share—'

King held up a hand. 'You're not pressuring me into anything. If I didn't want to talk, I wouldn't talk.'

'You probably shouldn't.'

'Says who?'

'The people who pay me, I'm sure.'

'They pay me, too,' King said. 'But they don't control me. That was the agreement.'

'You mentioned Slater...'

King nodded. A handful of details had slipped through the cracks over the eight months he and Rory had worked together.

'Who is he?' Rory said.

'We work together.'

'Same position?'

'Yeah.'

'He lives next door?'

'How'd you know that?'

'I passed him in the corridor once. He had eyes like yours.'

'They're different colours.'

'That's not what I'm talking about.'

King raised an eyebrow.

Rory said, 'Cold.'

'Right.'

'If he does what you do,' Rory said, 'how come I'm not training him?'

'Slater trains himself. He's always preferred it that way.'

'He must be confident to take it into his own hands.'

'More like blessed,' King said. 'He's a freak of nature.'

'And you aren't?'

'We've fought twice. He won both times.'

Still sitting, Rory said, 'Holy shit. How good is he?'

'About the same as me. Maybe, if I had to admit it, slightly better.'

'Can I train him? Just once? It'd be a privilege.'

A wry smile crept over King's lips. 'Slater doesn't like being told what to do. I don't think he'll ever conform to what's expected of him. He's not exactly a model athlete.'

'Where is he now?'

King didn't respond.

'Out on the town?' Rory said.

As the sun fell over New York, King said, 'How about that drink?'

3

Will Slater wasn't exactly sure how he ended up at Palantir, but he'd be damned if he wasn't going to make the most of it.

The deep tech house music throbbed through the underground club, most of its floorspace drenched in a combination of grimy darkness and toxic neon. It had the aesthetic of a grungy futuristic cantina, packed with horrendously expensive ornamentation made to look like it cost pennies on the dollar. The difference between a *truly* grungy venue and Palantir was the fact that you had to reserve an entry ticket four months in advance if you wanted a chance in hell of getting in.

Once you were in, you were expected to spend, and spend, and spend.

And then spend some more.

Or you'd get shown the door.

Sure, Slater had enough money to buy the whole damn building, but it hadn't been his intended destination. Before this he'd been drinking alone in a small hole-in-the-wall bar in Koreatown made to look like a speakeasy. Hunched over the oak countertop, deep in his own thoughts. The place was packed with Manhattan socialites gearing up for a big night out on the town, all more than willing to chat with strangers, but he hadn't come for conversation. He'd come to throw back whiskies somewhere that felt reputable, rather than drinking alone in his penthouse.

There was the attention, as always. He drew women like moths to a flame, and he couldn't pinpoint exactly why. He never put on a show to seize attention — particularly not tonight. He sat there and cradled his tumbler and sipped at the fine liquor and burned a hole in the countertop with his unblinking stare. Dwelling on the past. Dwelling on the times he'd failed.

Still, despite his guarded nature, two ladies in their late twenties approached him in quick succession. Both clad head-to-toe in designer-wear, both stunning. They put on a respectable performance of pretending not to see him until they were right next to him ordering a drink, but one of the benefits of his career was a knack for tactical awareness.

So he knew exactly what they were doing.

He didn't respond to their initial queries. He didn't let them break the ice.

He stared into his drink, as antisocial as he could ever remember being.

He let them float away of their own accord.

And then someone shook him out of his stupor in a way he least expected.

A guy in a charcoal grey suit that looked like it cost the equivalent of a mid-sized family car dropped into the stool next to Slater. He had his shirt open at the collar, exposing a muscular chest, and his expression was laid-back. Which didn't exactly fit the mould of high-strung, always-wired types that usually purchased twenty-thousand dollar suits.

The guy had curly brown hair and tanned skin and piercing blue eyes and an easy smile, and he didn't look anything like your typical investment banker or tech guru, which was what Slater had initially assumed.

So he had some initial curiosity, but then the guy said, 'You look like you're in killer shape, man.'

Slater half-smiled and shook his head. 'Sorry, brother. I don't swing that way.'

The guy froze in place, and Slater watched his brain make rapid calculations behind his bright eyes. Then the man laughed. 'No, no — that's not what I meant. Sorry. I've had too much to drink.'

'Haven't we all?'

'I just quit my job.'

'Congratulations.'

'Aren't you going to ask why?'

'I'm not exactly in a talkative mood.'

The guy raised both hands. 'Understood, my man. I'll leave you to it.'

Then he ordered a beer and took it straight back to a U-shaped booth crammed with eight other people. They all looked warm and inviting. Probably close friends. Echoes of the conversation floated across the room, and it was jovial.

The guy seemed hardly perturbed by Slater shutting him down.

Slater sat there, slightly more curious. This was New York, after all. The city of posturing. Everyone was in a collective dick-swinging contest, trying to out-spend their rivals. You had to have the better car, the better apartment, the better salary, the more impressive social circle. Which paved the way for the loudest, brashest types to strut around the bars and clubs like they owned them. That's what Slater had expected of the curly-headed man, but the guy had stayed true to his word and left him alone without the slightest provocation.

So when the man came back for another beer twenty minutes later, Slater said, 'Sorry about before. What's your name?'

'Pat,' the man said.

'I'm Will.'

Pat extended a hand. 'Seriously, man, if I'm bothering you...'

Slater half-smiled again. 'Trust me, you'd know.'

Still waiting for the bartender to deliver him a fresh bottle, Pat lowered himself into the same stool.

Slater said, 'Why did you quit your job?'

'Because it's all a bullshit performance to get to the top of the hierarchy.'

Slater paused. 'That's not something I thought I'd ever hear from a type like you.'

Pat raised an eyebrow. 'What type am I?'

Slater nodded to the suit.

Pat smiled. 'Appearances can be deceiving.'

'Can they?'

'For example, you look like a professional athlete. But you're not.'

'Aren't I?'

'I've been keeping an eye on how much you're drinking. You're not a professional athlete.'

'Maybe it's the off-season.'

'Maybe. But it's not.'

Slater shrugged, conceding the point. 'Okay, Pat. You got me. I'm not an athlete.'

'Then why are you in such insane shape?'

'I need to be for my job.'

'What's your job?'

'What's yours?'

'I'm officially unemployed,' Pat said. 'Remember?'

'What was your job yesterday?'

'Digital marketing. I started a firm. Landed some big clients. Made a lot of money. Sold for a lot of money.'

'Congratulations.'

'Thank you.'

'What are you doing with yourself now?'

'That's why I came over,' Pat said. 'You have that aura about you — you know what it's like to suffer. I'm training to qualify for Kona.'

Slater raised an eyebrow. 'Are you?'

'You know what that means?'

Slater said, 'Of course.'

Kona was the nickname in triathlon circles for the annual Ironman World Championship in Hawaii. It meant you didn't just have to finish an Ironman — a 2.4 mile swim, then a 115 mile bike ride, then a 26.2 mile run — you had to be the best in the world at it. It took a near incomprehensible level of willpower, and an astonishing capacity to suffer.

Slater said, 'You done an Ironman before?'

'Plenty.'

'Are you close to a qualifying time?'

'I will be. If I put in the work.'

'You realise what that will cost?'

'I have money.'

'That's not what I mean.'

Pat nodded. 'Roughly eight hours of intense physical training per day. Trust me — I know what I'm getting myself into.'

'Why would you do that to yourself? You're sorted. You

could put your feet up and sip cocktails on a beach for the rest of your life.'

'And then die fat and miserable and unsatisfied.'

Slater didn't respond.

Pat said, 'There's something beautiful on the other side of suffering. That's what I think I've finally realised.'

Slater didn't respond.

Pat said, 'And I got the feeling you're the only person in this place who would understand something like that. That's why I tried to start a conversation.'

'And what gave you that impression?'

'There's just something about you. You seem ... dangerous. But I think you can enjoy yourself at the same time. So why don't you come out with us tonight? I'm in a good mood.'

'You shouldn't be. You've got a long painful road ahead.'

'That's why I'm in a good mood.'

Slater paused.

Then smiled.

And slapped the man on the shoulder.

'I like you, Pat,' he said. 'Let's do it.'

Pat ushered him to their booth. On the way over, he explained, 'These are a few colleagues and friends. You'll like them.'

Slater nodded, and flipped a switch in his head.

Social butterfly mode: *On.*

But before he made it to the table, Pat clasped a hand on his shoulder and spun him round.

'You never told me what you do,' the man said.

Slater said, 'That was deliberate.'

Then he turned to the table and set to work greeting every single person in Pat's entourage.

A couple of hours later they were all at Palantir, reasonably drunk and sipping exorbitantly expensive alcohol in a VIP booth. Pat was leaving the socialite lifestyle behind with a bang.

But, as was the story of most of Will Slater's life, it didn't take long for him to find trouble.

4

Rico Guzmán couldn't pinpoint what exactly had fucked him up.

Either too much Dom Pérignon he'd lifted from the ice buckets in the centre of the booth, or too many blunts before they got to Palantir, or too much cocaine snorted off the marble countertops in the club bathrooms.

Oh, he thought. *There was the ecstasy, too.*

It didn't really matter what had done it. Fact of the matter was, he'd never felt this good before. Maybe the whole cocktail of drink and drugs had combined together in perfect quantities, which would be perfect for future reference if only he could remember the amounts he'd consumed. It had all become a blur over an hour ago, and his mood had swelled to a crescendo as soon as he'd returned from his third visit to the bathroom.

His booth was *packed.* He briefly thought about emptying out some of the newcomers, but he quickly realised he wasn't in any sort of state to utilise critical thinking.

He couldn't tell one of his guests from the other.

They all blurred together into a kaleidoscope of beauty and smiles and tanned skin and gyrating hips and jovial conversation. The lights in the club were dimmed low and the strobes were pulsating and the champagne was flowing. There were his buddies in their expensive black suits and open-necked shirts, all roughly his age — early to late twenties. Then there was the security — the fabled *sicarios* — in their cheaper suits, with their stockier builds, but they'd been expertly trained to keep as far away from the fun as possible. They were on the outskirts of the booth, melding into the shadows, keeping a close eye on their surroundings.

What broke up the machismo was the sea of gorgeous women — supermodels, all clad in tight-fitting dresses. Mostly blondes, with some brunettes and dark-haired girls thrown into the mix. They'd been herded into Rico's VIP booth as soon as he'd arrived, with the promise of free thousand-dollar champagne and as many drugs as they could feasibly put up their noses or on their tongues.

And everyone was making full use of the blank cheque.

Rico wasn't in New York often, so the burden rested squarely on his shoulders to make sure he and his entourage had a good time. It was rare that his father granted him permission to leave Mexico, but as a young scion with no concrete role in his family's business proceedings, he had little else to do but wait around until he was given the go ahead to live life at its most lavish.

He wasn't good at much, but he could damn well party.

So he lifted an open bottle of Dom Pérignon out of the nearest ice bucket and danced across to the closest model. She was stunning, even more so in the lowlight. Six inches shorter than him, even in heels, with a physique like something off the cover of a fitness magazine. She had broad blue eyes and white teeth between bright red lips, and she flashed her most alluring smile as he sauntered his way over. He could barely walk in a straight line, but he managed to gesture at the bottle in his hand. She batted her eyelashes at him and bent slightly at the knees.

Then she tilted her head back and opened her mouth.

He poured the champagne between her teeth, letting her suck it down. Then he took the bottle away, took a swig of his own, leant in and kissed her. She tasted warm and inviting, and she kissed back hard.

Rico knew it wasn't just his status that allowed him to womanise with such ease. He had his mother's good looks — his father was short and bald and fat, but the man was just as rich and powerful as he was ugly. He was the head of the Guzmán *pasador,* so he'd married a gorgeous Latino woman from Guadalajara, and together they'd had Rico. Thankfully, Rico had been blessed by the genetic lottery. Thick black hair swept back, a face like a movie star, pale green eyes with long lashes.

He used his blessings to spin the model around and gyrate against her, and together they descended into a bubble of pleasure. He had to use all the self-control in his arsenal not to drag her off to the bathroom and bend her over the countertop.

Instead, he thought he'd be a gentleman.

For once.

He whispered in her ear, 'Let's get a fresh bottle.'

She turned back around and purred, 'I'd like that.'

He drained the last dregs of the Dom Pérignon in his hand, then lowered the bottle to the countertop. He shoved his way over to the ice bucket, but it was empty.

So he strode straight for the booth's entrance.

One of the security put a hand on his chest. The man was a tried and tested *sicario* for Rico's father. Not to be fucked with under *any* circumstances. But Rico couldn't see straight, so he slapped the hand away. Hard. He didn't want the guy to have to go fetch him another bottle of champagne like he was a baby that needed coddling.

The *sicario* stepped in front of Rico. 'I can't let you out there on your own. You know the rules.'

'Fuck the rules,' Rico hissed. 'We need more Dom.'

'I'll get it.'

'The bar is right there.'

'I said I'll get it.'

Rico pulled the man close and said, 'If you don't let me go there myself, I'll tell my father you struck me.'

The guy went pale. Even in the throbbing darkness, punctuated only by dull flashing neon, Rico saw all the colour drain from his face. He smiled. It helped when your old man controlled fifty percent of the heroin and fentanyl that crossed the border from Mexico to America each and every day. You couldn't buy that sort of power in a hurry. You had to build it, rung by rung, until the whole ladder was complete. To do that, you had to kill a *lot* of people.

Raúl Guzmán was by all measures a psychopath, and he wouldn't take lightly to the fact that one of his men had hit the golden child unnecessarily.

So, despite the obvious security risks, the *sicario* backed down.

Rico smiled and pushed past. He could see the conflict in the man's eyes. The guy was in a Catch-22. If something happened to Rico, the Guzmán patriarch would never forgive him. He'd be tortured for weeks on end and then left to die. But if he disobeyed Rico's direct orders, then Rico would twist reality and the *sicario* would be as good as dead anyway.

Lose-lose.

Rico loved it.

He staggered out onto the dance floor, enmeshing with the throngs of upper-class civilians who'd emptied their savings just to get into Palantir. Rico would feel sorry for them if it wasn't for his total absence of empathy. They slaved away in cubicles for most of their lives so they could struggle to flirt with the opposite sex at an exclusive venue. The illusion of success. Rico simply asked his father for a credit card, then went out and seized everything he'd ever wanted.

It was a beautiful way to live.

He eyed the bar across the room, but he was seeing double. There was a row of booths behind him, all VIP, all brimming with the most attractive people in Manhattan. He oriented himself in the right direction and took a step forward.

There was someone in his way.

A guy had come out of one of the booths, like he wanted a moment to himself. He was African-American, built like a tank, with a shaved head and a cold gaze. He wasn't looking at Rico. He was watching the dance floor. Either looking for a girl to chase, or simply zoning out. Rico didn't care. The guy looked tough, and mean, but Rico was invincible. He was on a whole different level to these wannabes. Stern looks didn't faze him.

He figured, *Let's create some excitement.*

He dropped his shoulder low and stumbled forward and ran into the bald guy from behind, as hard as he could.

Thinking he'd at the very least knock the guy off the raised platform.

Make him stumble at least a few steps.

Make him look like an idiot.

Wipe the stern look off his face.

But the guy didn't budge. It was like he'd been concreted to the floor.

He turned slowly, raised an eyebrow, and seized Rico by the throat.

5

Unlike his colleague, King had enough restraint to enjoy a casual drink without getting carried away.

He couldn't pinpoint why. Every time he conducted a rudimentary character analysis he came away convinced that he should be more like Slater. They were men of extremes, after all. Their careers were likely to get them killed, their daily physical regimes were intense enough to make the eventual degradation of their bodies inevitable, and their ability to tolerate discomfort rested as a far outlier in comparison to not just the general population, but most of their peers too. So, realistically, approaching everything in life with that sort of intensity should have been a character trait.

One drink should turn to two, then five, then ten, then...

But it didn't.

Not often.

He and Rory sat under the red glow of an outdoor heater in an exclusive laneway beer garden in Yorkville. The drinks were overpriced, the expected tips were exorbitant, and the patrons were important businessmen and women. The first time King had showed up on the bar's doorstep, he'd been turned away because of his attire. He wore designer clothing but he didn't wear suits. Ever. It had taken serious persuasion to be allowed in, but then he'd become a regular. He didn't take his alcohol consumption to Slater's level, but at least he drank enough for a warm buzz and tipped handsomely.

Slater had never been here.

It wasn't his style.

Rory gazed around and said, 'I thought *I* was doing well.'

'You are.'

'Not like this.'

King shrugged and sipped at an unpasteurised brew. 'As soon as you get wrapped up in Manhattan's social contest it's a guaranteed loss. There's always someone doing better than you.'

'Then why are you part of it? From what I can gather, you could be anywhere in the country.'

'I like it here.'

'But you're not playing the game?'

'No.'

'You drink at nice establishments. You own some of the finest real estate in the country. I'm sure you eat at expensive restaurants. I'm sure you indulge.'

'Of course. It's a byproduct of living here.'

'I don't understand.'

'Which part?'

'You say you're not playing the game, but everything I see shows the contrary.'

'You train me.'

'I do.'

'You see what I go through on a daily basis.'

'That's a small part of your day.'

'You see anyone else working like that?'

'Only professional fighters.'

'I only drill striking with you,' King said. 'I'm a third-degree black belt in Brazilian jiu-jitsu, and I train every day at a Gracie gym near here. Then there's strength and conditioning. Then work at the nearest shooting range. Then every other avenue imaginable to hone my body — meditation, cryotherapy, infrared saunas, photobiomodulation therapy. It's a permanent relationship with suffering, and then a marathon journey to recover from that suffering. You spend long enough with that sort of routine and all this socialite-style posturing seems exactly like the farce it is. I guess I take part in it. But I'm detached from it.'

Rory took a swig of his beer and wiped foam off his upper lip.

King said, 'Does that answer your question?'

'It gives me a better idea of what you do for a living.'

'I think you already know.'

'Is that why we're here?'

'We're coworkers getting a drink after work.'

Rory shook his head. 'We're not coworkers. You're in a whole different league.'

'Depends what you mean by "league."'

'Are you a hitman? For powerful people? People who pay top dollar for human weapons?'

'In a roundabout way, yeah.'

Rory said nothing.

King said, 'How do you feel about that?'

'Without details — uneasy.'

'Would you like details?'

'If I asked for them, would you tell the truth?'

'Yes.'

'Why?'

'I trust you.'

'You don't know me well enough.'

'I think I do,' King said. 'Sure, we don't talk much. But I don't talk much to anyone. There's more to trust than conversation.'

Rory said, 'Continue.'

'You've seen me broken by fatigue. You've seen how hard I push my body. You've never tried to one-up me, or been too hard on me. You're the perfect blend of stern yet accommodating. I can tell you're an honourable man outside of our training. I don't need to interrogate you verbally to know that.'

'If martial arts hadn't humbled me,' Rory said, 'then I wouldn't be where I am today.'

'So ask away.'

'Who do you work for?'

'The government.'

'Military?'

'Not exactly.'

6

Slater stood solemn and quiet, surrounded by hedonism.

His head was swimming from the booze, but he hadn't lost control. Either he hadn't consumed as much top-shelf alcohol as he remembered, or he was just getting tolerant to these sorts of quantities.

He hoped it was the former.

So in a rare moment of clarity he shuffled his way out of the booth for a moment to himself. He crossed his arms over his chest and surveyed the dance floor, but he wasn't really paying attention to the throngs of gyrating socialites. He was thinking. And, for the first time in a long time, he was content. He figured he was the perfect level of drunk. Not messy enough to spiral out of control, but far detached from the sordid state that was his usual sober self. Here he could go deep into his own head, unobstructed and unafraid. So he did, and he didn't find many demons lying there dormant. Maybe he was more drunk than he thought. Maybe he wouldn't even remember this in the morning.

Then someone deliberately ran into him from behind.

He felt the brush of a shoulder against his back before the assailant committed their full weight to the charge. When it came down to reaction speed, there was a staggering difference between himself and 99.9% of the general population. So he understood what was happening in a millisecond and tensed up like a coiled spring, rooting himself in place. The shoulder became forceful as someone tried to shove him off the platform, but now he sure as hell wasn't going anywhere.

He felt the force reverberate back into the guy's shoulder, sending the assailant stumbling backward.

Slater turned around.

Saw a young good-looking kid, probably only a hair older than twenty, his eyes clouded with drink, his lips spread in an ugly smirk. He was everything Slater hated about New York. Not from the city, just visiting, treating Manhattan as a plaything to use and discard. Probably had a rich dad back home — wherever home was. The lighting was dark and pulsating, but Slater guessed he was Mexican.

Before Slater could use rational thinking to remember who the richest people in Mexico were, he reached out and snatched the guy by the throat and wiped the smirk right off his face.

Slater dug his fingers into the trachea, making him gasp for air. The kid's long eyelashes batted several times over as he gasped and clawed at Slater's muscled forearm.

But it was like slapping wet putty against concrete.

Slater had never seen a reaction quite like what came next. At least five men in suits poured out of the booth next to Slater's like they'd been electrocuted. They were all in various states of panic. Wide-eyed, tight-lipped, cold-gazed. Hard cruel men, the lot of them. Slater instantly recognised their kind.

Then he made the connection, and released his grip on what he imagined was the son of a powerful cartel kingpin across the border.

The music boomed and thrummed through the space, drowning out any conversation that wasn't shouted, so the scene played out before him like a silent movie. They surrounded the kid, who was pale and shaky and had red marks on his neck from Slater's grip. They hustled him back toward the booth and then squared up to Slater in a tight procession, all equally angry.

Slater knew a single moment of weakness could get him mobbed in a situation like this, especially when alcohol was involved. Genetic reflexes meant nothing when he was curled up under five bodies, getting the living shit kicked out of him.

So he moved like he'd been electrocuted too.

Jerked forward with fast-twitch muscle fibres of a pro football player.

He shoved the closest guy so hard that the man came off his feet instantly, as if he'd been hit by a car. The guy toppled back into two of his buddies, who had to use all their attention to catch him and keep him upright. Slater used the next half-second to lunge sideways and seize hold of the fourth man, grabbing him by the lapels with a level of intensity he probably hadn't felt in a long time. Slater used the moment of hesitation to push him backward, even harder than the first shove. The guy went sideways, crashed into the fifth man, and both of them went down in a heap.

Slater immediately turned back to the original trio, who were still scrambling for balance. He came within half a foot of them and then stopped short before they had fully righted themselves.

Above the roar of the music he yelled, 'Let's cool it.'

They didn't react.

But they didn't try to fight him.

He'd demonstrated a level of power they weren't accustomed to.

'I respect who you are,' Slater yelled. 'You should respect me. You saw what the kid did. I was well within my rights to react.'

No response from the suits.

Just the steady flow of drunk patrons all around them, and the deep vibrations of the bass thumping through the club. Sure, there'd been a sudden altercation right near the VIP booths, but it had happened fast. And it hadn't escalated. This wasn't a drunken brawl. It was a tense negotiation between two parties well-accustomed to violence. Not a group of inebriated finance yuppies swinging haymakers at each other because their day jobs didn't let them channel their cooped-up aggression into something productive.

Slater stepped in closer and said, 'How do you want this to go?'

'We need to set an example,' the first guy he'd shoved said. 'We can't be made to look like that. Not here.'

'But you can tell I'm going to be a problem. Or you would have tried something already.'

'It's better for everyone if we don't start a brawl.'

'Then go babysit your child,' Slater said. 'Pleasure doing business with you.'

Reluctantly, the group of five trickled back toward their booth. It didn't happen all at once — there was too much unaddressed machismo in the air. These men were enforcers for a drug lord. That carried certain expectations in and of itself. But Slater had ample experience with the cartels, and he wouldn't be shy if it came to conflict. There wasn't a bone in his body that would waver, even if it meant waging war with the entire faction out of a simple inability to back down.

And they could sense that.

So they backed down first.

Then the kid with the long hair and the ugly smirk shouldered past all five of them, drew a Colt M1911 from a holster underneath his suit jacket, and pointed it square between Slater's eyes.

7

Rory said, 'Off the books?'

King said, 'Yes.'

'Black operations?'

'Yes.'

'Were you ever in the military?'

'A long, long time ago.'

'What happened?'

'I was pulled out of the traditional military structure only a few years into my twenties. People far smarter than me identified certain talents in me. I'm genetically gifted.'

'With your athleticism?'

King shook his head. 'There's no shortage of athletes. It was always about reflexes.'

'Reaction speed?'

'Yes.'

'I picked that up. I've never seen anyone make adjustments in real time like you do. If I'm holding a pad a few inches away from where it should be, it's like you compute it in a millisecond and land the punch or kick in the right place every single time.'

'Is that why you said I should be a professional fighter?'

Rory nodded. 'Those abilities would pay dividends in the cage.'

'But now you understand why I can't.'

Another nod.

King said, 'They've paid dividends throughout my career. Trust me.'

'How so?'

'I should be dead a thousand times over. I'm not.'

Rory said, 'When are you going to stop?'

'I tried to stop.'

'What happened?'

'Nothing good.'

'You don't want to go into it?'

'Not particularly.'

'I thought you said—'

'Certain topics are off-limits.'

'I can respect that.'

King finished the dregs of beer at the bottom of the glass and folded his giant hands over each other on the tabletop. He sighed and said, 'Have you ever done anything other than fighting, Rory?'

Rory said, 'Of course. I'm training you, aren't I?'

'But that's still the business. There's something raw and primal and animalistic about it. If you were to get a job in retail, it wouldn't quite have the same ... pop. We all like to pretend that we look down on violence, but when you see it up close and personal, it's something so vastly different to anything else on this planet.'

Rory nodded.

King said, 'It's not like you *enjoy* it, so to speak. But you couldn't see yourself not being involved with it.'

Another nod.

Rory said, 'I've spent my life as a kickboxer. I couldn't stop. Even if I wanted to.'

'Apply the same logic to what I do, and there you have your answer.'

'You don't like the violence,' Rory said. 'But it's necessary for you to be part of it. Because you're good at it and you couldn't see yourself letting your talents go to waste. I'm sure you've helped countless people through your feats. I get it.'

'So when you burrow down to the core, we're in the same game after all.'

Rory said, 'People don't die in my game. Combat sports is not the real world. It's artificial. Made up for entertainment. When the ref says stop, you stop. I couldn't imagine translating my skills to the real world. That's far too messy.'

'All the more reason why I can't quit. Not many people have been conditioned to do what I do. I try not to be arrogant when I say that. Truth is...'

He trailed off, but he could feel Rory's eyes boring into him.

He'd never told anyone this.

Not Slater.

Not a soul.

Eventually Rory said, 'What?'

King lifted his gaze. 'This stays between us. No matter what.'

Rory drained his beer and nodded. It wasn't just any old nod. It conveyed respect and honour. The word of a professional mixed martial artist was as good a guarantee as anything. They knew too much pain and suffering to be superficial.

King said, 'I wish I'd never been born with the genetic advantages I have. They make me very adept at not dying, but sometimes I wish it'd all come to an end just for the weight it'd take off my shoulders.'

'That's a dangerous thing to say.'

'I'm not suicidal. Not even close. But this constant momentum weighs on me. I don't suppress it like Slater does. I just dwell on it. I have a partner in the same business I'm in, and she keeps me sane. But it's taking a toll. Not being able to stop. Not wanting to stop. Not taking the foot off the gas even for a moment.'

Rory said, 'It's not a predicament I'd want to be in.'

'So do you have the answers you wanted?'

'I have a million more questions.'

'Maybe another time. I have a date tonight.'

'With this mysterious partner of yours?'

'The one and only.'

'Who is she?'

'Her name's Violetta,' King said. 'She's probably the one who pays you.'

Rory raised an eyebrow. 'She's your boss?'

'She's my handler.'

'How'd you two end up together?'

'Unwisely.'

'How do you separate work and your personal lives?'

'It's difficult.'

'I won't pry.'

'Appreciate it.'

'Can I ask about Slater?'

King considered it. But ultimately he reached the right conclusion.

'No,' he said.

'Why not?'

'I get that you're interested in our world. But it's all very secretive. I don't feel comfortable sharing anything about Will Slater without his permission.'

'He's like you?'

'In a way.'

'How do you differ?'

King clasped his hands together. 'You and I are sitting here making light conversation over a single drink.'

'And Slater?'

'He's probably up to something a little more ... unruly.'

8

No one saw a thing.

The Colt was there, and then it wasn't.

If the kid had it in plain sight for any longer than a few seconds, someone in the crowd would notice the neon lights flashing off the gunmetal and react accordingly. As soon as enough people realised what was happening, pandemonium would break out.

But none of that happened because Slater stripped the guy of the weapon before anyone was the wiser.

He lunged forward and snatched hold of the kid's spindly wrist and bent it so hard he nearly broke the ulna and the radius in the same jerk. The guy's tanned face went pale and his eyes nearly bugged out of his head, and Slater used the sudden change in momentum to wrench the gun out of his grasp like it had never been there at all. Then, in one smooth motion, he tucked it into the back of his own waistband and dropped his leather jacket over it, hiding it from sight in an instant.

All five of the *sicario*s saw what happened.

None of them reacted.

And Slater understood.

This little shit is out of control, they were thinking. *Please teach him a lesson.*

Slater darted into range and looped a giant arm over the back of the kid's neck, draping his hand over the opposite shoulder, like an overly macho hug between two best friends.

He pulled the guy in close and said in his ear, 'What's your name?'

The kid stood there, flabbergasted by the turn of events. He tried to look behind him to see where his bodyguards were, but Slater grabbed the back of his skull as soon as he turned his head and shoved it forward, preventing him from getting a proper look. He pointed to the dance floor.

'Look out there, kid,' Slater said. 'What's your name?'

'Rico.'

'Rico, huh?'

'Get the fuck off me, man.'

'What are you going to do if I don't?'

'Where are—'

He tried to turn his head again. Started craning his neck, but Slater used the hand looped over one shoulder to slap Rico in the face. His palm *thwack*ed off the kid's cheek and his head bounced back into place.

'I took care of your bodyguards,' Slater said.

It wasn't true, but Rico didn't know that. Everything had happened so fast, and the kid was drunk or high or both, and the darkness was all-encompassing, and the music was pounding. He had no way of knowing whether his men were standing right there behind him, blissfully oblivious to his situation, or laid out on the club floor with broken faces and concussions.

If Rico gave it a moment's thought, he'd realise Slater hadn't had time for any of that.

But he didn't give it a moment's thought, because all he could concentrate on was the fact that a stranger had his gun and was in the process of humiliating him.

Rico's eyes flared up with rage. The sting would be creeping its way through his cheek. Adrenaline was now flowing through him, parting the clouds of inebriation. He was sobering up fast, and realising how stupid he looked, and starting to panic.

Slater said, 'You going to try and break free?'

'Dude,' Rico said, squirming in Slater's iron grip. 'I told you to get the—'

Slater slapped him again, but masked it from sight with the bulk of his frame. He made it look like any old drunken friendly hug. 'You got some nerve pulling a piece in here.'

'Yeah, well, I've—'

'Got no spine?' Slater said.

'What?'

'You've got no spine. You haven't done any of this on your own. You're using daddy's credit card.'

Rico visibly tensed.

Slater tightened the arm around the back of his neck. Turning it into a half-headlock. Making sure he didn't go anywhere.

Slater said, 'When I let go you might think you should try something. I'm advising you not to. You've already fucked up twice. Don't make the third time the charm.'

This time, the kid didn't squirm, and he didn't respond.

His shoulders slumped forward.

He recognised defeat.

Slater let go of him and shoved him back in the direction

of his booth. 'I don't know how you got that gun in here, but now it's mine.'

Rico sized up his surroundings. Slater watched his gaze sweep over his security, who were all standing there patiently with their hands folded in front of them. Like a procession standing at attention at a funeral.

Rico stared at them, incredulous, and then pointed a shaking finger at Slater.

Whether it was shaking from fear or adrenaline — that was hard to discern.

Maybe both.

'Get my piece back,' he shouted above the music. 'Papá gave it to me.'

None of them moved.

Slater watched them.

Put one hand behind his back, just in case.

Like a Wild West gunslinger ready to draw.

They looked at him. He knew they wanted to give it a shot. Rico's father would be none too happy if the kid relayed this story. Slater had reached a mutual understanding with them through implication alone, but there was no guarantee that would last.

He got ready to shoot five men dead in a Manhattan nightclub.

9

A waiter in a tailored suit floated over to King as soon as his glass was empty. 'A refill, sir?'

'Not tonight, Santino,' King said. 'I've got places to be.'

The man nodded and drifted away.

Rory said, 'Is that my cue?'

'I'm afraid it has to be.'

'Where are you headed?'

'I told you I have a date. With Violetta.'

'Must be nice.'

King said, 'I assume you do an awful lot of travelling if you float between MMA camps.'

A nod.

'Do you have a significant other?'

'Not currently,' Rory said. 'The last one ended badly. That was two years ago. Nothing's really eventuated since then. Nothing permanent, at least.'

'You're always on the move?'

'Pretty much. I take it you are, too.'

'Not as much as I was in the past,' King said. 'But it's still brutal.'

'How'd you find a way around it?'

King thought of his first encounter with Violetta. 'I found someone crazy enough to work in the same field I'm in. That was enough.'

'Has Slater done the same?'

King paused. 'He tried.'

'What happened?'

'What usually happens in our field.'

Rory bowed his head. 'Sorry to hear that.'

'You didn't know her. And you don't know him. What's it to you?'

'I know you. Aside from your vices, it sounds like you two are one and the same. Sounds like he would have been happy with her.'

'Yeah,' King said. 'He would have.'

Silence.

King said, 'But shit happens.'

'Shit happens,' Rory repeated.

He lifted the glass to his lips and finished it.

'I'll see you next week?' King said.

Rory nodded. 'I'm heading out to Vegas for five days, and then I'll be back. A fighter's camp out there needs me.'

'Get 'em ready for war.'

'Always.'

They stood up. The sun had set long ago, and it was approaching the hour where the night truly came alive. King checked his watch — 10:43. Violetta had made a reservation for seven at their favourite Japanese restaurant on the Upper East Side, but she'd messaged an apology hours earlier, blaming work for unexpected delays. In any other career, he might have suspected she was up to something. But with the business she operated in, news like that worried him for other reasons. Nine times out of ten it meant something real bad was happening somewhere in the world. She probably had skin in the game — a black-ops specialist on foreign soil, deep in enemy territory, suddenly compromised. He'd realised long ago that she might be the only person he knew besides Slater that shared a similar level of job stress.

Sure, her life wasn't directly on the line, but the second- and third-order consequences of her actions carried enough weight to traumatise her if she butchered a job. She truly cared about people. King had been with her for long enough to know that. Deep down in her core, she shouldered all the responsibility for the operatives she managed.

If they died in the field, it was her fault.

Which also worried King.

Because if the death of an operative under her supervision crushed her soul, how would she take it if the man she loved died under her watch?

Then he figured, *It'd be worse for me than it would be for her.*

I'd be dead.

He and Rory snaked their way out of the establishment, past the outdoor heaters and crimson decorative lights and overhanging vines and throngs of tipsy socialites. Then through the bar, where there were a few slightly more unruly characters throwing back neat whiskey and vodka, all of them manicured and moisturised and dressed as expensively as their counterparts out in the beer garden.

It was the same as every bar on earth.

The fact that its clientele resided in a different socioeconomic bracket didn't change a thing about human nature.

Everyone loves to dull the bad memories.

King felt a faint twinge of something. Some repressed

urge. Right then, he wanted nothing more than another drink. The pull for it tugged at his brain, gnawing at him.

Wouldn't you like to forget everything you've done?

Everything that's been done to you?

But out of habit he crushed the moment of weakness, and when he stepped outside with Rory into a cool, crisp New York evening, he was back to savouring the time he had available instead of trying to suppress the entirety of his off-duty life.

He couldn't say that Slater was doing the same.

He and Rory put their hands in their coat pockets and watched their breath fog under the streetlights and stared up at the infinite rows of windows in the skyscrapers all around them. There was something magical about New York. It was all concrete and brick and glass, and in the summertime the streets stank of fetid garbage, but at the same time there was a mysticism to it that didn't gel with the ultra-modern setting. King figured he could spend the rest of his life here. It was chaotic, but he'd always thrived in chaos.

He preferred noise and excitement to peace and quiet.

Always had.

Always would.

Still gazing up, Rory said, 'I don't know how you do it.'

'What?'

'Live here. You could live anywhere.'

'I take it you plan to retire somewhere else.'

'I've spent most of my life fighting,' Rory said. 'When I have what I need, I'm out.'

'How long?'

'Maybe a few more years.'

'Then I'd better make the most of you while you're around,' King said.

They both smiled.

Rory offered a hand.

King reached out and shook it.

'Be seeing you,' Rory said.

King nodded.

Then, in one all-encompassing moment, every square of light emanating from the windows above them flickered out.

As did the streetlights.

Their whole world plunged into darkness.

10

The bodyguards noticed Slater was ready to go down in a blaze of glory.

They must have seen the look in his eyes. They sized him up, alternating their gazes between Slater and Rico, and finally one of them reached out and snatched the kid by the arm and hauled him back into the VIP booth.

The other four followed.

A collective decision.

Not worth the trouble.

Slater turned back to his own booth. Pat was watching in awe from the corner of his booth. It was awfully difficult to mask emotions when you were drunk. Slater half-smiled at him and shooed him away. *Don't draw attention.*

Pat tipped back the remainder of a vodka shot and shook his head, flabbergasted. He must have been watching the whole time. Understanding the nuance of what was unfolding. Seeing Slater handle it like an artisan as he floated from one confrontation to the next with ease, chaining them together into a perfect sequence. Slater never really considered it from an outsider's perspective. Most people in modern society were afraid of confrontation to begin with. Not only was he fully comfortable in its grip, it was one of his specialties. He knew how to handle anything thrown his way. That could have escalated into something unstoppable, but he culled it before it got out of control.

Someone else noticed too.

One of Pat's friends stepped down from the booth and made her way over. Slater had spoken to her a handful of times throughout the evening. At one point, Pat had discreetly let slip that she was the reason he'd approached Slater at the Koreatown bar in the first place. She'd been interested from the get-go. And as he watched her approach, he couldn't help but admit he was interested back. She was only a couple of inches shorter than him, tall and long-legged with a model's graceful physique. She had rich eyes and an alluring smile, and speaking to her in the booth he'd been struck by the giddy sensation that there was nothing else going on in the world — just their conversation. She was one of the most interesting women he'd met in quite some time. She was Pat's risk analyst, and had been working for him for three years. Outside of work, she was a gym junkie. She trained Crossfit every morning and ran five miles every evening.

Once again, Slater found it always came back to the mutual penchant for suffering.

You had to find balance.

You had to hurt in solitude so you could fully enjoy the hedonistic moments like this. Otherwise you wound up in a place like Palantir fat and sweaty and out of shape, with a turbulent mind. Wherever Slater went, he was at peace. He could tell she was the same.

Her name was Serena, and now she waltzed right up to him and put her hands on his shoulders.

She brought her lips up to his ear and said, 'Did I just see what I think I saw?'

'Depends what you think you saw.'

'Are you in trouble?'

Slater flashed a glance at Rico's booth. It was still packed to the rafters, but the kid himself was nowhere to be found. Probably seated up the back licking his wounds. The security were stationed at regular intervals around the perimeter, but they were deliberately looking in any direction but Slater's.

They'd come to an understanding, evidently.

Slater said, 'I don't think so.'

She kept her hands where they were, and he liked it. It was the first move either of them had made. Despite the alcoholic haze, there'd been an undercurrent of agreement that they would both play hard to get.

Until now.

He kissed her. She smiled as he did, her lips against his and her white teeth bared, and then kissed back. The rest of the club fell away. They probed as best as they could with their hands given the public setting, and when they parted she kept her arms draped over his shoulders. She seemed ready to shed her dress at the slightest provocation. He gave silent thanks for the torture he put himself through on a daily basis. It made him irresistible to women of her calibre, and as far as he was concerned in his drunken state, that was all there was to life.

At least in this moment.

He said, 'I have a place.'

'Where?'

'Upper East Side.'

She raised an eyebrow. 'Someone's doing well.'

'Wait until you see it.'

'You're acting like that's a foregone conclusion.'

He shrugged, feeling her palms on his collar bones. 'Suit yourself.'

She offered a playful smile. 'You knew I was going to come back with you, didn't you?'

'I had a suspicion.'

'How'd you know?'

'I'm persuasive.'

'You are.'

'Has it worked?'

She kissed him again, then went up on her tiptoes to whisper in his ear. 'It sure has.'

'Should we get out of here?'

'Let's.'

He took her by the hand and turned away from the booths. He didn't bother searching for any sign of aggression from Rico's booth. The security were level-headed enough to know their place, and there were five of them. He'd won them over, so they'd keep Rico away from him if the kid had any malicious impulses. But Slater imagined he wouldn't. He'd been humiliated, and he wouldn't be feeling as drunk as he had a few moments ago. Sobering clarity sinks in as the haze of confidence falls away.

Making him realise, *That guy just took my gun and made my* sicarios *babysit me.*

So Slater looped an arm around Serena's shoulder and started to guide her toward the exit.

Then the music cut out with an audible *whump.* Compared to the deafening bass, the silence was eerie.

Concerned murmuring rose off the dance floor, and spread through the club like wildfire.

Slater paused.

A second later, the lights went out.

11

Dead quiet.

King didn't move a muscle.

He stood under the night sky, barely able to make out his surroundings. He could see the outlines of buildings, now akin to mammoth archaeological relics without any lights to demonstrate their modernity. The darkness was all-encompassing. Perhaps in the countryside it might have seemed normal. But Manhattan was a different beast. New York was the city that never slept — powered up twenty-four-seven, running around the clock, complete with shouts and horns and flashing lights everywhere you looked.

King listened intently to the silence.

But it only lasted a few seconds.

It was like the whole city paused in unison, staring around in awe at the blackout. Then, like clockwork, the cacophony of noise returned. Drivers leant on horns, pedestrians in the distance shouted to one another, and the general murmur of the city cranked up in decibels.

People were concerned. And they had every right to be.

Finally, King moved. He turned around and stared down the alleyway. He could see cars flashing past its mouth, their headlights still beaming. He turned back, and peered down to the other end. Same deal. But the buildings stayed dark. The streets stayed dark. It was like a great swathe of black, illuminated by a maze of interconnected roads and streets and laneways still teeming with vehicles.

Only half a dozen feet away but practically invisible, Rory said, 'What was that?'

King said, 'A blackout.'

'I know, but...'

'I know what you mean.'

'The power will come back on, right?'

King looked up at the skyscrapers.

Nothing.

Quiet.

Dark.

Dormant.

It had only been a few seconds since the lights had gone out.

It felt like hours.

Rory said, 'Jason?'

King realised the man had been speaking. He hadn't heard a word.

King said, 'What?'

'I've never seen you like this.'

'Like what?'

'So quiet.'

'I don't talk much.'

'This is different.'

King realised minutes must have passed. He was deep in his own head, skewered away, very close to something eerily similar to panic. And Rory was right. He couldn't remember the last time he'd succumbed to emotions like this. He tried to force them back down.

But this time he couldn't.

He said, 'How long have we been standing here?'

'Maybe five minutes.'

King's legs felt concreted to the ground. He pulled out his smartphone and fired it up. The screen glowed like a furnace in the total darkness.

He saw what he expected to see.

EMERGENCY ALERT.

Right there on the screen. Sent to every smartphone in the city probably. Possibly the entire New York Metropolitan Area, depending on how widespread the blackout was.

He read it.

POWER OUTAGE IN NEW YORK. AWAIT FURTHER DETAILS.

King held up his phone for Rory to see. 'This isn't good.'

'That's just the default protocol, isn't it?'

'I don't think so.'

'What do you know about power outages?'

'That they're never this big.'

'It could just be this block.'

'It's not.'

'How do you know?'

'They wouldn't have sent that alert out if they knew what was happening.'

Neither of them said a word. They listened to the sounds of the city. It wasn't pandemonium. Far from it. In fact, there was an undercurrent of excitement in the air. The murmuring was excited. King understood why. It was a Friday night, and half the city's socialites were a few drinks deep. Those prone to panic were more likely squared away in their apartments. Right now, with most of those out and about shrouded in a pleasant buzz, the darkness would seem exciting.

But not for long.

Rory didn't seem to like the quiet. He managed a laugh, but it came out hollow, with a tinge of nervousness. After all, he'd spent enough time with King to know the man was afraid of almost nothing.

So when the laugh died off, Rory said, 'Okay, what the fuck is up with you?'

King looked at him. His eyes had adjusted to the darkness. He could see the man's silhouette clearly. Again, he said, 'This isn't good.'

'It's been five minutes.'

'But soon it'll be ten. Then it'll be an hour.'

'You don't know that.'

'They sent out an emergency alert.'

'Which means?'

King rubbed his brow. 'That they'd been expecting everything to go to shit.'

'You can't be sure.'

'I work for the government.'

'You're an independent contractor. You don't know anything about what happens behind-the-scenes. You told me that yourself.'

'But I know what will happen if this lasts any longer than a couple of hours.'

'It'll be okay.'

'There's twenty million people in the New York Metropolitan Area.'

Rory lapsed into silence.

Thinking.

Finally he said, 'It's still only been five minutes. You need to relax.'

King said, 'Phones will be dead within a day. Flashlights and radios will go, too. There's not going to be any running water.'

Silence.

He said, 'How long do you think it'll take people to start panicking?'

Rory looked around.

Manhattan was dark.

The man said, 'Not long.'

'And when it starts, it'll spread like wildfire.'

The tendrils of a breeze whispered down the alleyway. King shivered in the night.

Rory said, 'Yeah, okay, this isn't good.'

'If this goes for any longer than an hour it's going to be bedlam.'

'Surely New York can stay calm for longer than that.'

'One person starts looting and everyone will join in. It's the mob mentality.'

'After an hour? Surely emergency services will maintain—'

'Think about how many people are trapped in elevators right now.'

Rory said nothing.

King said, 'And that's just the start of the problems.'

Silence.

'Hospitals.'

Silence.

'Gridlock.'

Rory said, 'What do we do?'

King didn't respond. In that moment he understood his insignificance. Together they could maybe help a dozen people. There were, potentially, twenty million who would soon be thrust back into something similar to the dark ages if this situation didn't resolve itself. Twenty million people living in the modern age, most of them completely dependent on cellphones and meal delivery services and...

'Shit,' King said.

Rory said, 'You should call your girlfriend.'

'Yeah,' King said. 'I should.'

'What do you want me to do?'

'I ... don't know.'

Rory offered a hand.

As a gesture of farewell.

King stared at it.

'What are you doing?' he said.

'This isn't my world.'

'Yeah, but—'

'Do you need me?'

King paused.

Then said, 'I guess I don't.'

And shook his hand.

'If this lasts as long as you think it will,' Rory said, 'then there's going to be panic. Just like you said. We both know what that leads to. You're going to be needed.'

'Are you sure you—?'

'I train fighters. I don't fight. Especially not in the real world. People have guns and knives in the real world. That trumps what I do.'

King didn't respond.

Rory said, 'But not what you do.'

King nodded.

Rory said, 'I'd just get in the way.'

'Where will you go?'

'I don't know.'

'Will I still see you next week for training?'

Rory tried to smile.

Once again, it was hollow.

But he said, 'There's that familiar optimism.'

King said, 'We'll figure this out. Don't worry.'

'Oh, I'm worried,' Rory said. 'Because I've never seen you worried.'

Then he turned and walked off into the darkness without another word.

Leaving King to his own devices.

Leaving him alone in the city that, for the first time in years, had gone to sleep.

12

No one immediately panicked.

Everyone was drunk, and alcohol had the uncanny ability to make you nonplussed about future consequences. As Slater lost his vision the drunken haze peeled away, replaced quickly by pure adrenaline, but to almost every other patron in Palantir the lights going out was a mere inconvenience. There were laughs of derision, and half-hearted *aw-shucks* complaints, and excited murmuring between groups. Slater's ears whined in the sudden silence, still affected by the thrumming music that had cut out only moments earlier. He heard a couple of particularly drunken customers start whooping and hollering in the darkness, but it was muffled. It'd take a few minutes for his hearing to fully return.

Serena was gripping him tight around the waist.

Maybe she'd sensed the fact he was on edge.

She said, 'Are you okay?'

He couldn't see her. It was pitch black. His mind immediately wandered to potential dangers. Had one of Rico's friends or business associates cut the power? Were there *sicarios* lunging toward him right now with switchblades in their hands?

He reached back, felt the cool touch of the Colt against his waist, and placed his hand gently on the grip. Then he stood still as a statue and stiffened, waiting for the slightest provocation. His eyes were wide as saucers. He fought to acclimatise to the darkness, but there wasn't a window in sight to let in even a sliver of natural light. There would be no adjusting.

The inklings of panic started to drift through the crowd. He felt the atmosphere palpably shift. It never took much. Maybe one person had started to hyperventilate in the corner of the room and it had set off a chain reaction. No way to know for sure. But suddenly the murmurings became more concerned. Some people raised their voices. The whooping and hollering stopped. There was a smattering of requests for an exit. First quiet and noncommittal, then louder.

Then, louder still.

Suddenly everyone was squirming and shuffling about, pressed against each other on the dance floor.

Slater hadn't sensed anyone trying to bullrush him.

He started to realise this wasn't a deliberate ploy to catch him off-guard.

Not everything revolves around you.

By now he was close to dead sober, despite the mountains of booze in his system. He could tap into the cocktail of stress chemicals at will — it was second nature to him. Right now the alcohol served no purpose, so he thrust its effects away as adrenaline rushed through his system.

He whispered into Serena's ear, 'I'm going to need to handle this.'

She said, 'What?'

He said, 'Don't get frightened.'

Then he stepped away from her, waited for the briefest lull in the crowd's volume, and then screamed at the top of his lungs, '*Everybody quiet!*'

When he needed to, he could roar like nobody's business.

Everyone shut up in unison.

Like tape had been wrenched across all their mouths at once.

Slater yelled, '*I'm a cop! Everyone relax. No one panic.*'

There was still a smattering of drunken murmurs and whispers, but apart from that everyone seemed to be obeying. Nothing like the loss of one of your senses to shock you into submission. They would do what he said. Hopefully he could prevent a stampede.

'*Everyone get your phones out and turn your flashlights on.*'

It was obvious in hindsight, but there were only a handful of beams illuminated when he made the command. Then, in the space of ten seconds, Palantir lit up with dozens of bright white lights skewering toward the ceiling, casting sweeping shadows over the decor. It added an eerie vibe to the club, but it was better than pitch darkness.

Slater shouted, '*Everyone make your way* slowly *toward the exit. No faster than a shuffle. Do* not *run or panic.*'

The crowd obliged.

He could hear the slightest indicators of movement amidst the sea of white light — like an interconnected body of water flowing in one direction. Clothes rustling against each other. Hands probing for shoulders. But no one ran. And no one panicked. Serena's fingers touched Slater's hips and he led her along with the tide, aiming for the exit. By now, he was calm. There wouldn't be a stampede. That was the most important thing. Most people underestimate how destructive a panicked crowd in a tight space could be. He gave the patrons of Palantir silent credit for their calmness. No one was shouting and screaming. Everyone seemed to collectively understand the need for cooperation — at least until they were out on the street.

Slater found the exit and followed the masses down a tighter corridor, illuminated brighter than the cavernous main space by the abundance of flashlights. Then they were in the entranceway, where unnerved bouncers were standing around looking dumb. They didn't know what to do. Slater found it a little disconcerting. Surely they should be trying to restore calm and make sure that all the patrons were safe—

Then Slater stepped outside, and realised it wasn't just their building that had been hit.

Every skyscraper he could see, every streetlight in the laneway...

All dark.

'Oh, *shit*,' he said.

Serena gazed around in wonderment. 'Wow. You ever seen anything like this before?'

'It happened in 2003,' Slater said. 'But I wasn't in-country back then.'

'Where were you?'

Slater didn't respond.

She said, 'Are you really a cop?'

'No.'

'That was quick thinking, then.'

'I guess I'm half a cop.'

'And the other half?'

He didn't answer.

He peered all around, drinking in the night, ignoring the masses and crowds all around him.

Then he looked at her.

'Serena, I have to go.'

She furrowed her brow. 'It's just a power outage. Surely we can still—'

'I'm sorry,' he said. 'I had fun tonight. Take care of yourself.'

He turned and disappeared into the crowd.

Then pulled out his smartphone and stared at the screen.

And froze.

The networks were down.

That wasn't normal. Almost all the major cell towers relied on backup generators in case of outages exactly like this. For the networks to go down, those generators would have to be deliberately targeted...

His blood ran cold.

Is this an attack?

Thankfully, his own phone had been modified by Violetta's tech team to provide satellite capabilities in the event he was ever out of range.

He breathed silent thanks for her hindsight, and called Jason King.

13

King didn't answer.

He was already on the phone to Violetta LaFleur, making use of the same satellite technology.

She picked up immediately and said, 'Where are you?'

'Yorkville. How bad is it?'

'Where in Yorkville?'

'The beer garden we've visited before. Just off 85th and Second.'

'Okay,' she said. 'Are you with Will?'

'No.'

'Have you heard from him?'

'No. I assume he's close to a blackout himself.'

She didn't laugh.

That's when he knew it was serious.

He said, 'Where do you need me?'

'Go back home right now. I'll meet you there.'

'At the penthouse?'

'Yes.'

'That'll be eighty flights of stairs. Is that really necessary?'

'Your building has an emergency generator system installed, so you'll be okay to use the elevators. Give thanks that you live in one of the most exclusive residences on the Upper East Side.'

He said, 'How did you know that and I didn't?'

'Because ever since the attack on your penthouses last year, we've been monitoring the building for you. You and Will know how valuable you are to us. Those extra security measures we discussed also included knowing every feature the place has.'

'How long's the emergency generator going to last? Especially for a building of that size.'

'Long enough.'

He paused. 'Do you know what's happening?'

'Yes,' she said. 'And we need you both.'

'For what?'

'Get back home,' she said. 'I need to go. It's chaos over here.'

'Understood.'

'And Jason?'

'Yes.'

'Please don't get yourself killed on the way back.'

'Why on earth would that happen?'

'I don't know,' she said. 'I just... I don't like this. Don't drop your guard.'

'I never do.'

'See you soon.'

She ended the call.

He lowered the phone and loitered in the alleyway. He hadn't moved since Rory had walked away. Most of the beer garden's patrons had filtered past him on their way out of the dark bar, illuminating the way forward with the flashlights on their phones. But by now all the beacons of light were gone, flowing through into the city streets where urgent energy was flowing like a river. All King could think was, *That's going to kill their batteries real quick.*

And then what?

Two days, he figured.

That's how long it would take until real problems would arise.

And those problems...

...well, he couldn't even fathom how severe they'd be.

He twirled the phone in his hand, then opened the settings and killed anything running in the background that wasn't absolutely necessary. He needed the battery to last as long as possible.

Then the screen changed, replaced by an incoming call notification.

The contact name was one word.

SLATER.

King answered and said, 'How many drinks have you had?'

'I'm fine.'

'That doesn't answer my question.'

'I said I'm fine.'

'You sound lucid enough.'

'I'm not the drunk you think I am.'

'You're still skirting around the question. That tells me everything I need to know.'

'I've had a lot,' Slater said. 'Is that what you wanted? Can you even tell that it's affecting me?'

'No, I can't. But I'd say that's because of your tolerance level. That doesn't make you any less drunk.'

'Cut the bullshit and tell me where you need me.'

'What makes you think I know?'

'You've spoken to Violetta, I'm sure.'

'Yeah.'

'And?'

'Get back home,' King said. 'I'll meet you there.'

'In the lobby? I'm not taking the stairs for no good reason.'

Great minds think alike, King thought.

He said, 'There's an emergency generator in the building.'

'How the hell do you know that?'

'I don't. Violetta told me.'

A pause, then a laugh. 'What would we do without her?'

'Who knows,' King said. 'Where are you?'

'Palantir. At least, I was.'

'I thought you said you were having a quiet one.'

'*I was.* Got carried away.'

'That seems to be a recurring theme.'

'Host an intervention for me later. What do you know about this? What did Violetta say?'

'Not a whole lot. But she said enough.'

'It's bad, right?'

'It has the potential to be.'

'I thought as much.'

'Any craziness happening where you are?'

A pause, then Slater said, 'I nearly got into a fight with the son of a drug lord. It would have got ugly real fast. But that was before the power went out. Nothing of note has happened in the last ten minutes.'

King said, 'Christ. Just make it back home in one piece.'

'Yes, sir. Anything else?'

'I don't think so.'

'Is this why she had to stay back at work?' Slater said.

'You told me dinner got pushed back so you were going to train with Rory. Did she know this was coming?'

King hesitated.

He hadn't considered it.

He said, 'I don't know. I'll find out.'

'She couldn't tell you over the phone?'

'As you can imagine, she's dealing with a lot of issues right now.'

'Is she meeting us in person?'

'Yes.'

'Then we're probably going to be needed.'

'We *are* needed. I just told you that.'

'Right.'

The hints of inebriation, slipping through the cracks in the façade.

King said, 'How fast can you sober up?'

'I'm already sober. But I'll buy a bottle of water on the way home.'

King shook his head, flabbergasted. 'I don't know how you do it.'

'Practice.'

The line went dead.

He put the phone back in his pocket and left the alleyway, stepping out onto 83rd Street. A churning sensation rippled through his gut, and he paused and placed his hand on the nearby brick wall to steady himself. It wasn't the beer. He could handle much more than a single pint. And it wasn't the fact that he and Slater were needed. Sure, that meant violence and chaos, but that was to be expected in this line of work.

What really worried him was the scope of the blackout.

He didn't know much about contingency plans.

He just knew everything would go to hell if this lasted too long.

And if Violetta had known something was coming, then that meant it was pre-planned.

It meant it was deliberate.

King set off into the city streets, pushing through throngs of pedestrians waving their phone flashlights around like they were at a rave. The piercing glare of stationary headlights cut through the gridlock traffic. Without functioning traffic lights, the city had come to a standstill. It all combined into an uncanny atmosphere, like nothing he'd ever seen before in Manhattan.

A sea of pinpoints, the white artificial lights like specks against the greater backdrop of the dark city.

Unnerved by how alien it all felt, he broke into a jog toward the Upper East Side.

Rico pushed a pair of fingers into his closed eyes, trying to thrust the headache away.

It achieved nothing.

He blinked hard and said, 'What is this shit?'

There weren't many people around. His rich scion friends from Mexico were twiddling their thumbs in the corner of the alleyway, and all the girls had seemingly vanished like magic. No reason to hang around when the power was out and the usual luxurious hedonism couldn't be maintained. The fridges weren't running, so the Dom Pérignon was getting warm. They'd bailed at the first opportunity.

One of Rico's bodyguards said, 'The power's out. Might be affecting the whole city. The networks are down, too.'

Rico lifted his gaze. 'What did you say?'

'You heard me.'

'The last part.'

'The phones. They don't work.'

'So you can't call my father?'

'That's right. He won't be happy when we miss our check-in, but he'll understand later. This blackout will make the news. If it lasts any longer, it might make international headlines.'

Rico didn't hear any of what the man said after, *"That's right."* The pain needling behind his eyeballs receded. Only temporarily, but it went away for long enough to clear his head. And that's when he recognised the opportunity. Possibly the last he'd ever have to disobey, to be reckless, to have *fun.*

Because in truth, this life was wearing on him. Pleasure meant nothing if you had too much of it. When he was younger he thought all the "money doesn't buy happiness" talk was bullshit. Never in his wildest dreams had he imag-

14

Rico Guzmán wasn't having a good time.

There were a number of reasons, and if he put some conscious thought into dissecting exactly why he felt so terrible, he might have had a touch more self-awareness. But conscious thought didn't get a vote. It was dark and chaotic and he felt like shit. He had a throbbing headache, and blotchy purple bruising had formed on his neck, and the overbearing sensation of disorientation had him in its grasp.

To make matters worse, he no longer had his Colt, and he definitely didn't have the trust of his bodyguards.

Which made him angry.

He stood out the front of Palantir, surrounded by the *sicarios*, who were doing a respectable job of pretending they were window dressing in suits and not trained stone-cold killers. Better for the general public to think they were some rich kid's unnecessary security rather than a cohort of assassins tasked with protecting the precious son of the esteemed Guzmán patriarch.

ined it might get old to drink and do drugs and have sex with beautiful women — but it could, and it had. Not old enough to stop doing it — its allure was undeniable — but something he couldn't put his finger on had been nagging at him for a long time, and now he understood what it was.

The chaos of life.

He'd never truly felt it. He'd caught snippets of it from time to time, but most of his raucous behaviour was carried out in a controlled environment. He was the golden child, after all, and his father understood that. There was a lot of leverage to be exploited if one of Guzmán's rivals kidnapped his son. So the *sicario*s and the bodyguards and the henchmen went with him everywhere, and they watched him drink and smoke and fuck his life away. It was odd to outsiders, but he'd become used to them always being there, always watching like hawks, always sober, never partaking.

So, really, the partying wasn't too crazy.

Because there was never the potential for anything *really* crazy to happen.

Like tonight.

Rico had received a taste of the chaos inside Palantir. Even though he'd been humiliated, stripped of his weapon and degraded in front of his own security, at least he'd felt alive in the process. Everyone thought he'd been skulking when he retreated to his booth after the bald guy had thrown him around like a puppet on strings. But really, he was savouring the adrenaline.

He was savouring the excitement.

So it clicked. He realised, *The power's out. We're uncontactable. When am I going to get an opportunity like this again?*

He eyed the *sicario*s.

They eyed him back.

He knew they knew.

But what were they going to do to stop him?

The eldest bodyguard said, 'Don't even think about it, kid.'

Rico was sick of it. All of it. Being told what to do, being told where to be, being told who to associate with. He might have listened to them if they'd been as loyal as puppy dogs. But they weren't. They'd let the stranger humiliate him, and backed down from a fight. So he had no reason to hang around in their miserable company. They could fend for themselves and deal with the consequences when they got back to Mexico and had to explain to his father why he wasn't with them.

He didn't hesitate any longer.

He ran off down the alley and disappeared into the darkness, the remnants of coke and weed and booze still in his system, making him ambivalent to the consequences.

He heard his father's men give chase, but he was genetically gifted with athleticism, and he used it.

He made it out into the busy street and vanished into the crowds of pedestrians.

Alone.

No supervision.

He audibly whooped with excitement. He couldn't remember the last time there'd been nobody keeping tabs on him. He looked up and around, saw all the towering skyscrapers draped in shadow, like obelisks in the night. He'd never seen New York like this.

He'd never seen anything like this.

Savouring the anonymity of the crowds, he remembered the bag inside his jacket pocket, forgotten amidst the turbulence of the last thirty minutes. He hadn't even thought about how he'd keep the party going, but now he gave thanks for it being there. Anything to delay the inevitable hangover. That'd ruin all the fun.

He took the small plastic ziplock bag out of his suit, opened it up, and dipped his pinky finger into the cocaine within. He was surrounded by people, but no one saw. Most of them had their phone flashlights firing, but the beams weren't directed at Rico. They were aimed at the sidewalks beneath them, or up toward the sky. Almost everyone was awestruck by the dormant skyscrapers.

So when he scooped out a fingertip's worth of the white powder and put it straight up his left nostril, no one batted an eyelid.

Even if they did see, no one would care.

Every socialite in New York City did coke. It wasn't a special sight, not compared to what was going on all around them.

It hit immediately. He widened his eyes and rubbed another fingertip's worth into his lower gums. He felt his heart beat harder in his chest, speeding up only slightly but *thudding* like it was turbocharged.

He smiled.

Life was good.

He was free.

He picked up speed, trying to find a quieter section of the city.

Looking for some trouble.

15

Slater stayed true to his word.

He bought two bottles of water from a street cart that had been hastily set up to accommodate the needs of the tens of thousands of people flowing out of buildings. The sidewalks were clogged with gesticulating civilians, and no one was getting anywhere in a hurry. Crowds had started to spill out into the roads themselves as everyone realised the gridlock traffic wasn't easing up. It left drivers and passengers trapped in their cars, surrounded by hordes of pedestrians darting left and right across the roads. And this was just the start. Slater knew almost every vehicle in the city would be abandoned within hours. The reality was, no one was getting anywhere in these sorts of conditions. There were no functioning street lights. There were probably thousands of people trapped in elevators, so emergency services wouldn't be focused on the roads.

No, for now, you could walk or you could sit in your vehicle with nowhere to go.

Already, people were locking up their cars and leaving them in the middle of the streets.

Slater sculled one bottle, sucking down twenty ounces of much-needed fluids, and then cracked open the second one. He dropped the first in a trash can and then broke into a jog, figuring his best bet was to sweat out some of the alcohol on the way back to the Upper East Side. It'd dehydrate him within minutes if he didn't replenish his fluids, but he planned to keep buying water bottles along the way until his head stopped swimming and his equilibrium returned.

He had a feeling he'd need it.

It wasn't comfortable, but nothing in his life was. He'd always favoured efficiency over comfort, and this was the shortest route to a clear head.

He kept running, trying to make sure no one panicked when they saw him blazing past. He worked his legs like pistons until he got his heart rate up to an appropriate level, and then he maintained that pace all the way from Midtown to the Upper East Side. Perspiration beaded on his forehead and soaked his undershirt. Instead of deterring him, it only motivated him to run faster. He kept pounding the pavement until he was drenched, and then he stumbled to a halt at an intersection packed with pedestrians and sucked down the second bottle of water.

He found another street cart, and bought another bottle.

Then it was back to the same head-throbbing, heart-pounding blur of motion. He was barely paying attention to street signs, or his surroundings. He knew by instinct where the Upper East Side lay, and he steered himself there using his subconscious alone. He needed to. He could barely think straight through the haze of booze. He had the uncanny ability to mask his inebriation, but he knew how he felt on the inside, and he was by no means ready for an intense debrief with King and Violetta.

When the demographic changed from excited civilians

of all socioeconomic backgrounds to frantic businessmen and women in suits and skirts and coats, he knew he'd made it to the Upper East Side.

He wondered what people made of him. He was dressed expensively in designer-wear, including a seven-thousand dollar leather jacket from Dolce & Gabbana, but he was coated in sweat and panting for breath with every step.

It helped that he was still feeling the effects of the booze. He didn't give a shit what people thought of him.

He didn't pay much attention to his surroundings. His mind was dull and unfocused, grappling with the change in circumstances. One moment he'd been dancing with a beautiful woman, planning a sleepless night with her at his penthouse, and the next he was running back home on foot, downing bottles of water, perspiring freely, trying his best to return to a coherent state so he could be of use to his country's government in a time of mass panic.

He drank down the entire third bottle, found his building's street, and jogged across the road, weaving between stationary cars. The Upper East Side was a more lavish area, but a blackout didn't discriminate. Streetlights and traffic lights weren't working here, either. Everyone was just as concerned as they were in Harlem.

Sure enough, his building was illuminated. There were only a smattering of windows glowing up the side of the eighty-storey structure. In normal circumstances, the lack of light would have made it seem desolate. Now, surrounded by total darkness, it was a beacon. A soft glow emanated through the floor-to-ceiling glass windows in the lobby, and Slater peered through to see a handful of the building's staff milling behind the reception desk, looking mighty uncomfortable.

They'd opted to use as few lights as possible. Slater

admired the decision. The less attention drawn to them, the better. The last thing they wanted was angry mobs outside the front door, demanding to be let in. As a result, the lobby had been plunged into shadow.

Slater pulled to a halt on the other side of the street and doubled over to catch his breath. He wanted to appear presentable, even though he was known to the staff. It would be just his luck to be turned away because he looked like a sweating madman. So he wiped the perspiration off his face with the shirt under his leather jacket before straightening up.

He stepped down off the sidewalk.

Something whistled past his ear from behind, fast and hard.

He flinched.

Half a second later the guttural *cough* of a suppressed gunshot spat from the lip of the alleyway behind him.

He heard it, and threw himself to the sidewalk with reckless abandon, nearly breaking his nose in his haste to flatten to the concrete.

Lucky he took such drastic measures.

More displaced air washed over him.

Thwack, thwack.

Once, twice.

He rolled, tumbling end over end like a man possessed until he reached the safety of a big metal dumpster overflowing with trash. He hurled himself behind it, sacrificing the skin on his hands for greater speed. When he leapt up into a crouch with his heart in his throat, he realised how disoriented he was. His vision tilted to the left as he righted himself. With one hand he seized the edge of the dumpster for support, and the other reached back for the Colt.

You drunk, he thought. *You fucking drunk. It's about time it got you killed. You deserve this.*

But there were no follow-up shots.

Just the pitter-patter of footsteps, receding into the distance.

His attacker, fleeing.

A throaty cackle rang out, eerie in the dark.

Slater froze in place. He didn't often hear laughter in the midst of a firefight.

And after the cackle, a high-pitched male voice.

'You did this!' it screamed, the words echoing off the dumpsters. 'You took everything from us, motherfucker! This is your fault! This—'

The man didn't finish the last sentence. He devolved into more raucous laughter, this time uncontrolled. Slater didn't move a muscle. He stayed right behind the dumpster. Mostly because the guy was already running away, and there was no point prolonging a firefight unnecessarily. But partly because of the volatility. The guy sounded certifiably insane. No matter how unskilled he might be combat-wise, you couldn't predict what a madman would do. There was a chance he was crazy enough to have no regard for his own life.

So Slater stayed put, and a shiver ran down his spine.

Because of the weird setting, and the total absence of streetlights, and the echo of laughter, and the absence of civilians on this particular stretch of sidewalk.

When the laughter faded into nothingness, Slater stood up.

You did this.

Dread enveloped him.

Tentatively, he raced across the street for his building's lobby.

16

Dark.

All dark.

King was inches away from the floor-to-ceiling windows of his penthouse. Eighty floors up, with an unparalleled view of Manhattan and Central Park.

It was like something out of a dystopian movie. He couldn't pinpoint exactly why it filled him with tension. In all likelihood, the government would mobilise its resources to fix the issue at the source, and power would be restored before the following evening. Sure, right now there was no running water, no phone coverage, no ability to communicate with anyone through anything other than the radio. But it'd all be okay in the morning.

Right?

'Right,' King muttered to himself.

He stood in the dark, too. There was a desk lamp switched on in the corner of the cavernous space, giving just enough illumination to see the silhouettes of his furniture, but it felt wrong to have the overhead lights on when the rest of the city had been plunged into the dark ages.

It certainly made things a touch more ominous.

Someone knocked at the front door.

King stopped twirling the satellite phone between his fingers. He eyed the big slab of oak at the end of the corridor, but he didn't immediately move to answer it. He found himself rooted to the spot, deep in thought. For the first time in a while, he didn't want to step out of his comfort zone. It'd either be Slater or Violetta. Neither option enticed excitement.

Ordinarily he was jumping at the bit for combat and pain and suffering and war, but now...

Now, it felt different.

Then the knocking became more urgent.

He shook himself out of his stupor, walked to the door, and opened it.

Slater was standing there, gun in hand. He was sweating freely, his shirt damp, practically soaked all the way through. His leather jacket had drops of perspiration on the sleeve. But he seemed alert enough. His bright green eyes were piercing and unwavering, as usual. King had seen them turn foggy in the midst of a binge drinking session, but that didn't seem to be the case now. He figured the man had sprinted all the way from Palantir to sweat out the booze.

Smart move.

King would have done the same.

They had a mutual inclination for the fastest solution to the problem, no matter how uncomfortable you had to get in the process.

King looked down at the Colt.

'Whose is that?' he said. 'That's not yours.'

'It's the kid's from Palantir. Why don't you have any lights on?'

'Doesn't feel right. What kid from Palantir?'

'The cartel kid. The one I told you about over the phone.'

King shook his head from side to side. 'Sorry. I'm out of it. Got a million things on my mind.'

'I'd have a million things on my mind too if ... you know.'

'You were sober?'

'I'm getting there.'

'You look like you've been for a swim.'

'I ran from—'

'I figured.'

'You going to let me in?'

'Right,' King said, shaking his head for the second time. An attempt to wrestle himself out of his stupor.

He stepped aside, and Slater strode past. Together they made their way into the living area. Slater placed the Colt on the arm of the Eames chair in the corner of the loft-style space and threw himself down into the chair itself. Then he touched two fingers to the damp shirt material under his jacket and said, 'You got a spare change of clothes?'

King nodded and went to the bedroom. He came back with a few garments he figured would lend themselves better to athletic endeavours. Dark combat khakis, a long-sleeved compression shirt and a pair of Gore-Tex boots. He threw them over, and Slater stripped down.

King wasn't fazed. They'd been side-by-side through some of the most hellish circumstances imaginable. They weren't exactly shy around each other.

As Slater changed, King surveyed the landscape. Nothing had changed. He checked his watch — it had been an hour since New York went dark. He grimaced and turned back to find Slater wearing his clothes like a glove. King was three inches taller, but they both shared the same physique. Athletic specimens, built like pro sprinters with more muscle. It took serious discipline to balance the raw power needed to manhandle people using their bare hands with the cardio necessary to run long distances if required. There was a calculated science to it, and they'd been training for both those eventualities most of their adult lives.

Slater moved to the kitchen, opened the fridge, and came out with a gallon jug half-filled with a pre-made concoction, bright blue in colour. It was a mixture of electrolytes, stimulants, and … a few ingredients usually off-limits to the general population.

You simply couldn't train like King and Slater without the aid of certain enhancements.

Right now, King could see Slater needed shaking out of his half-drunk, half-hungover state.

He downed half the contents of the jug, then put it back in the fridge and closed his eyes to compose himself.

King could see him feeling the effects of the stimulants almost immediately.

After this many years in the game, they'd nailed their nutrition and supplementation to a tee.

Slater crossed back to the armchair, dumped himself down in it, and let his stomach set to work digesting the cocktail he'd sucked down. King could see his belly distended from sculling so much water.

Then Slater said, 'Someone shot at me on the way here.'

17

Slater watched King's face.

The man said, 'What?'

'You heard me.'

'Where?'

'In the alleyway across from our building.'

'Who?'

'I don't know. He was in the shadows.'

'You didn't hunt him down?'

'He was insane.'

'Insane how?'

'Laughing. Cackling to himself. Probably just a junkie who got his hands on a firearm when the lights went out.'

'You don't really believe that, do you?'

'No,' Slater said, rubbing his brow. 'No, I don't.'

'Did he know you lived here?'

'How am I supposed to know that?'

'I mean, was he following you all the way here, or was he lying in wait?'

Slater shook his head. 'He wasn't following me. I ran all

the way here. Would have been pretty obvious if a junkie was on my heels the whole time.'

'So then he knows we're here.'

'It's one guy.'

'You wouldn't have brought it up if it didn't concern you.'

Slater kept rubbing his brow. Didn't immediately react. Then said, 'Yeah, I'm concerned.'

'Did he say anything?'

'He said we did this.'

'Did what?'

'I don't know.'

'The blackout?'

'I doubt it.'

'Like — we're responsible for it?'

'He was a junkie,' Slater said, trying to reassure himself more than King.

King said, 'A junkie who knew where you were. Who shot at you.'

Slater shivered involuntarily.

King paused, 'You okay?'

Slater looked up. 'You'd think I'd be numb to it by now, but I'm not.'

'Numb to what?'

'He got close to hitting me.'

'How close?'

'Inches.'

'Christ.'

'That rattles you. No matter how much experience you have.'

'I know.'

'You think he's going to be the only one to shoot at me tonight?'

'We don't know what this is yet. We don't know how long it's going to last.'

'What's your estimation?' Slater said.

King raised an eyebrow. 'What do you mean?'

'How long until this gets really bad?'

'Two days.'

'You think? That soon?'

'I don't know enough about it.'

'When are we going to find out more?'

King held up the phone in his palm.

'When this phone rings,' he said.

It rang.

Started shrilling in his hand like he'd planned it all along, and with an ominous scowl on his face he lifted it to his ear and swiped across the touchscreen.

Slater sat perfectly still and watched King's face. The man stared ahead, listening hard. He muttered a few agreements. Slater spent the time assessing his condition. His vision wasn't wobbling anymore. He wasn't detached. He could feel the dried beads of sweat on his forehead, the clamminess of his hands, the chill of the penthouse. When the space was brightly lit and filled with guests, it provided a level of comfort few apartments could match. It inspired awe. But here and now, drenched in shadow with its high ceiling and polished floor and the two of them alone in the cavernous space, it felt far too big.

Far too vulnerable.

King finished up the conversation and hung up.

He said, 'We can't stay here.'

'Why not?'

'She didn't go into detail.'

'Are we really going to get into this again?'

'What?'

'We had problems with that in Nepal. And before that, too. She's consistently sparse on the details and it drives me—'

'She's downstairs.'

Slater paused. 'Oh.'

'In the lobby.'

'Right.'

'She's going to give us all the details she has in person. She doesn't trust this line.'

'It's encrypted.'

'So was the power grid. It didn't stop them losing it.'

Slater didn't immediately respond. He processed it. Then he said, 'Are you serious?'

'Completely.'

'That's bad.'

'That's why we're needed.'

'You don't seem like you're losing your mind over it.'

'I'm trying to compartmentalise. You should too.'

Slater wiped his brow. Gnashed his teeth together, then reached out and gripped the edges of the armchair. Used them to haul himself to his feet, and then he started pacing back and forth in front of the windows, head bowed, mind racing.

King said, 'There's nothing we can change by worrying over this. All we can do is act.'

'I'm not a fucking robot,' Slater said. 'You tell me some rogue entity has seized control of the power grid and you expect me to just nod and ask what's expected of us next?'

'Yes,' King said. 'That's exactly what I expect you to do. I expect the same from myself. We're government operatives. This isn't play school.'

Slater knew the reason for his stress. It was the fading of the alcohol, the return of clarity, the sudden realisation that shit was about to hit the fan. Deep in his inebriation the whole blackout had seemed like a sick joke. Now it was real, and the consequences were prevalent.

He turned to King and said, 'Are you sure it's a cyberattack?'

'That's what she said. I expect we'll get more details when we're downstairs. We're wasting time.'

'Let's go then.'

They set off toward the door in unison, but halfway there the phone shrilled again.

King answered.

Slater watched his face fall.

18

As the phone rang, King read the contact name: VIOLETTA LAFLEUR.

She'd been straight to the point before, but that was nothing out of the ordinary when work was the subject of conversation. This was an ominous situation, but it was nothing that couldn't be resolved by level-headed thinking. His entire career had been a series of impossible tasks resolved time after time through concentrated effort. So he wasn't panicking yet.

Not until he picked up the phone and heard her rasping for breath.

Before he could speak, she panted, 'Get downstairs. And arm yourselves.'

His face fell.

He saw Slater notice.

He said, 'Are you in the building?'

'Yes. The lobby's been breached. The staff are dead. I'm taking cover, but there's—'

No time, King thought.

He said, 'Stairs?'

'Elevator.'

King turned to Slater and said, 'Elevator. Now.'

Slater didn't hesitate for a moment. He lurched forward, threw the front door open, raced out into the corridor and disappeared from sight.

Just before he vanished, King saw him reaching back for the Colt in his waistband.

King doubled back into the kitchen, yanked one of the drawers open in the kitchen island and came out with a Sig-Sauer P320. It was a weapon he'd become intimately familiar with during his time in Nepal, and after surviving against a horde of Maoist insurgents from the foothills using the very same handgun, he'd kept one in his kitchen as a backup plan in case his home was ever breached. Now he pivoted and raced to offer Slater backup, keeping the phone pressed to his ear the whole time.

'How many?' he said as he sprinted out the front door.

Violetta started to answer, but she was cut off by gunshots from her end of the line.

The call went dead.

Then more gunshots blared outside the apartment.

King tucked the phone away, lurched to a halt outside his penthouse and surveyed the scene.

He needn't have bothered with the backup.

Sometimes he forgot who Will Slater was.

There were four bodies against the far wall of the elevator, its metal walls now drenched in blood. They were all men, their faces masked by balaclavas and their torsos clad with body armour. They were dressed in casual-wear underneath the Kevlar vests — denim jeans, and button-up shirts rolled past their forearms. That way they could blend in as they approached the building on foot. More importantly, there were Heckler & Koch G36C compact assault rifles in their hands. None of them had the chance to fire a shot. Slater had been waiting there, zoned in like a madman, and he'd put a bullet in each of their skulls before the four of them could blink. He was standing over them now, panting with adrenaline, checking each corpse for signs of life.

His back was still turned to King.

King said, 'Are you hurt?'

'No.'

It was all that needed to be said. Neither of them were in the mood for prolonged conversation anymore. The stakes had become horrifically real. There were people coming to kill them. It wasn't a foreign sensation for either of them, but it never failed to put them in a savage mindset.

Because, at the end of the day, that's what they were.

Savages trying to stay alive in a brutal world.

King heard something. The clatter of a footstep, echoing off concrete walls. Coming from behind him.

The stairwell.

He called to Slater, 'Gun. Now.'

Slater understood. He darted into the elevator, picked up one of the G36C rifles, twisted and threw it underhand down the carpeted hallway. King tucked his Sig Sauer into his waistband and, a moment later, caught the rifle double-handed. He made sure the thirty-round magazine was locked and loaded and ready to go, then pivoted toward the stairwell and thundered a boot into the door frame.

Perfect timing.

He caught a man on the other side of the door as it swung into the stairwell, awkwardly pinning the assailant in place, halting his momentum. The guy shouldered it back in King's direction, but by then King had the advantage. He threw his full weight into the door and sent the man tumbling off his feet. Then he stepped into the narrow gap created in the doorway and brought the G36C up to his shoulder and seized hold of the foregrip and took careful aim and pulled the trigger.

Put three rounds into the guy's throat, because he was wearing the same Kevlar vest as his buddies in the elevator.

The rounds tore through his neck and killed him instantly, and the momentum sent him toppling back over the railing. He plummeted into darkness.

King swept the barrel over the rest of the spiralling stairwell and found three men racing up toward him. Two of them had already drawn a bead on him with HK rifles of their own.

Move.

King fell back, reacting in a split second, his brain firing on all cylinders. His reflexes barely saved him. Rounds tore up through the stairwell and shattered the plexiglass window of the door beside him. He landed on his rear in the corridor and vaulted backwards, using his own momentum to roll to his feet.

Behind him, he heard Slater snarl and charge forward.

Slater tore past him, dropped to one knee, leant round the corner, and unloaded the ammunition of another stolen G36C into the stairwell.

19

King probably thought Slater had elected to spray-and-pray, but he was far from the type to throw caution to the wind unless it was absolutely necessary.

He'd fetched one of the compact HK rifles off another body in the elevator, and as soon as he'd turned around to help, he'd seen King tumbling back out of the stairwell amidst a wave of gunfire.

So he'd sprinted forward, putting his own wellbeing aside to protect his closest friend. It was second nature for both of them. If they couldn't rely on each other in the pulse-pounding heat of war, they were as good as dead. He was now in the line of fire, as close to death as humanly possible. And some small part of him relished it. He was maximally alive, filling a doorway that could be riddled with bullets at any moment. Focus like this simply wasn't possible without external stimuli — in this case, a stairwell filled with armed hostiles looking to pump lead into him until he flatlined.

So he zoned in and aimed and fired. He took the utmost

care with his shot selection, even though a couple of bullets missed him by mere inches the moment he stepped into the doorway. He ignored them — they hadn't struck him, and therefore they didn't matter. Nothing mattered except—

Aim.

Fire.

He killed one man, then a second, then a third. Bodies collapsed against walls and blood flecked the concrete. The gunfire was deafening in the stairwell. Every unsuppressed shot sounded like a bomb going off. Slater temporarily lost his hearing, but he didn't need hearing.

Just sight.

A fourth man tried to leapfrog his buddy's corpse a couple of flights down. But he was jumpy and nervous and deafened, and he certainly hadn't been expecting a firefight in such a tight enclosed space. He'd seen his coworkers die, and if this was a mercenary force then the guns-for-hire had probably been working together for years. Even if you had no morals and sold your soul to the highest bidder, you still formed connections with your fellow brothers-in-arms.

Even the bad guys have attachments.

Slater knew that all too well. Which explained why the fourth man panicked and stumbled and tripped over his friend in his haste to get upstairs. He was probably angry, trying his hardest to get his hands on the men that had killed his friends.

He didn't get the chance.

Combat is a ruthless game.

When he tripped and fell forward and splayed across the cold stairs, Slater didn't show him mercy. Instead he shot the man through the top of his head with a single well-placed round from the G36C.

Not the movies, he thought.

No time to consider taking prisoners and debating what to do with them for hours on end.

No, this was the real world, and in the real world, you focus on just one thing when there's bullets coming at you.

Survival.

Four men dead. A fifth lay at his feet, shot by King before Slater had even got to the stairwell.

The coast was clear.

Slater moved like an automaton, going through the motions in the only way a man well-accustomed to putting his life on the line could. The usual reaction to getting shot at by automatic rifles and winning a close-quarters skirmish against nine men across an elevator and a stairwell would be to collapse in pure ecstasy, in disbelief that you'd survived. But Slater didn't do that. Instead he stepped back into the carpeted hallway and found King striding toward him with a collection of spare magazines for the G36C rifles.

King tossed three over, one by one, and tucked two of his own three into his waistband. Then he reloaded with the one in his palm.

Slater did the same.

They didn't say a word to each other. They slotted full magazines into their weapons and focused on bringing their heart rates down and waiting for their hearing to return. Both outcomes happened, one after the other. First the heart rate slowed, then the tinnitus faded. They looked at each other and nodded once, silently coming to an agreement.

The stairs.

Not the elevator.

They had more opportunities to survive if they took the manual way down. Sure, the elevator would be faster, but if there were more mercenaries waiting for them in the lobby, it would come down to fifty-fifty odds when the doors slid open. A Wild West gunfight. First to shoot, wins. They'd probably win, given their unnatural reflexes, so it wasn't exactly fifty-fifty, but if they had the ability to avoid such a tense showdown they might as well.

They wordlessly agreed on the best course of action, and set to work executing it. Slater turned and kicked the stairwell door open again and aimed his HK rifle down the three flights in his field of view. Then he whistled softly.

Clear.

King ran past.

Descended those three flights of stairs, keeping his rifle trained on the space in front of him the whole time, and then took up position at the edge of Slater's field of view.

King whistled softly, too.

Slater ran to King, then swept down three more flights as King stood still as a statue, ready to provide covering fire as soon as he was needed.

Six flights covered.

Seventy-four to go.

Utilising the same tactic, they crept down the skyscraper's core.

20

King had a premonition that he'd be the first to reach the ground floor.

He hadn't done the math — really, there was no way he would focus his attention on something so banal when there could be mercenaries swarming into view at any moment — but he had a gut feeling.

And he was right.

Violetta was here somewhere. The last thing he'd heard from her end of the line was gunshots. He hadn't been able to ascertain whether she was the instigator, or the one getting shot.

That's what made him slip up. He was desperate to know. He and Slater acted like automatons in combat, but the human brain is a fickle bitch. Even the most hardened soldiers are still human. He could be blessed with all the talent in the world, but he still had emotion. And emotion makes you dumb. Not that anyone observing might have known the difference. He was still moving like a freight train, his guard up, his rifle aimed at the dead space in front of him.

He stayed constantly in motion as he reached the bottom of the stairwell, creeping out into the lobby as he swept the barrel from one corner of the mammoth space to the other.

He noticed several things at once.

They all hit him, one after the other, like electric shocks to the brain.

First, the body.

He knew the night guard, Malcolm. The guy was close to fifty, with a wife and three kids in Brooklyn. Rapidly approaching the twilight years, but still in decent shape. He was ex-army, having served what he labelled a "long and unimpressive career" before being released into society to fend for himself. A security gig in a building like this paid handsomely, and he must have stood out from the pack somehow, so King had always doubted the man's career was as dull as he claimed. From what he could tell, Malcolm was a man with a tremendous work ethic and a firm moral compass, who stayed true to his word even if it made him uncomfortable. All the qualities King admired. He'd even invited the guy up to his penthouse for a few beers over dinner just a couple of months ago. They'd talked for hours, and King had managed to skirt around the finer details of his career the entire time. He recalled liking Malcolm. There weren't many security guards as self-disciplined and honourable as he was.

And now the man was dead. Lying facedown in a pool of his own blood on the marble floor of the lobby, maybe a dozen feet from the big reception desk. The light was still low in the lobby, accentuating the shadows, and the crimson had a surreal glint to it.

That's where the emotion came into play.

King registered the sight of the corpse, and realisation

rippled through him, and he hesitated for a fraction of a second.

Just long enough for the two remaining mercenaries to get the jump on him.

One of them materialised from behind a column, along with Violetta. The guy wasn't wearing a balaclava. He had sandy red hair and a hint of stubble and a pale freckled face. Irish, probably. He had a burly exposed forearm around Violetta's throat. It was rippling with muscle. Her long blond hair, ordinarily smooth as silk, was now slick with sweat. Her face showed fear, but her eyes were coolly detached. They glowed, blue and intense in the dark. The redhead had a gun pressed to her head, but she wasn't hyperventilating, or even panicking.

She was ready.

But King wasn't. Because the second merc stepped in from the left, emerging from the shadows, and trained his weapon on King from the side.

King froze in place. Just enough of his torso was exposed. He was half-in, half-out of the stairwell. He'd been capitalising on the momentum of descending eighty flights of stairs, and it had made him too hasty. That, coupled with the sight of a dead friend and the understanding that someone he loved deeply was being held hostage, had led to the tiniest fraction of a mistake.

In this game, that's all it took.

He had his own rifle aimed squarely between the redhead's eyes, but there was no doubt if anyone pulled the trigger they'd all wind up dead.

King didn't hear a thing behind him. He didn't know where Slater was. He didn't know if either of the mercenaries had even seen him.

The redhead said, 'Drop it.'

King said, 'No.'

'I'll shoot her.'

'I'll shoot you.'

Silence.

King said, 'You didn't come here to die. Let's compromise.'

'This bitch killed three of my friends,' the guy snarled. 'Cut them all down with a Glock before we could react. What is she — Special Forces or something? They were my buddies. I grew up with them.'

King nodded at Malcolm's body between them. 'He was my friend.'

'I didn't do that.'

'He's dead all the same.'

'We came for you. And the other guy. Where is he?'

'Behind you.'

The redhead didn't turn around. But King could almost see the hairs on the back of his neck bristle. The shadows sure didn't help. King imagined the cogs in his brain turning, running over and over again with hypotheticals. Like, *Could it be?*

And Violetta knew that was her cue.

She was five-eight, slim at the waist and curvaceous in the hips, with thin arms. Not the sort of physique you'd expect to be effective in combat, especially against a six-two angry Irish thug dressed in tactical gear with a loaded gun in his hand. But fighting isn't really about strength. It is in a cage, with a referee, which is why weight classes exist. But when Violetta threw her head back like it was a bowling ball and pulverised the mercenary's nose with the back of her skull, it came as no surprise to King that it worked flawlessly.

Because physics were the same no matter how big or small you were.

A nose is fragile, and a skull is hard.

The crack actually echoed through the lobby, as spacious and silent as it was. It was a brutal noise, bound to make almost anyone squeamish. In his peripheral vision, King noticed the merc to his left get distracted. Once again, only for a half-second, but it was enough. The man's gaze flitted sideways to determine the source of the broken bone. Was it his buddy in a pickle, or had the redhead simply decided to teach Violetta a lesson to speed up the proceedings?

He realised it was his buddy with a now-broken nose, and immediately jerked his gaze back in King's direction, because now the situation was serious. But suddenly there was someone behind King, filling up the rest of the doorway. An African-American man, materialising out of nowhere.

Three things happened at once.

First, Violetta deliberately jerked her head forward, in the opposite direction to her initial headbutt, and the momentum was enough for the redhead's aim to slip. Suddenly the barrel wasn't skewered into the side of her head, and when he pulled the trigger reflexively the bullet missed her head by a couple of inches, passing through the space between his chest and the back of her head.

Second, King shot the redhead in the face.

Third, Slater shot the other mercenary in the face.

Two bodies clattered to the floor with twin *thwacks*.

Violetta stepped away from the redhead's corpse and quietly dusted herself off.

She said, 'Thanks.'

King breathed a sigh of relief.

21

Slater eased himself out of the doorway and surveyed the lobby for the first time since it had been breached.

It was a mess. A disaster zone. The big slab of marble that constituted the reception desk was riddled with bullets and scorch marks. There was the body of the night guard in the middle of the space, and a dead woman in uniform behind the desk. Her face was pale and her eyes were glazed over. There were two bloody holes in the centre of her chest. Slater turned away from the macabre sight and took in the chipped columns, the overturned furniture, the soft wind trickling in through the space where the floor-to-ceiling windows used to be, the dead mercenaries scattered across the ground. The redhead hadn't been lying. Violetta had gunned down most of the backup on her own.

Without her, he and King mightn't have been so lucky.

She said, 'Are either of you hurt?'

'No,' he and King said in unison.

This time it was her turn to sigh with relief. 'Okay.'

She went quiet.

King said, 'Don't beat yourself up. You were outnumbered.'

'You're outnumbered every operation. You two still manage.'

'We're... a little different.'

'You think I can't take care of myself?'

Slater swept a hand across the space. 'You seemed to manage okay.'

'Not really. When you got here, I had a gun to my head.'

'Like I said,' King said, 'don't beat yourself up.'

'Hard not to. I'd be dead if you were a minute slower.'

'Probably not.'

She raised an eyebrow.

King said, 'He seemed intent on using you as a hostage. They were here for us. Not for you.'

'Oh, well, I feel miles better.'

'You're our handler. Not an operative. And you still killed three of them.'

'Yeah,' she mumbled, and turned to survey the scene.

It didn't seem real to her.

Slater said, 'Have you killed anyone before?'

King threw a quick glance in Slater's direction, and gave a subtle nod.

Then he raised his hand and drew it once across his throat. *Not now.*

Slater nodded back. *Understood.*

Violetta looked up and said, 'I'm not a spring chicken.'

'Let's not get into that,' King said.

'Probably a good idea. You two, come with me.'

'Where?'

'Away from here.'

Slater scanned the bodies, noting their body armour and the casual-wear underneath. This had been planned. A strategy had been formulated and executed by parties unknown. He and King were targets, just like they'd been targets many months ago in this very same building. They weren't nearly as beaten and battered as they had been at the end of that particular skirmish, but the same principle applied. Someone wanted them dead, and it coincided with a blackout.

Coincidence? he thought.

As Violetta fetched her Glock from behind one of the overturned chairs, Slater said, 'Is this about us?'

She checked the magazine was full, slammed it back home, then looked up. 'What?'

He jerked a thumb toward the street. 'Everything happening out there. Are we the reason?'

Violetta stared at him. 'Are you being serious?'

'The timing adds up.'

'If this was just about you two, you think they'd take out all of New York City?'

King stiffened. 'Is that what happened?'

'Didn't you know? Everyone got the same emergency alert. There's more than eight million people affected.'

'How?'

She looked at King. 'What do you mean?'

'The networks are down. How'd you get that alert out? I didn't even think about that.'

'We got it out before they went down. It was close. Whoever's behind this killed the cell towers half an hour after they killed the lights.'

'*Why* are the networks down?' King said, disgruntled. 'Aren't there backup generators in place to keep the cell towers operational? I thought all that was put into place after one of the hurricanes.'

'It's complicated,' she said. 'We don't entirely understand it. Right now, the phone companies can't communicate with critical cell towers. It's like they were targeted, too. Like this was one giant cluster bomb of disorientation designed to go off at once, to sow the seeds of panic.'

'What's happening here, Violetta?'

Silence.

King said, 'What *is* this?'

'Nothing good. I'm not about to brief you here. There could be more of them on the way.'

'Do you know why they're coming for us?'

'No.'

'Do you have an idea?'

'Maybe.'

'Are we testing your patience?'

'Yes.'

Slater said, 'Let's go, then.'

'Drop the rifles and get handguns,' she said. 'We need to move on foot. I don't want the pair of you causing a mass panic by openly wielding fully automatic assault rifles in plain view.'

'It's dark,' King said. 'We'll be discreet.'

She stared daggers at him.

He dropped the G36C.

'Understood,' he said. 'You're the boss.'

Slater didn't like it. 'Have you looked around? You think whoever wants us out of the equation is going to stop at one wave? Do you remember what happened before Nepal?'

'Yes,' she said. 'Please don't start this here, Will.'

'I—'

'You have a problem with authority. And you might have

a personal problem with me, too. You think I favour King because we're together. Right now, none of that matters. We only need to cover a few blocks, and I'm not about to have you parading through the streets with HK rifles. People are on edge enough as it is. And the streets are clogged. In those circumstances you're both a better shot with a handgun that with a rifle. Now pick up a pistol and follow me.'

Slater mulled it over, but by now he was almost completely sober, and common sense took over.

He said, 'Okay.'

Violetta blinked. 'Really?'

'What?'

'You're complying.'

'You don't think people can mature?'

'Maybe some people,' she said. 'You? Not so much.'

King half-smirked.

Slater gave him a death stare.

King wiped it off his face immediately.

'Where are we going?' King said.

'We have a temporary HQ, not far from here. A covert set-up in an empty office building. Fully discreet. No-one knows of its existence. The pair of you can treat it like a safe house until we get this sorted.'

'Was it created for a reason?'

'What do you mean?'

Slater said, 'He means — did you know this blackout was coming?'

'Not the blackout, specifically.'

'But you knew something was wrong.'

She looked at them both. The silence was ominous.

'Yes,' she said.

Then she put the hand holding the Glock inside her

coat, shielding it from view, and set off for the building's entrance.

As if on cue, the dim light in the lobby spluttered out.

In the darkness, King and Slater exchanged a look.

It said everything that needed to be said.

Then they followed.

22

Rico was halfway through a mugging when gunshots exploded into earshot, just down the street.

He nearly leapt out of his skin.

He'd stumbled all the way to the Upper East Side from Palantir, wired to the eyeballs from the cocaine, barely noticing the frantic crowds all around him. He thought he noticed passersby getting slightly more perturbed by the blackout, but he chalked it up to his adrenaline firing on all cylinders and forced it out of his mind. He couldn't care less if the whole goddamn city started freaking out. It didn't affect him one iota.

He'd spent a considerable amount of time searching for the perfect location to cause some trouble, and found it in a quiet street just off Second Avenue, home to a smattering of luxury residential buildings. It hadn't taken him long to find a target.

He'd cornered a couple in their sixties not long after arrival, shepherding them into the shadows with sharp jerky movements. They were old and unaccustomed to the harsher side of life, and they'd obeyed like sheep. She was in a fur coat and he was in a three-piece suit that barely hid his gut. Rico figured they'd been on the way home from the theatre or an expensive dinner when the lights went out. They were pathetic, in his opinion. Dinosaurs stuck in their ways, moving through life on autopilot. He hadn't even pretended to own a weapon. He'd just stuck his chest out and acted unhinged — which, frankly, didn't take much effort given the amount of substances in his system — and demanded their wallets.

They'd been in the process of handing them over, both of them on the verge of breakdowns, when the gunshots went off like fireworks in the distance.

Rico flinched so hard he gave himself a heart palpitation. He felt the organ lurch and jerk in his chest, which added to the sudden shock. He gave thanks that it was dark, and that the elderly couple didn't see him go pale. He touched a hand reflexively to the left side of his chest to make sure he wasn't about to have a heart attack, but everything returned to normal within seconds.

Recovered from the jarring sensation, he snatched the two wallets and shooed the couple away. They hurried off down the street, in the opposite direction to the gunshots. Rico thought he heard a sniffle from the wife, and maybe from the husband, too.

It put a smile on his face.

He tucked the wallets into his pockets without going through them. He had all the time in the world for that later. Right now, he was fixated on the firefight playing out a hundred yards down the street. Men with rifles flooded toward a building with floor-to-ceiling glass windows and shot them out, shattering the panes with deafening rounds. He couldn't make out their features. They were dark silhouettes against a dark backdrop, and they bled inside like creatures of the night.

Then something struck a dumpster a dozen feet to his left, and a moment later the muzzle flare emanated from within the lobby itself.

He'd been shot at.

Rico's heart spiked again.

This time, it palpitated longer.

Seized by sudden terror, he threw himself behind the dumpster, clutching his chest. Sweat broke out under the collar of his shirt, but he didn't notice. He was fixated on the space ahead, his eyes glazing over. Fear unlike anything he'd ever felt before struck him, turning him cold. His heart zigged and zagged in his chest. He gripped his pectoral muscle tighter. His eyes went wide.

Really? he thought. *This is where it all comes to an end?*

He thought his life flashing before his eyes was a cliché, but it happened.

Well, not all of it. Only some parts. Only the parts that mattered, the parts that had contributed to his current predicament.

Like every time he'd stumbled into a bathroom and snorted lines, or taken ecstasy and ignored the tightness in his chest. Each memory flashed across his vision in a rapid-fire montage, and he realised, *Yeah, I probably deserve this.* He'd been pretending the warning signs weren't there for far too long.

But it subsided. It took some time, and when his heartbeat finally returned to normal he became aware of other sensations. Like the sheet of perspiration he was coated in, and the clamminess of his hands, and the paralysing fear gripping him tight. Then, one by one, those sensations faded too, and he found himself seated behind the dumpster panting and fighting the urge to vomit.

No more, he told himself. *No more drugs. At least, not for a while.*

He realised he very well could have been sitting there for an hour. Pure fear is a fugue state. It feels like an eternity, and it also feels like the blink of an eye.

Fighting to keep all the alcohol down, Rico crawled on all fours out of cover, wondering if the gunshots had been some crazed hallucination induced by a vital organ on the verge of shutdown. But he stumbled his way to the mouth of the alley and saw the glass windows still shattered. He hadn't been dreaming it. But the street was silent. His ears weren't ringing, so perhaps the violence was over...

Then a couple more shots rang out, and Rico froze up. A few minutes later, a trio of individuals stepped out of the lobby and set off down the street. There was no artificial light whatsoever, and he could only make out their silhouettes, but something about the way one of them moved seemed familiar—

Then they were gone.

Rico stayed on all fours, barely moving a muscle. The sweat was drying on his skin, turning cold. His pulse was steady, but hard, thrumming in his neck and chest.

He tried to figure out what to do next.

Then a voice only inches behind him whispered, 'Hello.'

He jolted so hard he nearly induced another episode.

He turned to see a guy roughly his age staring at him, with a shaved head and wide, unblinking eyes. The kid looked like a skeleton. He was gaunt and his skull seemed hollow.

He was on his knees in the middle of the alleyway, watching Rico like a cat watches a bird.

The scene was indescribable.

Rico flapped his lips like a dying fish.

The walking skeleton said, 'I'm Samuel. What's your name?'

23

King stepped across the threshold before Slater, staying on Violetta's heels.

He didn't think of steering their conversation toward anything personal. They were an item, but whenever work interfered they tucked that side of their relationship firmly aside. No ifs, ands or buts. No exceptions. And this...

This was definitely work.

Shards of glass crunched underfoot as he stepped out onto the sidewalk. The giant window panes that had previously constituted the entire lobby wall facing the street were now shattered into thousands of pieces by the mercenaries' gunfire. King scanned the street, up and down, as soon as he was out in the open. There was no one in sight. Any pedestrians had promptly scattered. There was no pandemonium. Nothing close to what would have happened if the firefight played out on a normal Manhattan evening. These circumstances were different.

Maybe a few hysterical civilians who'd seen or heard the shootout unfold might have run off screaming bloody murder, but they would have quickly been swallowed by the general hysteria reigning across the city.

No, it was just quiet.

Violetta said, 'This way.'

She wasn't looking at them. Her eyes were everywhere at once, scanning every visible window and every dark shadow for signs of hostility. King did the same, and he knew behind him Slater would be following suit. He mirrored Violetta's stance, keeping his Sig Sauer P320 in his hand and readily accessible, hidden from civilian sight only by the fold of his leather jacket.

But there were no more reinforcements, and no reason to worry. It had been a once-off invasion, quashed as soon as it had begun. King didn't bother trying to figure out what that meant.

He knew almost nothing at this point, and speculation was just wasted time.

They moved in a tight unit, and they didn't speak. They covered the length of the street in the darkness. Better to keep things discreet. They reached the end of the street and merged into Second Avenue. It was like transitioning from a ghost town to a major city at peak hour. There were thousands and thousands of people crammed into the long avenue, flowing in several different directions at once, each in various stages of excitement. Some were giddy, some were scared, and some had no visible reaction to the blackout.

Almost everyone was looking up. That's where the awe lay.

King barely noticed. All his brainpower was consumed by risk assessment. He was scanning every face, searching for the slightest hint of hostile intention. He knew it was useless — if the mercenaries truly knew his position, they'd be watching him from one of the blacked-out windows. But it was impossible to follow anyone in a crowd like this, especially one so frantic.

They trekked south-west, toward Lenox Hill. King noticed someone by his side and looked over to see that Slater had caught up.

Above the incessant murmur of thousands of civilians, Slater said, 'No one's freaking out yet.'

'People are scared.'

'Scared. Not panicked. There's a big difference.'

'I know.'

'You said two days.'

'Yeah.'

'Are you sticking to that?'

'Yeah.'

'She won't tell us anything until we're secure, right?'

'Not yet. She takes protocol seriously.'

'It sounds like malicious code.'

'What?'

'Don't worry. I'm speculating.'

'You mean a deliberate attack on the power grid?'

'Yeah.'

'Aren't there systems in place to prevent that?'

'I don't know.'

'You seem to know what you're talking about. Could it be done?'

'We'll find out, won't we?' Slater said.

Together, they bored holes into Violetta's back. Desperate for answers. But she didn't turn around. She was in a hurry, laser-focused on the task at hand. She shouldered pedestrians aside as best she could in her haste to reach their destination. King and Slater almost had to strain themselves to keep up.

Then, all of a sudden, she veered off Second Avenue,

deep in Lenox Hill. They moved away from the crushing throng of pedestrians and found some space to breathe. King followed her carefully as they passed a couple of art galleries and an expensive hotel, all dark. Then they reached a walk-up residential building that seemed barely inhabited, even when the lights were usually on. It looked like tenement housing, with old brick walls and arched windows and dirty glass and a rusting metal fire escape trailing up the exterior.

There was a visible water tower on the roof.

King pointed up and it and said, 'Most residential buildings in New York have those, right?'

She followed his gaze and said, 'Most of them should. It used to be a requirement because of the water pressure you'd need to pump water up to the top. Why?'

'That's good, then,' he said. 'The taps might work for more than two days in those buildings.'

She didn't respond. Just thought about it, and nodded curtly.

Slater said, 'And then?'

'And then they'll go dry like the rest of them.'

Violetta didn't react. But the ramifications seemed to sink in, if only for a moment. She'd clearly been running all systems go ever since the power went out, including flirting with death in the lobby of King's building. Now, in a rare moment of quiet, with her adrenaline coming down, it seemed she had time to consider the consequences.

She reached out and placed a hand on his shoulder.

Then she looked from him, to Slater.

She said, 'We need the two of you now more than we ever have. This is going to be a disaster of historic proportions if we don't fix it.'

They nodded.

The gravity of the situation seemed to get heavier.

The atmosphere bristled.

She said, 'Follow me.'

Then she walked up the short flight of concrete steps to the tenement building's lobby and opened the door.

She ushered them into the dark.

24

Slater had no idea what to expect.

They crossed a rundown lobby, then went four floors up a chipped and cracked staircase in pitch darkness. He figured the building was uninhabited. Maybe cordoned off by the city for health and safety reasons, and then delayed back to market so the government could use it discreetly. They reached the fourth floor and came to a door with frosted glass at head height. By then, their eyes had adjusted to the dark.

Violetta reached out and knocked once.

The door flew open, and a gun barrel protruded from the shadows. It came inches away from touching her forehead. She was too close to get out of the way, but she didn't try to.

The voice on the other end of the firearm breathed out. 'Good. You're back.'

She turned and ushered Slater and King through the doorway. 'After you, gentlemen.'

Very professional.

Her demeanour entirely different.

Slater figured she was overcompensating to try and mask the fact that she and King were in a relationship.

Professional conflict of interest, and all that.

Slater went first, and found a middle-aged guy behind the gun barrel, with two guys behind him in turn. The three-man cohort seemed restless and thrown-off yet professional all at once. They wore navy blue suits with white shirts open at the collar. They were all Caucasian, and all of them had short hair, only a little longer than military buzz-cuts. Like they'd got out of the army several years ago but never lost the habit. They were built bigger than the average serviceman, with extra muscle sculpted out of additional downtime. They were all hard and mean under the surface, but their auras were accommodating enough. They still eyed Slater as he stepped in all the same. Subtle machismo. None of the three stepped aside to let him through, meaning he'd have to weave his way around them like he was in a maze.

He figured they were federal agents with egos.

He stopped dead in his tracks and stared right back at them.

King stepped through the doorway and did the same.

The guy with his firearm in his hand said, 'Are you the infamous duo?'

'Depends,' Slater said. 'Define "infamous."'

'The ones she hasn't been able to shut up about for the past few hours. Are you even military?'

Violetta said, 'Cool it,' from the landing.

Slater understood intimidation, and posturing, and peacocking. He could read the three of them like a book. They seemed fairly important, so they probably *were* feds, but they were disgruntled at having been called out to safeguard a place like this. Which meant they had probably been told very little.

So they didn't understand Violetta's importance, or what this temporary HQ even constituted, because it was well above their pay grade. And, as feds, there wasn't much above their pay grade in terms of counter-intelligence. So the world of black operations was a foreign one to them, which made them a last resort for Violetta. She must have known they were close by and leveraged her power to call them in as bodyguards.

They weren't used to being bodyguards.

And they wouldn't understand why King and Slater were even necessary.

So Slater put all that together and said, 'We might be the infamous duo. But you don't need to know anything about that. You weren't hired for that.'

They bristled.

Slater said, 'You're here to guard this door.'

More bristling.

King said, 'We wouldn't want to distract you from such an important task.'

Cold silence.

Slater slapped the lead man on the shoulder and said, 'Best of luck with it, boys. You've trained your whole lives for this.'

Then he went through the maze, working his way around them to get past, but he brushed them aside with just enough subdued aggression to let them know he wasn't a pushover. The third guy was both the biggest and the angriest, and he saw what was coming after Slater touched his two co-workers en route. So the guy stepped forward fast, trying to add a little *oomph* to the impact when their shoulders inevitably clashed.

But Slater changed direction in a split second and worked his way past the other side, missing the third guy entirely, which made him look like an idiot for having such a strong reaction.

He stood there, aware that he'd been humiliated but unsure exactly how.

King didn't meet any of the same resistance on the way down the corridor.

Slater turned at the end of the hallway and watched Violetta thread her way through the procession. On the way past, she stared at each of the feds in turn and rolled her eyes. Like, *Really, gentlemen?*

Slater masked a smirk.

'Where to?' he said to Violetta, which was another subtle dig at the feds.

Where are we going that they're not allowed?

Violetta pointed to a nondescript door at the very end of the hallway. It matched the rest of the building's interior. In poor condition, with sturdy foundations. Everything was chipped and cracked and faded and worn, but if you locked a door in this place, it would hold. Perfect for discreet operations.

Slater stepped up and knocked. There was a pause, and then the *thunk-thunk-thunk* of three bolts sliding across one by one, and then the door inched open a crack.

It was too dark inside for Slater to see anything.

He said, 'We're with her.'

He figured they'd get the message — whoever they were.

They did.

The door closed again, a chain came off, and then it opened just wide enough for Slater to squeeze his broad frame through. Keeping the inside of the room out of sight of the feds. Another precaution they'd be none too happy with. Slater stepped inside, turned to let King through, and then Violetta squeezed in last.

An Asian man wearing a T-shirt tucked into slacks closed the door behind them. Slater admired the back of the door — the bolts he'd heard turning were enormous. Shiny and thick and made of steel. The entire door frame was reinforced with some sort of impenetrable concrete that most definitely hadn't been there to start with. It was an impressive contraption, and it'd take a dump truck with a battering ram fixed to the front to get through.

Which meant what lay behind the door was important.

Slater turned to admire one of the first black-ops HQs he'd seen in the flesh.

25

Rico was already back to his usual, fun-loving self.

The strange thing was, he didn't much care about being shot at. Something about a potential heart attack was just viscerally terrifying, no matter how reckless you were. He'd *felt* his body collapsing from the inside, the primary organ simply ceasing to work. And then it was all back to normal, and relief flooded over him. Besides, there was still enough coke in his system to subdue the panic unless he was outright traumatised.

And he wasn't.

The pleasant haze settled back over him, and he almost didn't care that a gaunt wide-eyed guy had snuck up on him in the process.

He got to his feet, and the man who'd introduced himself as Samuel did the same.

Rico said, 'Hey. I'm Rico.'

'Nice to meet you,' the guy said, and gave a sinister smile.

Rico still wasn't sure if he was dreaming.

He said, 'What are you doing here?'

Samuel held up one hand, turning it to the faint moonlight. He had something in it.

A gun, Rico realised.

A 9mm Glock, by the looks of it.

Rico said, 'Where'd you get that?'

'It's mine,' Samuel said.

'Nice.'

'Have you seen two men?'

'I've seen a lot of men,' Rico said. 'You know how many people there are on the streets right now?'

'I'm looking for Jason King and Will Slater.'

'No idea who you're talking about.'

'Oh, well,' Samuel said, tutting to himself. His brow furrowed, and a frown appeared on his face. 'That's unfortunate.'

'What are you doing here?' Rico said again.

'Just having a good time,' Samuel said. 'It's fun with the lights out.'

'It is,' Rico said.

But the tendrils of sobriety were creeping into his consciousness. He didn't like that one bit. It made his current situation all the more harrowing. His skin salty, his heart racing, his mind hazy. Alone in the middle of Manhattan, without his usual safety net. No guards, no security. Probably in deep shit with his father. Standing opposite a lunatic who looked like something out of a horror movie, making strange conversation. He didn't want to think about any of that. He wanted to dull it.

He said, 'Samuel, you got any drink on you?'

Samuel smiled and extracted a flask from the pocket of his jeans. He opened it and took a long swig. At least two or three shots worth, if it was straight spirits.

He didn't blink once.

He said, 'It's whiskey. You want some?'

Rico said, 'Yes.'

He reached out and took the flask from Samuel, then put it to his lips and sucked down a giant mouthful. It was warm and he tasted caramel and vanilla. Maker's Mark, probably. He'd drunk himself into a stupor more times than he could count using every form of alcohol under the sun. He could pinpoint a brand when the taste seemed familiar. It was second nature by this point.

The effect hit him in seconds, although that probably meant it was placebo. Drink, and your brain convinces you you're drunk well before the stuff actually hits your system. But he didn't care what was real and what wasn't. It felt real to him, and he settled back into the same groggy stupor. The consequences of his actions receded from the forefront of his mind.

Good, he thought.

This is all still a dream.

Samuel said, 'I'm no longer needed.'

Rico said, 'What?'

'I was part of something. Now it's over. Now I don't have anything to do. I figured I might go kill somebody.'

This has to be a dream.

'Who?' Rico said.

Samuel shrugged. 'I thought I'd come here first, but I didn't find who I was looking for.'

'Jason King and... who was it that you said before?'

'Will Slater.'

'Who are they?'

'Enemies.'

'What do you mean?'

'I don't like them. They took everything from me.'

'What do they do?'

'I don't know. They're just bad people.'

'Did they hurt you?'

'In a roundabout way.'

'Do you know how to find them?'

'No.'

'Do you know what they look like?'

'No. I know they're big guys. That's it. It's frustrating. I shot at a big guy before. Someone at the end of an alleyway. I just ... wanted to shoot at someone. Anyone.'

'Who was he?'

'Someone. Anyone,' Samuel repeated. 'All I saw was that he was big. I could only see his silhouette. I thought it might be God delivering one of them to me. But I couldn't hit him. I tried to shoot him a few times, but then I couldn't see him anymore. So I ran away.'

Rico didn't say anything. There was nothing to say. The whole spiel was bizarre.

He stayed quiet and waited for Samuel to speak again.

'So, anyway, I'm pissed off,' Samuel said, 'and I want to do something about it. Who are you?'

'Just a visitor,' Rico said. 'Not in town for long. I was at Palantir — you know the club?'

Samuel shook his head.

Rico said, 'Bottom line is, I'm pissed off too. Some dickhead took my gun and slapped me around in front of all my friends. I have a reputation to uphold, you know? Piece of shit needs to get what's coming to him.'

'Did you get his name?'

'No.'

'Know where he is?'

'No.'

'Damn.' Samuel paused and turned his face to the night sky. The bone around his eyes was protruded, and the sockets were deep and hollow. The shadows plunged into them, lending him an even more macabre expression. Eerily, he looked back at Rico and said, 'You on drugs?'

'Yeah.'

'You got some?'

'Yeah.'

Rico reached into his jacket pocket and came out with the small baggie of cocaine. An involuntary shiver rippled through him. Something close to phantom pain gripped his chest. Not a heart attack, not a palpitation — just his brain delivering a warning. *Don't you dare.*

He handed it over. 'Here you go.'

Samuel took it and stared long and hard. 'You don't want it?'

'I've had plenty.'

'Thanks.'

Rico held up the flask. 'Mind if I take this, then?'

'Go ahead.'

They ingested their substance of choice in unison. Rico lifted the flask back to his lips and drained the whiskey. There was plenty of it, and his throat burned as he finished the last drop. He lowered the flask to see Samuel rubbing white powder into his huge gums. There was residue peppered across his left nostril from where he'd snorted some, too.

Rico smiled.

Samuel smiled back. His smile was a hundred times more sinister.

He stepped forward, wrapped a friendly arm around Rico's shoulders, and roared with manic laughter.

Then he said, 'Let's go kill somebody.'

Rico shrugged, deep in madness.

'Okay,' he said.

Why not?

With an arm looped over each other's shoulders like long lost brothers, they set off into the city.

26

King had to admit he was underwhelmed by the HQ.

But that was the nature of the twenty-first century, wasn't it?

Black operations were a different beast entirely. Separate from the official military structure, informal, without all the stringent rules and regulations and codes that dictated what could legally be accomplished. Today's warfare took place on screens, in algorithms and in lines of code. The world of combat and warfare was now a place where the most important individuals in uniform were the ones who weren't in uniform at all. They were the tech prodigies, dressed casually, responsible for keeping the peace from behind a desk. There were maybe a dozen of them here now, surrounded by enough hardware to destabilise emerging markets, if that's what was required.

King didn't pretend to know what he was looking at. He saw rows of desks set up in a space fashioned out of three tenement-style apartments laid end to end. The dividing walls had been knocked down long ago, creating a massive interior room with the same floor space as an empty church. The light was low, emanating only from the screens and a couple of weak desk lamps. Arched windows faced out, offering a plain view of the street below and the opposite apartment block. Inside the room, King saw stacks of CPUs and triple-monitor set-ups manned by an assortment of men and women that couldn't have had a median age far above thirty.

They were operating at warp speed. He didn't know whether they were hopped up on Adderall or other, more refined stimulants engineered by a separate wing of the government, but he certainly suspected they were. He'd never seen anyone work so fast. Not a single person looked at him or Slater as they stepped into the room. Their pupils flashed across the monitors like a bug watching flies. They tabbed from program to program, and when their fingers touched their keyboards intermittently they typed at a speed he could barely comprehend. There was the faintest murmuring between them when they opted to talk to each other, but it was interspersed with long periods of silence and intense focus.

King kept his voice low and said, 'This is the future, huh?'

'They're trying to figure out what's happening,' Violetta said. 'And doing anything they can to prevent it.'

King noticed Slater was equally slack-jawed, even though King was technologically challenged in comparison. Slater said, 'What are we even needed for these days?'

Violetta said, 'You'll see. Follow me.'

She led them to the very end of the room, where partitions squared off a space the size of a respectable corner office. She ushered them inside, where they found a plain desk and four dull office chairs. King took one on the left-hand side, and Slater took the other. Violetta sat across from them, and switched on a weak desk lamp.

King said, 'So you've got an emergency generator, too.'

'It's kind of necessary.'

'You knew this was coming.'

'Kind of.'

'How?'

Violetta sighed and interlocked her fingers on the surface of the desk. She said, 'Can I be honest with you?'

Slater said, 'We damn well expect you to be.'

She said, 'An incident of this magnitude has never happened before on this planet. Right now, every software engineer in the country employed by us, as well as a significant portion that aren't, are trying to work out our options. That includes the NSA, the DIA, feds, the CIA. All of the big ones, and a handful that don't officially exist, including us.'

'Okay,' King said.

'You don't seem very concerned.'

'Are we supposed to be?'

'I just need to hammer home—'

Slater said, 'You don't need to hammer anything home. We're not amateurs. Maybe something of this magnitude hasn't happened before, but it's all the same to us. Every time we're needed, our life is on the line. That's the greatest magnitude you can get. So don't beat around the bush and just tell it like it is, Violetta.'

She said, 'Okay. This is your official briefing.'

They nodded, one by one.

'Right now, we don't know who's behind this,' she said. 'We don't know what they want. We don't know who they are. They're hackers, and they're rogue. They're not affiliated with any terrorist organisation. They've used malicious code to seize control of every transformer in a number of critical substations. We only realised they were inside once they had complete control. That's what the computer worm was for. They hoodwinked the engineers at these substations into thinking everything was normal, and—'

Slater said, 'You mean like draping a veil over the whole thing? Putting up a façade?'

Violetta nodded.

She opened her mouth to continue, but Slater said, 'Are you getting at what I think you're getting at?'

She looked at him. 'Do you know about Iran?'

'Yes.'

'Then, yes,' she said. 'That's exactly what I'm getting at.'

'They did *that* to us?'

'It's not Iran who did it,' she said. 'They wouldn't know how.'

King held up a hand. They both stopped talking. He said, 'Could you enlighten the pre-schooler in the room, please? I know a lot of what happened in Iran, but I don't think I'm following what you two are talking about.'

Violetta said, 'The engineers sitting in the operations centres of our substations didn't see it. As far as they were concerned, everything was running smoothly. The way these systems *stay* running smoothly is to have the right balance between the supply and demand of electricity. If that balance is achieved, all is well. But it doesn't take much to tip the scales.'

'Surely there are safeguards against that,' King said. 'You're not seriously telling me that it was invisible until—'

'Yes,' Violetta said. 'That's exactly what I'm telling you.'

King looked across at Slater, but he didn't seem disbelieving. Far from it. He looked resigned, and beat down, and battered.

Before the operation had even begun.

Violetta said, 'That's what the code did. It got into the system, and then parts of it got right to work. Cloaking its very existence. Taking over the electronic readings, and spitting out false feedback. No one knew a thing until they had enough control to lock out the power companies.'

No one spoke.

Violetta said, 'And then they shut down all five boroughs of New York. With the snap of their fingers.'

King said, 'This is ridiculous. It sounds like the plot of a sci-fi movie. It's not that simple. I'm technologically challenged, but you can't be telling me malicious code can do all of that.'

'Of course it can,' Violetta said.

'How can you be so sure?'

Through clenched teeth, Slater muttered, 'The U.S. did it first.'

King looked over.

Didn't speak.

Violetta said, 'He's right. It can be done. We'd know.'

King stayed silent.

She said, 'We did it to Iran.'

27

The gravity of it all compounded Slater's headache.

Ever since Palantir had gone dark, he'd known about the possibilities of a hostile attack. They'd always been there, floating in the back of his head, whispering sweet nothings to him, trying to convince him that the world as he knew it could very well come crashing down around him. But he'd forced it aside until he met with Violetta, because there was no use fretting over something that might not be real.

But it was very real, and his worst suspicions were confirmed.

He envied King. The man hadn't put it together yet. He was one of the most intelligent people Slater had met, and he was in no way naive, so Slater didn't blame him or think he was an idiot. It seemed incomprehensible if you didn't know the finer details.

Slater, unfortunately, was wise to the finer details.

Across the table, he exchanged a solemn glance with Violetta. Their eyes met for an instant, but they communicated everything.

Who should be the one to tell him?

Slater nodded his head an inch in her direction.

You.

Violetta didn't react, but her eyes registered the passing of the torch.

King wasn't an idiot. He noticed.

He said, 'What?'

She sighed.

Slater said, 'You'll be able to explain it better than I will.'

'Tell me,' King said.

She said, 'In 2008 we attacked Iran's nuclear program. We worked with Israel to do it. We used malicious code as a digital weapon. It had never been done before on a scale like that. We pulled it off.'

King said, 'Pulled *what* off?'

'It was called Stuxnet. It was a computer worm. We unleashed it inside nuclear facilities in Iran. We shut down nearly a thousand centrifuges, and the engineers at the plants never knew it had happened until it was far too late. Stuxnet fed the engineers the wrong feedback. It showed everything in the green, when really we were eating away at the infrastructure from the inside. That's the simplest way I can put it.'

King didn't visibly react. Slater chewed his lower lip and waited for Violetta to continue.

She said, 'That's what happened to the power companies.'

'Which power companies?'

'Every single one of them that has a stake in the New York Metropolitan Area.'

'Why here?'

'We don't know.'

'What's their motive?'

'We don't know.'

A pause.

Then King breathed out and said, 'Holy shit.'

The stakes seemed to be dawning on him for the first time.

Slater sat back and waited for the inevitable follow-up.

King said, 'Why don't more people know about Stuxnet?'

Violetta said, 'It's out there. Books have been written about it. But no one cares, because no one in power will talk about it. Not us, and not Iran. Think about it. Why would we? And why would they? We don't want to publicise it any more than they do. It makes them look vulnerable, and it shows that we were willing to do something that hadn't ever been integrated with policy before. At least, not publicly.'

'Digital warfare?'

'Yes.'

King said, 'Okay. Work backwards, then. Who has the resources to do this?'

'That's the problem.'

'Sounds like there's a few problems.'

'We did some digging,' she said, 'and we realised that almost any rogue entity could have pulled this off. They just had to know where to aim.'

'You can't be serious.'

'Does this seem like the right atmosphere to start cracking jokes?'

Now, Slater sat forward.

He'd been listening without interjection, deep in his own head, piecing things together.

Now it all clicked.

'That's why they were able to do it,' he said, his jaw slack. 'Because of the power companies.'

'Yeah,' Violetta said.

King said, 'Explain.'

Slater hunched forward and stared at the floor. He waited until he'd formed a clear narrative instead of spewing word vomit. If self-discipline had taught him anything, first and foremost it had shown him the benefit of patience.

'Correct me if I'm wrong,' he said to Violetta, 'but the power industry isn't regulated by the government.'

She nodded.

He said, 'So that means it's cutthroat, suited for competition. And competition means moving fast. It means getting a leg up over the other guy. Which sometimes means being cheap.'

Another nod.

Slater said, 'So there's not really much of a barrier for entry, is there? If you were up to date on every scrap of groundbreaking technology, you could get past the old-school computer systems without much of an issue?'

A third nod.

Slater said, 'You'd just have to know where to aim, as you said. Which wouldn't be easy to figure out, but you *could* do it, if you were driven enough and had the resources.'

A final nod.

King said, 'It can't be that easy.'

'It is,' Violetta said. 'And they did it. And nobody realised it was possible until it was too late.'

King said, 'Look, I get it. It makes sense. It's a simple sequence of events. The power industry wants to be independent from the government. That lets them cut corners, because there's no oversight. They have terrible cybersecurity as a result. They pass it off as a non-issue, thinking no one would be smart enough to take advantage of the gaping holes in the system. And then it happens.'

Silence.

King said, 'That exact scenario happens over and over again. Look at history. Something is impossible until it happens.'

All quiet.

King said, 'I just can't believe we were so stupid.'

'We were,' Violetta said. 'And now we have forty-eight hours to get it back. Or all five boroughs are headed for disaster.'

Slater exchanged a wordless glance with his counterpart.

Two days.

Accurate, after all.

Slater said, 'What happens in two days?'

'Nothing good.'

'Lay it out for us.'

'It would take almost that long to give you a list of all the consequences,' she said. 'But I'm sure you can imagine how fast things will head south.'

'Have you started evacuating New York?' King said. 'If you know for a *fact* this is hostile.'

Violetta stared at him. 'Evacuate over eight million people?'

Silence.

She said, 'How?'

Silence.

She said, 'To where?'

Silence.

'There's no plan,' she said. 'Trust me, I've spoken to everyone who might know. Scale like this is unmanageable.

It might have been, if there were concrete plans in place, plans for this very scenario. There aren't.'

You could cut the tension in the air with a knife.

Neither Slater nor King felt the urge to speak. They were hypothesising, leaving the quiet to amplify and intensify until Violetta seemingly couldn't take it anymore. She sat forward, drawing closer to them, and said, 'We have leads. We have potential solutions. It's not the end of the world yet. But we need to move, and we need to move now.'

'Who's we?' King said.

'The pair of you.'

'I thought as much.'

She raised an eyebrow. 'What — you want me out there in the field with you?'

'You're more than capable of handling your own,' King said. 'You killed three men tonight.'

She didn't speak.

'Sorry,' King said.

She lifted her head, pulled her composure together, and said, 'That's the reality of this line of work. If I thought I was going to be shielded from the front lines I never would have signed up for the job.'

To take her mind off what she had done, King said, 'Can you give us a rough overview of what happens in two days?'

She brooded.

Chewed her lower lip.

Then said, 'Absolute chaos.'

28

Rico stared at a sea of abandoned vehicles.

There was no longer anyone in the city with enough patience to try and wait it out in their cars. The bumper-to-bumper traffic had ground to a standstill hours ago. Pedestrians thronged through the gaps between the dormant cars and trucks and taxis, having realised there was no risk of getting sandwiched between them. Manhattan's streets were now a stationary maze, easily navigable by foot but inconvenient for anyone looking to move fast.

The darkness didn't help.

Phone lights glowed like stark pinpoints across the cityscape. Rico knew he might have been imagining it, but the amount of lights seemed fewer and farther between than at the beginning of the blackout. Maybe people were realising this might last longer than they thought. It would be wise to conserve their batteries if there was no hope of charging them for the foreseeable future.

He stopped his thoughts dead in their tracks, aware that he was sobering up.

He didn't like that one bit.

Samuel said, 'What are you doing? Why are we stopping?'

Rico drifted his gaze over. His vision swam — the after-effect of the drugs — but he could see the wide-eyed kid beside him clearly.

He didn't like that either. Right now, numbness took precedence.

Then, like a holy sign from the gods, he looked in the other direction and saw a liquor store beside them. It was a cheap mom-and-pop operation, but that didn't matter. It had spirits in bottles in the windows, and that was currently his number one priority. There were no lights on, and the door appeared locked, but that had never stopped anyone who put their mind to it.

Rico said, 'I need a drink. Get your gun out.'

'Here?' Samuel said, looking around.

Now paranoid.

Rico lunged forward and seized him by the back of the neck. He pulled the kid in close and hissed, 'You getting cold feet?'

Samuel eyed him with the unhinged menace of a psycho. 'No.'

'Prove it.'

Samuel nodded. Still wired to the eyeballs. Not much time had passed. He took the Glock out of his waistband, pointed it square at the small glass window in the liquor store's door, and fired a shot.

The report exploded, unsuppressed, down the street.

A few people screamed. Most just scattered. Even though his senses were dulled, Rico could see the outlines of civilians fleeing like wraiths. If there'd been power, and lights, and order, and control, the gunshot might have been a bigger deal. But there were none of those things. Just the steady realisation settling over the city that perhaps this wasn't a temporary problem after all. Perhaps each and every resident of New York would soon be fending for themselves. Perhaps civilised society was hanging on by a thread.

Rico knew that concept would fill him with dread if he was sober.

He reached through the broken window frame, taking care not to cut his wrists on the jagged pieces of leftover glass, and turned the lock on the inside of the door. Then he pushed down on the handle and stepped inside.

Samuel followed.

His footsteps echoed. The atmosphere was muffled. Almost as dark as outside, but claustrophobic. Rows and rows of shelves, stocked with bottles of booze, barely illuminated by a mixture of moonlight and the haloes of phone flashlights filtering in from the street. The atmosphere was positively ethereal. Rico couldn't see much, but his new friend was armed, and that gave him all the confidence he needed. He sauntered deeper into the store and fetched a bottle of whiskey off the nearest shelf.

Rolled it over in his palm, scrutinising the label.

Then he nodded with satisfaction and turned back to see Samuel shivering.

In both fear and excitement.

His eyes were wider than ever.

Rico followed Samuel's gaze and found an old man at the other end of it. Hispanic, with brown weathered skin and almost no other discernible features. It was hard to make out much of what was happening in the lowlight, but Rico could see, plain as day, that the guy had a pump-action shotgun in his hands. He was aiming it at Samuel's belly. Samuel had his Glock pointed at the old man's head.

The shop owner, no doubt.

A standstill.

Samuel laughed, and the sound ricocheted off the walls.

No, not a laugh, Rico thought.

More of a cackle.

Suddenly Rico sensed the depravity of his new friend.

Samuel was genuinely enjoying this.

Rico's heart throbbed, three beats a second.

Samuel said, 'Put that down, buddy.'

The owner growled, 'Get out of my store.'

'We will. As soon as we're done getting what we need.'

'No. Get out now.'

Samuel feigned mock horror. 'But my friend here needs a *drink*.'

'Fuck your friend. Tell him to put that bottle down and get out.'

'Tell him yourself.'

'I'm not playing around,' the owner said. 'Out. Now.'

Samuel's right hand stayed rigid gripping the Glock, fixed in place. But his left started shaking. It trembled and the fingers jerked up and down like marionette strings. Rico noted it, and figured the kid was more unstable than he thought.

Samuel's eyes went wider than ever.

Samuel said, 'Do you know who I am?'

'No,' the old man said.

'Do you know what I'm capable of?'

The owner didn't respond. Clearly he'd reached the limits of his patience. He wasn't about to indulge in faux-gangster dialogue, and Rico started to sympathise. Irritation nagged at him, and he took a step forward to get closer to Samuel.

Under his breath, he muttered, 'Let's go, man. I've got what I need.'

'No,' the owner said, his voice terse. 'Put the bottle down.'

But Rico wasn't about to do that. He needed to avoid clear thoughts like an addict needed the hot spoon.

Samuel cocked his head to one side, his left hand still vibrating. Then, keeping his aim unmoving, he turned to look at Rico and said, 'Get a load of this motherfucker. He clearly doesn't know. But you know. You know...'

Rico didn't say anything.

Know what? he thought.

Samuel turned back to the shop owner and said, 'See how there's no lights? See how it's all dark? I did this. Me. I run this city, old man. I helped create this and if you think for one second I'm going to let you tell me what to—'

Then the shop owner did something incomprehensibly stupid.

Midway through Samuel's tirade, the old man lunged forward. Lowering his own shotgun. Stretching one hand out, fingers reaching, palm open. Trying to get a hold of Samuel's Glock.

Listening to the spiel, he must have figured the kid was deranged and opted to try and diffuse the tension by wrestling the gun away.

Bad move, Rico thought. *He's deranged, but he's not detached.*

The owner only made it halfway to the Glock before Samuel pulled the trigger and shot him in the chest.

It was hard to see where exactly the bullet impacted in the dark. The body fell face-first to the cold tiles and lay still. Rico didn't look down. He was no stranger to the thrill of doing things that were off-limits, but this was...

He couldn't put it into words.

It just felt wrong.

Samuel regarded the body, then motioned to the unopened bottle of whiskey. 'All yours now. Drink.'

Rico didn't need to be asked twice.

This isn't happening. This isn't real. Make it feel like an illusion.

He cracked the seal, twisted the top off, brought the open neck up to his lips and drank greedily. The liquid was warm, and it burned. It was beautiful. He knew that within minutes it would dull those pesky emotions — guilt and fear.

He lowered the bottle and noticed Samuel watching him silently. Like a hawk.

Rico shivered.

He felt the need to speak.

To say something.

Anything.

'That was bullshit, right?' he said. 'About the lights. About you being involved. You were just baiting him.'

Samuel laughed.

The same harsh, discordant cackle.

The kid said, 'Maybe you *don't* know...'

Then he turned and skipped merrily out of the liquor store, twirling his gun like a child's plaything as he went.

29

Violetta spent close to ten minutes laying it out.

Every piece of the snowball of panic that would accumulate as time ticked by.

It would start when bottled water became inaccessible and all the immediate supplies were looted from stores. Groceries and pharmacies would be desolate within a couple of days. No amount of emergency aid from other states would be able to replenish food and water supplies in time. Not for eight million people. When the water towers ran out, every tap in New York would be fundamentally useless. Maybe in the outer boroughs the residents might be able to maintain order for another day or two, but here in the heart of Manhattan it would be pure chaos. People would turn on each other when they realised they might very well starve or die of thirst if their circumstances didn't change soon. The smartphones that had become the lifeblood of civilisation over the last decade would all be dead, and even those who could keep theirs charged with back-up power banks would find them useless without a cell signal. Half the city wouldn't know what to do, and then survival instincts would kick in.

Whoever made the first move to attack and loot their neighbours would start a chain reaction that would spread like wildfire.

In the glum aftermath of her speech, King said, 'What emergency services are being mobilised? What scale are we talking?'

She said, 'That's not my focus. There's whole departments going haywire right now coordinating all of that. Every effort is being made to—'

'You don't have to talk to us like that,' Slater said.

She looked at him. 'Like what?'

'Like you're making a public service announcement.'

'I'm just saying that—'

'King is asking whether we were prepared to handle something like this.'

'Obviously there's—'

King said, 'Violetta.'

She stopped dead.

He said, 'Tell us the truth. It won't change anything. It's better if we know.'

She tapped the table with a single finger.

Over and over and over again.

Then she said, 'Okay. We're fucked. The main thing the government is focused on is bringing in back-up transformers in case this lasts longer than expected, which it very well could. But there's a thousand logistical problems with that — transformers are enormous, and they can't be transported easily, so it's a nightmare. No one — not me or any of my peers — expected something on this scale to happen. If it doesn't get fixed, the United States is wholly unprepared for the aftermath. Our best bet is flying in power trucks on

DOD planes so we can start replacing the lines, but that's a nightmare, too, as I'm sure you can imagine.'

Slater said, 'So this *needs* to be rectified before the forty-eight hour window is up.'

'Yes.'

'Or all of New York goes back to the Stone Age.'

'Yes.'

'And if New York goes back to the Stone Age, it'll be even harder to fix this with power trucks when it's every man and woman for themselves. The streets will be a wasteland within a week.'

'Yes.'

Slater didn't follow up.

There was no need.

The stakes were there, loud and clear.

Instead he said, 'I get it. You could go on all day about hypotheticals, and contingencies, and possibilities, but that's not what we're here for. We're here to fix it before any of that shit is even necessary. So let's start doing that.'

'That's why I collected you personally,' she said. 'Realistically you might be the last chance of stopping this. There's the digital way of shutting it down, which doesn't seem feasible. And then there's storming in there and demolishing it at the source. Doing things the old-fashioned way. And the pair of you might be the best on the planet at that.'

King managed a wry smile. 'The old guard still has some advantages.'

'But that's pointless,' Slater interjected. 'If we need to physically be there, what are the chances that—?'

She held up a hand, cutting him off.

He stopped.

She said, 'There's things you don't know. There's things I haven't told you.'

Slater's eyes widened. 'What do you have?'

'An address.'

'How'd you get it?'

'Do you think my guys are twiddling their thumbs out there? There's an inevitable trail of breadcrumbs in any cyberattack. Don't ask me to go into detail. It's as much of an impossible labyrinth to me as it is to you.'

'Where's the address?'

'In the Bowery.'

Neither of them said a word.

King said, 'Here.'

'Yes.'

'Why would they do that?' Slater said. 'Who on earth would set up their base of operations in the very same place they're instigating a blackout?'

'There's any number of explanations,' Violetta said. 'Most of them aren't good for us. The obvious reason is—'

'That it's a fake address,' King finished. 'A dummy lead. A dead end.'

'Right.'

'But if it's not.'

'On the off chance that it's not, I need elite level-headed operatives who can get in there and think on the fly. It's an old bank building in the Bowery. Probably fortified. Any guess what might happen if I amass half the NYPD and park them out front?'

'A standoff, probably.'

'Does it look like we have time for a standoff?'

'No,' King said. 'It sure doesn't.'

'Besides,' she said, 'every cop in the city has a hundred things on their plate right now. Hospitals, elevators, street presence — you name it.'

'Yeah,' Slater said. 'We figured that.'

'So we need you. I need you.'

'You, and who you represent, I'm sure,' Slater said.

'All the way to the very top,' she said. 'The order's been passed down. The pair of you have total flexibility and freedom. Any further questions?'

King said, 'No.'

Slater said, 'No.'

'Any flaws you can find in my reasoning as to why you're needed?'

Together, they said, 'No.'

'Then congratulations,' she said. 'You're on the clock.'

30

Rico and Samuel stood on 5th Avenue's sidewalk, at the precipice of Central Park.

The space was like the belly of the whale, dark and quiet and all-encompassing. Rico kept his ears tuned for the sounds of distress, but he heard nothing. There was the incessant hum of commotion behind them, and off to the sides.

But ahead … nothing at all.

The void.

People were avoiding the park, he knew. At least there was safety in numbers on the streets of Manhattan. In Central Park, fear of the unknown reigned supreme. It made sense to want to be surrounded by fellow city-dwellers in the same predicament. You could bounce worries and excitement and nervous energy off one another.

If you venture into the park, all goes quiet.

Rico might not have liked the quiet twenty minutes ago. It may have unnerved him.

Now, though…

Now he didn't care.

He was drunk.

He stumbled in a half-circle and saw Samuel locked in a staring contest with the void. The man's eyes were drab and soulless, but those features washed past Rico. Nothing affected him. He'd run away from the *sicarios* to look for something different, and Samuel was something *entirely* different.

Rico said, 'You want to go in there?'

He knew he was slurring.

Samuel looked over. 'Not really. I just like the quiet.'

'Do you?'

'Yeah.'

'Did you get much quiet? You know ... before all this?'

Samuel didn't blink. Stared daggers into Rico's soul. Said, 'Naw, man. No quiet at all.'

'Who are you?' Rico said, still slurring, still franker than usual. Alcohol helps you cut to the chase, after all. 'Before this. What did you do?'

Samuel said, 'For the last six weeks I've just been killin' people, man.'

'Who?'

'All types of people. Landlords, witnesses, people sniffin' around.'

'Why?'

'Got told to.'

'Who told you to?'

Samuel narrowed his gaze. 'You a cop?'

Rico laughed. Put his hands on his hips and shook his head in amazement. 'You serious?'

'I don't know, man. You might be.'

'I just watched you kill a guy. Don't you think I would have arrested you?'

'Maybe you believe me,' Samuel said. 'About playing a

part in this blackout. Maybe you're trying to get more out of me, man. Maybe you want me to keep talking, and then you're gonna swoop.'

Rico's head swam. He said, 'Want me to prove I'm not a cop? Is that what this is?'

The darkness seemed to pulsate around Samuel.

Too much to drink, Rico thought. *Too, too much.*

But he'd said it.

He'd pushed the metaphorical snowball down the hill.

And now it was picking up momentum.

An object in motion stays in motion.

Newton's first law.

Samuel's eyes lit up. He leered. Handed over the Glock. 'Yeah. I want you to prove it.'

'What do you want me to do?'

But they both knew. Under the surface of their conversation was the darkness. It was raw and untamed, and it hovered there, waiting for Rico to step down into it. All he needed to do was widen his gaze, begin looking for a victim...

Reluctantly, he looked away from Samuel. He didn't want to. But he was in too deep. He felt the cold grip of the pistol in his hand and slipped a finger inside the trigger guard. He spent a moment surveying the street, but the lack of light provided enough anonymity to commit any sort of crime he wanted. All he had to do was aim, fire, and run.

Into the park.

Samuel knew it too. He hadn't instructed Rico to do anything, but there was an unspoken agreement. An unbreakable allegiance, if they each killed someone.

Why are you doing this? Rico thought as he looked around.

His pulse rose again, putting more stress on his heart. By

now he could barely feel it beneath the veil of alcohol. He was numb to sensation and thought. Immediate consequences didn't exist.

He spotted a guy walking in their direction, head down, hands in coat pockets, headphones in. He was in his late thirties and seemed like he was doing well for himself. The coat was expensive and the shine of his shoes reflected in the dull moonlight. Rico understood his demeanour. He saw a guy trying his hardest to pretend the blackout wasn't happening. If he couldn't see the lack of light, then it wasn't there. He was probably the anxious type, unnerved by the change in routine, intent on making it home to the safety of his apartment where he could wait it out in the dark, alone but reassured.

Shame, Rico thought.

He raised the gun and pulled the trigger three times.

Hands came out of pockets, and the coat fell open, and the shoes caught on the sidewalk, and the man fell forward.

Hit the ground with the sort of *thunk* that can only come from a lifeless body.

Rico didn't see anything else.

He just ran.

High-tailed it into Central Park, letting the shadows swallow him up, breath rasping in his throat, heart pounding in his ears. He could hear Samuel's boots scuffing on the pavement behind him, hot on his heels. He wasn't sure how long he ran for, but when he staggered to a halt he'd worked up a thin coating of sweat over his face. He sat down hard on the kerb, even though he couldn't see a thing. Planted down on his rear and gripped his knees and sucked in giant lungfuls of air.

Samuel sat down alongside him, barely out of breath.

Rico let out a sharp exhale, but an involuntary sound

came out with it. It turned into a ragged sigh, which he certainly didn't intend.

It made him seem weak.

Samuel said, 'Have you done that before?'

'Killed someone?'

'Yeah.'

'Yeah, I've killed a few people back home.'

'Where's home?'

'Juárez.'

'You got a powerful daddy?'

'Yeah. How'd you know?'

'It adds up.'

'What about you?'

'My whole family was powerful. Like your daddy.'

'"*Was?*"'

Samuel let out a noise somewhere close to a growl. 'They ain't shit no more.'

'What happened?'

'Everything was taken from them. They got into a war with a pair of thugs. And those two thugs stripped them of everything.'

31

From the makeshift office, Violetta led King and Slater across the main space, past the rows and rows of desks manned by the same intensely focused workers.

King kept his mouth shut. He'd survived in his field for so long by figuring out early on that he wasn't the master of everything. In the earliest years of his career, he'd opted to go silent when he was out of his depth and absorb knowledge like a sponge. So he wasn't saying a great deal. But he sure was thinking it.

It was impossible not to. All the meditation in the world couldn't prevent his mind from racing. He'd never grappled with something so daunting. Dealing with the possibility of mass civilian casualties — like a bomb going off — was one thing, but at least that was instantaneous.

Bang.

Over.

This was a different beast. It would be a steady decline into madness. Maybe some of them would make it out of the boroughs before panic gripped them, but not everyone. Innocent lives would be lost at a staggering rate when the shit hit the fan.

And this address, if it was accurate, might spell the difference between the lights coming back on, or staying off for good.

That opened up another hundred questions, but he quashed them.

Now was not the time.

Violetta pulled to a halt in front of a V-shaped desk in the corner of the room, separated from the rest of the rows by at least a dozen feet of empty space. There was a guy in his forties sitting in a black office chair with an air of importance around him. His back was hunched as he faced his triple-monitor setup, but it didn't seem like his natural posture. More conducive to a man who'd given up on appearing professional in the midst of an unprecedented crisis.

King stood quietly behind him, and Slater pulled up alongside.

Violetta stepped forward and tapped a finger gently on the table.

'Alonzo,' she said.

He jolted in his seat and rotated. He was Hispanic, with a neatly trimmed goatee and thick curly hair falling forward over his forehead. He had thick bushy eyebrows and a face that might normally appear kind and patient. Now, it was wracked with stress. He had heavy bags under his eyes from lack of sleep.

He looked King in the eyes, then Slater, and said, 'You're the muscle?'

'Yeah,' Slater said, folding his arms over his chest.

Alonzo eyed Violetta. 'They're as good as you say?'

'They're the best we have.'

'They'll need to be.'

He ran both hands through his hair in distress.

Violetta said, 'Give them a rudimentary explanation of how you got the address, and what it means.'

'Right,' Alonzo said, processing the request with a couple of blinks. King instantly knew his type. Intensely straightforward, no excuses, no bullshit. Totally analytical. The best kind of intelligence operative. The man would tell it how it was. He wouldn't cut corners. He wouldn't add window dressing. And he wouldn't downplay something, no matter how disastrous it might sound.

King said, 'Just give it to us straight.'

Alonzo said, 'There's a very slim chance that the people responsible for this are operating out of an abandoned bank building in the Bowery. I only got the address three hours ago, but as far as I can tell it's legit. They sure as hell didn't want me to have it. It took some serious manipulation of the trail I had to work with.'

Slater said, 'You mean what they left behind when they seized control of the system?'

'Yes,' Alonzo said. 'Good. You've got the gist of it. No one can do something on this scale and be a ghost. But these hackers that we're dealing with ... they're seriously fucking good. As in, some of the best I've ever seen, and I've been at the cutting edge of this technology for the better part of twenty years. Nothing they did was off-the-charts impressive, but they executed every step flawlessly, and now we're shut out. There's nothing we can do to get control back. They did their recon, they found the flaws, and they exploited them. The fact of the matter is, it doesn't matter how good we are as government operatives. We're now working with old-school systems in an ageing industry, and that doesn't leave any room for us to be creative. These guys we're fighting are brilliant. But if they were that smart, then they probably knew they couldn't truly mask their location. Not with the sort of back doors we have available. So, what I'm saying is...'

'They probably know that we know,' King said.

'Yes,' Alonzo said. 'And I don't think it's a fake address. I can't see how they'd do that. Not the way I got it.'

'Could it be something you can't see?' Slater suggested.

'No,' Alonzo said. 'I'm the best, and I hire the best.'

Matter of fact.

Straight to the point.

No unnecessary detail that he and King wouldn't understand anyway.

King nodded, satisfied. He liked the man already.

Alonzo said, 'So here's what I'm getting at. I can't see any other solution to this clusterfuck of a situation other than to do things the old-fashioned way. I'm sure Violetta already laid that out.'

'She did,' King said.

'Well, I'm here to reinforce it. The two of you are going to have to go into the Bowery, get inside that building, and find whoever the brains behind the operation is. It's probably going to be a whole team of rogues. You can't let a single one of them escape. You're going to need to persuade them to hand over control of the substations. I'm not going to walk you step-by-step through how to do that. I'm sure you know.'

King's heart sank in his chest.

He tried not to show it, but Violetta noticed.

Probably because Slater was sporting the same signs of distress.

She said, 'What?'

'I figured we'd just need to smash up some hardware,' King said. 'You sure there's not another way around it?'

Alonzo said, 'If you destroy their computers, that doesn't achieve anything. They're still in the system. They're still the only ones with access. They need to manually hand it back over.'

'We're not going to be able to do that,' Slater said. 'I'm telling you now.'

'Why not?'

'Whoever did this knew exactly what they were doing,' King said. 'They had reasons for it. They knew their location would be compromised. They're willing to die for the cause. In comparison to everyone in this room, Slater and I don't know shit about technology. But we know people.'

Slater said, 'We could torture them to within an inch of their life and they wouldn't give up.'

Alonzo said, 'If you made it hell for them—'

'They'd break,' King said, 'but they wouldn't reverse it. They'd tap away at their keyboards and do something to stall. We wouldn't know what we were looking at. But they'd never hand it back over. Not while they're alive.'

Alonzo stared at them.

Didn't respond.

Violetta stared at them.

Didn't say a word.

Then Alonzo leant forward and said, 'I don't know how else to put this.'

They waited.

He said, 'You're going to have to. Or tens of thousands of people will be dead by the end of the week.'

Slater nodded.

King nodded, too.

Dread crept into the atmosphere.

Violetta said, 'Let's get you geared up, then.'

With his stomach twisted in a knot, King followed her and Slater through a doorway.

32

E*verything was taken from them.*

Rico said, 'What did your family do?'

Samuel said, 'Went out and got what they wanted. Didn't care what the law thought about it.'

'Mine does that, too.'

Samuel looked over. 'Maybe we're similar.'

'I don't think so.'

'Why's that?'

'You do important things, by the sounds of it. You know ... like, kill people. I don't get to do any of that shit.'

'You just did.'

'Not for my family.'

'You're not involved in their business?'

Rico scoffed. Reached up and wiped sweat off his forehead. 'Of course not. Why do you think I'm here?'

'Your English is good. You come to America often?'

'I had lessons when I was younger. But, yeah, I'm here quite a bit. Nothing else to do.'

'There's nothing to do back in Mexico?'

'My father doesn't tell me shit. I don't see him.'

'You want shit to do?'

'I'd *kill* people for him if that's what he wanted. Like you do. That's got to be the life. Out on the edge, walking the fine line. I love it.'

'Ain't feel like much of anything if we're being honest,' Samuel said.

His voice sounded hollow.

Like he was speaking into an abyss.

Rico said, 'I need a taste of it. I can't go anywhere in Mexico. I'm too *valuable.* Papá's rich and powerful, so I'm what his enemies would use for extortion. So, yeah, I'm in a nice house, with a few nice cars and some toys, but it don't mean shit. I can't do anything. I can't even party over there. The cartels attack each other in the clubs now. They're hyper-violent. There's no more unspoken agreements. Nowhere is safe. So I have to come here to party.'

'That's all you do over here?'

'Yeah.'

'Do you like it?'

'It's alright. It gets old, cause I can't help thinkin' about the future. My brother's eight years older. He's mature, apparently. Smarter, if you're all about booksmarts. He'll probably take over the cartel when Papá bites the bullet. And that leaves me with fuck all to do, you know? Got all I'd ever wanted, but at the same time it isn't worth a damn thing.'

'I wish I partied more, before...'

'Before the killing?'

Samuel lapsed into silence. Rico thought he heard a sharp, rattling inhale.

Like the kid was trying to keep his composure.

Samuel said, 'I was always fucked up. But they made me

do some bad things, man. Bad, bad things. Now I'm all the way fucked up. There's no going back.'

'Who made you? Your family?'

'What's left of them.'

Rico mulled over that, then said, 'The two men that ruined your family. They're the two you were searching for earlier?'

'Yeah.'

'What did they do?'

'We used to be feared. Used to own this city. Not anymore. All thanks to them.'

'Who's *we?*'

Samuel smirked. 'You've got a lotta questions. What's your name?'

'Rico Guzmán.'

'Guzmán.' Samuel rolled the name off his tongue. 'That must be a powerful name in Mexico.'

'It is.'

'I wish it were mine.'

'And I wish I was involved in family affairs like you seem to be. If only we could swap lives.'

'You don't want my life,' Samuel said. 'Not for a second.'

'And why's that?'

'Because we contributed to this,' Samuel said, waving his hand around in the darkness. 'And there ain't no happy ending to this.'

Rico stared.

Tried to look deep into Samuel's eyes to figure out if the kid was telling the truth, but there wasn't much to see. It was too dark, too obscure. On a whim, Rico lurched to his feet, but he'd forgotten how drunk he was. He staggered a few uncontrollable steps into the middle of the path, and laughed as he righted himself. Samuel laughed too.

Rico said, 'You got any of that coke left?'

'A bit.'

'Take it. Then come with me.'

Still seated, Samuel withdrew the baggie and snorted another hit. Rico didn't see it, but he figured it must have been a sizeable amount, because Samuel leapt to his feet like he'd been electrocuted. He let out a primitive roar. The deep bellow echoed through the park, reverberating through the quiet. Rico knew it might have been his imagination, but he thought he heard birds scatter, disturbed from their slumber.

'Let's go,' Rico said. 'Walk and talk.'

They set off south, aiming generally for the south-east corner of Central Park. From there he figured they could cut across the Upper East Side again, maybe prey on a few wealthy stragglers who hadn't made it back home to their cushy apartments yet. There was still opportunity rife for the taking. And then...

Where are you going? a voice in Rico's head whispered. *What's the final destination?*

How does this impulsive rampage end?

He didn't know. He didn't care.

There were no bodyguards to his left or right. No one responsible for his safety and wellbeing, besides himself. And that was all he really wanted.

He thought he heard Samuel skipping alongside.

'What are you doing?' Rico said.

'Having fun. You ain't never had fun before?'

'Not real fun. Not like before.'

'You like that feeling?' Samuel said. 'You like shooting a man dead?'

Rico thought he'd recoil at the reminder, but he didn't. In fact, he found himself strangely calm. 'Yeah. I like it a lot.'

'Then what are you doing as a slave to your father, boy?' Samuel said. 'Why you listening to him? Why don't you run out there into the big wide world? Build something on your own.'

'Is that what you're thinking of doing?'

'Nah,' Samuel said. 'My time's up.'

'Let's pretend you actually had something to do with this blackout,' Rico said. 'Humour me. Why'd you do it?'

'I didn't.'

'You just said—'

'Said I contributed,' Samuel sneered. 'You gotta listen better, Guzmán. I ain't the mastermind.'

'Who's the mastermind?'

'If I told you,' Samuel said with a psychotic glint in his eye, 'I'd have to kill you.'

Rico believed him.

His head still swimming, he clammed up and kept staggering toward the edge of the park.

Samuel skipped merrily beside him the whole way.

33

Slater followed King and Violetta into a drab hallway with paint peeling off the walls and cold leeching through gaps in the window frames.

He heard footsteps behind him, and spun to see Alonzo following in stride.

Violetta looked over her shoulder, too.

Slater said, 'Is he supposed to be here?'

She said, 'There's nothing we know that he doesn't.'

Slater nodded.

That was all he needed to hear.

Alonzo gave a knowing smirk.

Violetta brought them to a door at the end of the hallway and said, 'This is the armoury.'

Slater looked at her. 'After you.'

'You and Alonzo go ahead.'

Slater folded his arms over his chest and turned from Violetta to King. 'Thought you two were keeping your personal lives out of this.'

'We are.'

King said nothing.

Slater shrugged. 'Doesn't affect me either way.'

He opened the door and stepped through into another abandoned apartment. The interior had been entirely stripped away, leaving a notably sanded patch of floor where the kitchen island had previously resided, and a whole lot of threadbare carpet around it. The space smelled simultaneously of tenement housing and metal. The metal was thanks to a collection of gleaming racks that had been carted in when the black-ops crew had moved in. The racks were home to an assortment of firepower, ranging from assault rifles to shotguns to handguns, all sleek and matte black and state-of-the-art.

The government had spared no expense.

Slater recognised a collection of the same thin bullet-proof vests he and King had used in San Francisco to help prevent a massacre of epic proportions. They were U.S. Armour Enforcer 6000s, and could be disguised underneath casual clothing to allow the wearer to blend into ordinary civilian surroundings. That way, you didn't need to pad up like an armoured mercenary and draw the attention of everyone in sight as soon as you stepped out into bustling Manhattan. Not even the lowlight would mask the presence of body armour, so he gave thanks for her hindsight.

Wordlessly, he shed his leather jacket and peeled the compression shirt over his head. The lighting was weak in the room, but there was still a lamp glowing in the corner, and every scar on his exposed torso was visible. He'd almost forgotten Alonzo was in the room.

The man said, 'How long have you been doing this?'

Slater immediately knew what had led to the question. He glanced down at his hard-packed abdominals and noted the faint remnants of hundreds of nicks, cuts, scratches, wounds, and broken bones. All healed now, but they'd left behind a body sporting considerable wear and tear, despite his astonishing physical condition.

He said, 'Too long.'

'So you work directly for Violetta?'

Slater finally turned to face the man. Alonzo's face, surprisingly, was creased with a mixture of concern and genuine interest. Slater didn't quite know how to categorise the guy. Obviously intensely knowledgeable, probably a literal genius with technology, no doubt the best in his field. You *had* to be at this level of the game, to be allowed in the door.

Slater said, 'Sort of. I don't know how to describe it.'

'She's explained,' Alonzo said. 'But I didn't know whether she was feeding me bullshit or not.'

'What'd she tell you?'

'That you and King were the best solo operatives in government history, and that you both "retired" around the same time. She didn't elaborate, but I got the sense you stirred up some serious shit when you went out. Am I far off the mark?'

'Not very.'

'And now you're back doing this because you don't know what else to do.'

'Is that what she thinks?'

'It's what she said. But I don't know how truthful she is with me.'

'I know a million things I'd rather be doing than this.'

'Then why do it?'

Slater didn't answer directly. He said, 'Could ask you the same question.'

To make a point, Alonzo lifted his cashmere sweater up, exposing a pale hairy midriff complete with love handles and an absence of abrasions. 'You see many battle scars?'

'Not all scars are external.'

Alonzo dropped his shirt and stared at Slater in pensive silence.

The seconds ticked by.

But Slater didn't take the bait. Someone less patient might have jumped to fill the void, but he was comfortable in the quiet. He waited for Alonzo to process what he needed to.

Then the man said, 'You're a whole lot smarter than I thought you'd be.'

Slater shrugged. 'Same ball game. Different positions. You could make a fortune in the private sector with a whole lot less work, just like I could. There's no shortage of billionaires looking for bodyguards with impressive résumés, and there's no shortage of companies looking for tech wizards like yourself. Fortune 100s would be jumping at the bit to snatch you up. But you're here, probably overloaded with stress, sacrificing your mental health and your sanity for your country. Because you want to do the right thing, and you're talented, and you know you're talented, and you don't want those talents to go to waste. Same as me.'

Alonzo said, 'I've never met an operative who didn't think I was an out-of-shape pen-pusher.'

'Well, you've met one now.'

A pause.

Then Alonzo said, 'Maybe that's what makes you the best. You and King both. You don't judge anyone. So you're probably humble enough to be ruthless self-assessors, which allows you to improve on your flaws. I've met my fair share of SF guys and black-ops guys who were never able to evolve. Ego always gets in the way. It's the silent killer. You think you're top shit so you don't work hard to get better. Or you only focus on your strengths.'

Slater nodded. 'I'll be working hard to get better until the day I die.'

'As will I,' Alonzo said. 'Guess that's what makes us, us.'

Slater didn't respond.

Alonzo said, 'There's gossip about you two in our world, you know?'

'I figured there might be. Good or bad?'

'The word "luck" gets thrown around more often than not. Especially after some of the stories that circulate about what the two of you have accomplished. But now, meeting you, I don't think it's luck. I think you just ruthlessly prepare for everything, so you have very few weaknesses. I've always thought that of high performers. I guess I try to apply it to my skillset, too. It helps me stay ahead of the tech guys on the other side, trying to destroy what I'm tasked with protecting.'

'Thanks for the character analysis,' Slater said with a smirk.

Alonzo said, 'I'll leave you to it. Thanks for the chat.'

'Anything I need to know about the building?'

'I'll send schematics to your phone over the satellite network. Other than that, it's on you and King. I'm just as in the dark as you two are.'

Slater glanced outside. 'Quite literally.'

Alonzo turned to place a hand on the doorknob, and then hesitated. He turned back one last time.

'Give 'em hell,' he said. 'You might be our last shot.'

'Seems to always be that way,' Slater sighed.

Alonzo nodded solemnly, then slipped outside, leaving Slater alone with all the pressure in the world.

What's new? he thought.

He picked up one of the bulletproof vests and shrugged it over his frame.

34

King waited for the door to close behind Slater and Alonzo, then turned and pulled Violetta in close.

She mumbled, 'You said—'

He pressed his lips to hers, and all went still. The quiet of the hallway amplified by ten, so silent they were able to hear each other's breathing as they interlocked their mouths. When they parted, King kept his forehead resting against hers. She didn't move, or protest. He could tell she had her own eyes closed, too.

Finally, after what felt like years, he stepped back.

She said, 'Was that smart?'

'I needed it.'

'We agreed that no matter what—'

'If Slater and I fail,' King said, 'then a rogue band of terrorists packs up their gear and flees in separate directions, and we stay locked out of the grid for good. Which, as far as I can tell, is an absolute disaster in both the short and long term. Right?'

'Right.'

'Then excuse me for needing to alleviate a little pressure. Sometimes I need a shoulder to rest on.'

She reached out and took his hand. Gripped it tight. She said, 'You're going to be okay.'

'*I* might be,' he said. 'But it's a lot likelier that we survive, and still fail.'

'You're not going to let that happen.'

'No,' King said. 'I don't think I will.'

She looked at him. 'If you're saying what I think you're saying—'

'When's the last time there were stakes like this?' he said. 'This is monumental. That disaster with China, all those months ago ... at least it would have been a steady decline. This is going to escalate rapidly. It's going to be a nightmare. So if there's an opportunity to put myself in harm's way to stop this ... I'm not going to hesitate. I'm going to take it. You need to be okay with that.'

There were a million responses in her eyes, swirling there deep in the blue, but she didn't vocalise any of them. She just said, 'I've always understood that.'

'I know that's always been the case,' he said. 'But I think, this time, it's clearer than ever.'

She nodded.

'In the grand scheme of things,' he said, 'we don't mean much. Not in comparison to what'll happen if we fail.'

'So don't fail.'

'I don't plan on it.'

She jerked her head at the closed door. 'How is he?'

'Slater?'

'Yeah.'

'He's okay, all things considered.'

'Is he drunk?'

'He was.'

She sighed. 'Christ.'

'He's not anymore.'

'Oh, I'm sure.'

'Trust me,' King said. 'He's talented at drinking himself into a state, but he's just as talented at getting his head back in the game when he needs to.'

She stared at him hard. 'Tell me something.'

'Okay.'

'Be honest.'

'Sure.'

'Are you keeping something like that from me? I wouldn't judge you.'

'A drinking problem?'

'I know what you've seen and done, and I know what Slater's seen and done. I guess what he does to himself in his spare time is understandable. But you ... I don't know, I've never seen you get carried away. If you do, you don't need to hide it from me. I'm telling you — I'd be the first to understand.'

'I'm not hiding anything,' King said. 'If I succumbed to it, you'd be the first to know.'

She half-smiled, probably reflecting on their workload. With the amount of her life she dedicated to black-ops, and the amount he slaved away at conditioning himself into a human weapon, there was little downtime between their schedules. They spent most of it with each other. It'd be difficult to mask a crippling alcohol addiction within those hours.

She said, 'Have you ever wondered why he falls into it and you don't?'

'Sometimes,' he said. 'But I'm usually interrupted by training. Then I don't think about much at all.'

Another half-smile.

But it was hollow.

King glanced at the door. 'Did Alonzo want to speak with Slater?'

Violetta shrugged. 'If he did, it's between them.'

He stepped over to her, put a giant arm over her shoulders, and held her reassuringly. She looped her arms around his waist, resting them on his rigid abdominals, and kept them there.

Together, they waited in silence.

There was little to say.

It had all been said.

Five minutes later the door opened, and Alonzo stepped out. King tried to read his face, and came away perplexed. The tech genius sported an expression somewhere between pride and contentment, which didn't exactly gel with the circumstances. King said, 'What'd you two talk about?'

Alonzo glanced at him. 'Not a whole lot. Just trivial stuff. You take care of yourself, friend.'

He sounded like he truly meant it.

Then he was gone, making a beeline down the hall for his desk.

Violetta stepped away from King when Slater appeared, sporting a distinctly thick new layer underneath his compression shirt. King knew exactly what it was. In one hand Slater had two big duffel bags, and in the other, a second Enforcer vest. He passed it over, and King set to work putting it on.

'What's in the bags?' Violetta said.

'MP7A1 submachine guns with suppressors and extended mags.'

'You don't want long range?'

He gave her a withering look. 'It's Manhattan.'

'You're the expert.'

She looked up at King.

He nodded. 'It's the right call. It'll be close quarters.'

She checked her watch. 'You two need to get moving.'

'What time is it?'

'Nearly two a.m.'

King pinched his eyes. He'd stripped off his own shirt, exposing the same battered, hard-as-steel physique as Slater's, and now he dropped the vest over it. He was a little taller than his counterpart, a little wider, a little denser. Harder muscle, a bigger frame, more of a giant than Slater.

He knew it didn't matter.

The two times they'd succumbed to their base instincts and started brawling, Slater had come away the victor. That would always be in the back of King's head, and always gave him the burning, white-hot determination to train every single day.

A constant pursuit of betterment.

Slater passed over an olive Glock 22 and an appendix holster, and King fixed both to the underneath of his shirt. Drawing from an appendix holster was as natural as breathing to him, and he knew he could have the firearm in hand in less than a second. King noticed Slater had fixed his own holster to the outside of his compression shirt and draped his leather jacket over the top.

Violetta said, 'You have all you need?'

They both nodded.

Vests. Handguns. Submachine guns.

And their brains and fists.

All you could ever ask for.

'Let's go,' King said, opting not to waste another second.

The longer they stalled, the more time they had to think.

The more time to realise how much weight was on their shoulders.

As one, they moved for the exit.

35

Slater went first, storming straight past the feds.

None of the trio were pleased that neither Slater or King even glanced their way. It was intentional on Slater's part, subtle yet aggravating. They didn't feel important. They were being kept out of the loop. They thought they mattered in their usual roles, but now they were discovering just how out of their depth they were.

In a vain attempt to provoke, the ringleader said, 'Do you really think you're being slick with those vests?'

Slater stopped. 'What?'

'You both look ridiculous. Cover them up a little more, for God's sake.'

Slater knew the best treatment was dead silence, but Violetta didn't have quite as much patience. 'What the hell do you think you're doing speaking like that?'

The ringleader glanced her way. 'Ma'am, I was only—'

'You were only *nothing,*' she hissed.

King placed a hand on her shoulder. 'It's okay. Let them let it out. They're frustrated they've been relegated to door bitches.'

She glanced up at him. 'Oh. I see.'

Slater smirked. The interaction was so beautiful he almost thought it might have been rehearsed.

It shut the feds down in a way they never anticipated.

One of the guys opened his mouth to retort but Slater walked off, refusing to allow him the time of day. King followed right behind him, with Violetta on their heels, who shot daggers at the feds the whole time.

In the stairwell, they could speak freely.

Violetta said, 'I don't want to cloud your minds with details. But you should know that I'm in the process of coordinating with the NYPD to arrange a cordon around half the Bowery.'

'I thought—'

'It's going to be ragtag, but it's something, at least. If these hackers are half as talented at defending their turf as they are at using malicious code, then a few clusters of night-shift cops aren't going to achieve a damn thing if they try to storm the building. So, for now, a cordon. From what I'm told, the police are a nightmare to try and coordinate right now. A chunk of them aren't listening to orders because there's immediate problems right in front of them. People trapped in elevators, hospitals in chaos, countless injuries. You name it, they're trying to fix it. It's noble, but their best bet right now would be to prioritise this and get the lights back on.'

'Sounds like a logistical nightmare,' King said.

'It is. So I want the pair of you to treat this like you're the last resort. Because you most likely are. But on the off chance you can't trap them and they flee, we might have reinforcements in place to scoop up the stragglers.'

'No offence,' Slater said. 'But that was never going to reassure us.'

'I didn't expect it to,' she said. 'It sure as hell doesn't reassure me. I'm not responsible for the NYPD.'

'I can't blame them,' King said. 'I've been taking matters into my own hands my whole career. Hell, we did it in Nepal. They just want to help.'

Violetta said, 'I'll send an info dump to both your phones en route to the Bowery. Go on foot. It's the fastest way. It's gridlock out there.'

'We know.'

'Move fast. Breach the building, find whoever has the ability to reverse all of this, and make them do it. Seem simple enough?'

Slater didn't respond.

King didn't respond.

She said, 'You've pulled off harder tasks before.'

'You don't know that,' Slater said. 'Because you don't know how hard this is going to be.'

'Go,' she said. 'No wasted time.'

Slater shifted the weight of the duffel bag, feeling the reassuring bulk of the MP7 within. He noticed Violetta's eyes linger on King, and his on hers. He turned away. He could rib them all he wanted, but in the end it was extraneous. They cared deeply for each other, and he'd almost had the same thing with an operative named Ruby Nazarian.

She wasn't around to reassure him now.

He tightened his grip on the bag and reached for the lobby door. Bracing himself against the cold, the wind, and the dark.

Turned back. 'Ready?'

King nodded.

No words.

Just action.

He threw the door open, and they left Violetta behind in the lobby, striding fast for the Bowery.

36

'You got money, then?' Samuel said as they reached the Grand Army Plaza.

Ordinarily bathed in dull streetlight, even in the middle of the night, the plaza was now shrouded in shadow. Dark, empty and soulless. The Soldiers' and Sailors' Arch speared a hundred and thirty feet into the air, dwarfing everything in sight, but Rico saw it only as a mammoth silhouette against the night sky. He staggered underneath it, aiming for the intersection beyond, suddenly unnerved by the darkness behind him.

There wasn't a civilian in sight, and if there *was* anyone in the vicinity, they were keeping a low profile. Probably for the best, given the blackout did nothing but aid predators in places like this. Rico's mind wasn't on that. Anyone tried to approach and intimidate him, he'd fuck them up. He still had the reassuring weight of the Glock in his hand, but even if he didn't, he'd be oblivious to the short-term consequences.

The perks of overindulging in illicit substances.

Samuel said, 'Did you hear me?'

'What?'

'You got money?'

'Yeah, I got money.'

'That's nice.'

'Don't tell me you don't have money.'

'Nah. Never have, never will.'

'You were a powerful family. That sort of wealth doesn't just go away in a—'

'*I* wasn't *shit,*' Samuel hissed. 'I had the family name. But I was always the fucked-up one. Nobody said it to my face, but everyone knew. I was the outcast. The psycho. You'd think that'd drive me away from the rest of the family, but nah, they had their uses for me. That's the worst part, you know? They're the big bad gangsters, but I'm the troubled one cause I like killin'. I figured there shouldn't have been anything wrong with that. Not after what I knew about their businesses. But I ain't kept a part of their businesses. Not now, not ever. They come to me and say, "Hey, we need this guy killed," and I'd go right along and do it. And I wouldn't even get a "thank you." I was the puppy dog, you see. Do this, do that, you've got no conscience, you can get it done for us. I thought, when we all fell apart, that they'd just leave me alone. I thought, even if they came back and wanted me to do things for them, I'd be smart enough to say no. So I just started keepin' to myself and doing what I felt like doing, not what someone else is telling me to do. But I ain't ever been the smart one. They came back, just like I thought they would, and they convinced me, real easy. And it's not like anything changed. Still kept out of the business. Still kept away from the cash. Still the outcast. Still stigmatised. So I ran. That's why I'm here, Rico Guzmán. Cause I'm doin' something for myself for the first time. What do you think about that?'

It was a lot to process. A tirade of epic proportions, no doubt spurred on by Samuel's first encounter with a certain fine white powder. Rico strolled quietly beside the wide-eyed kid as he let out all his bitterness and hostility toward his family, and when Samuel was done Rico couldn't help but relate to parts of it.

He told Samuel that, in no uncertain terms.

'I've never been a killer,' Rico said. 'I'm the opposite. No one's ever trusted me enough to put a gun in my hand. I'm the young idiot. The liability. But my family treats me the same as yours does to you. I'm kept away from the secrets. I'm not told a thing. I want to be. Maybe ... maybe if I killed like you do ... maybe they'd take me seriously.'

Even in the dark, Rico saw Samuel's eyes light up.

'Fuck them,' Samuel snarled. 'Fuck your family. And fuck mine. But I sure do like this killin' talk. I done a lot of it these last six weeks. A whole lot of it. But never because I wanted to. I was only doing what I was told. But ... you want the truth?'

'Yeah,' Rico said, and took another gulp of whiskey from the flask he'd funnelled the remainder of the bottle into. 'Yeah, I want the goddamn truth.'

'I liked it a whole lot more when I watched you do it.'

'You mean — before?'

'Yeah,' Samuel said, a wide grin on his face. 'When you shot that guy. I could see it on your face. Plain as day. It's new to you. It's novel. It gives you an excitement I can't get.'

Rico smiled, too.

Maybe craziness was infectious after all.

They were still walking, powering down 59th Street in a blur. By now they were probably halfway across the Upper East Side. Somewhere in Lenox Hill, Rico figured. Now there were pedestrians all around them, congregating in groups for perceived safety, murmuring to one another. Neither Rico nor Samuel noticed them. They were a dark blur on a dark background.

Samuel suddenly seized Rico's wrist — the one with the Glock. He'd been carrying it in plain sight the whole way from Central Park, and no one had noticed. There were bigger things on their mind than the blurry outline of a handgun. No one had even been looking for it.

Samuel held it up in front of his face. 'Nothing stands out more than someone who doesn't give a fuck.'

Rico listened.

Drank in the words.

Bathed in them.

That's what he'd been missing the whole time. All the partying, all the drinking — it was the actions of a rebellious teenager. Sooner or later he had to do something to evolve. Something to set him apart from the young cartel playboys. Something he could take back to his father and boast about.

Samuel said, 'How about you do some serious killin'?'

Slowly, Rico nodded.

Samuel said, 'Who do you want to kill?'

Rico looked around up and down the street. They were at the corner of 59th and Third. The Ed Koch Queensboro Bridge was a few hundred feet to the east. The Upper East Side was north. South was Midtown and Lower Manhattan. All the possibilities in the world. A city of millions, their lives ripe for the taking. Who did he want to target first? Adrenaline rippled through him, stirring a vigour he hadn't truly felt before.

Then he saw two men crossing the street.

He first noticed the big duffel bags they were carrying — it was the first thing that set them apart from the rest of the swarming civilians. Next was their physiques — they were both enormous men, with broad shoulders and purposeful strides. That made them stand out in its own right. But the third thing was the most important.

Rico recognised one of them.

It was the bald guy from Palantir, the man who had stripped him of his weapon and humiliated him in front of everyone he knew.

Determination flooded him in a wave.

He seized Samuel by the shoulder and pointed a shaking, accusatory finger across the street.

'Look,' he hissed.

'I see them.'

'I know one of them. I fucking hate him.'

'What'd he do?'

'Messed with me. Nobody does that. Not anymore.'

Samuel leered. 'Good, kid. You're learning.'

'Let's fucking *get them.*'

Together, they took off in pursuit.

37

They walked fast.

And they walked hard.

Just how they approached everything in life.

They swept through Midtown, then Koreatown, increasing their stride as they warmed up, keeping their eyes peeled for any sign of trouble. But in circumstances like this it was impossible to keep track of everything. There were hordes of people out on the streets now, and for most of them the initial excitement of the blackout had worn off. King saw faces barely concealing panic — some were more contained than others, but there was a definite undercurrent of stress now. It might have thrown him off if he didn't have tunnel vision, focused entirely on the sidewalks ahead. He was scanning every face and discarding it — superficial emotions like fear and unease didn't stand out. Everyone was feeling the same, as far as he could tell. And he knew it would only get worse.

When the lights stayed out for good, what was considered "civilised" would descend into something savage real fast.

King had spent enough time around the savages of the world.

Halfway through Koreatown, he noticed Slater staring into a dark hole-in-the-wall bar as they strode past it.

King said, 'What is it?'

Slater shook his head in apparent disbelief. 'That's where I started my night.'

'Bet it feels like a year ago.'

'And at the same time, it feels like the night hasn't even started yet.'

King said, 'How do you want to play this?'

'No point speculating until we see the building in the flesh.'

'That's exactly what I was going to say.'

Slater glanced over. 'You know ... we work well together. Maybe we should have started this cooperation thing a lot sooner in our careers.'

'Maybe,' King said. 'Or maybe we get killed tonight and that statement seems dumb in hindsight.'

'Not if I can help it.'

They kept walking. A hundred feet, then another hundred, then another, and suddenly Koreatown morphed into the Flatiron District. The crowds fell away, and their absence created a grimy atmosphere. King looked around and realised it must have been a snowball effect. When the lights went out, people were unnerved, and their instincts must have kicked in. They'd congregated in the busiest sections of Manhattan, grateful for the supposed "safety in numbers," and as soon as the quieter parts of the city emptied out, the stragglers scattered like ghosts in the wind.

He figured everything south of the Flatiron District would be even more desolate.

At least the emptier streets allowed for better observation. King could scan every passerby in an instant, and it allowed his mind to quieten too. He didn't have to rapidly process a dozen people at once, looking for any sign of a threat. He spotted every silhouette well in advance and ticked them off the list.

It was halfway through the Flatiron District that he realised he hadn't been keeping track of his six.

But Slater beat him to it.

The man had already thrown several glances over his shoulder, and now he looked back and his gaze lingered. King noticed. He turned, too, and saw nothing but shadow. You could have all the surveillance training in the world, and darkness was still darkness. He couldn't see a thing.

But it seemed Slater could.

Still keeping stride, the man murmured, 'Go left. Now.'

'What?'

'*Left,*' Slater hissed.

He seized King by the crook of his elbow and veered him off Fifth Avenue. Out on the main avenues there was the faintest aura of light — a few shops had backup generators, and the outer halo of illumination gave them *something,* at least.

But in the alleyway they veered into, it was pitch black.

Slater pushed King a couple of feet into the mouth of the laneway, and then let go of his arm. Slater handed over his duffel bag containing the MP7, freeing both his own. King froze on the spot, two bags in his left hand, and waited.

In the quiet King reflexively lifted his shirt, seizing hold of the Glock with his right hand. The handgun was large for its positioning against his appendix, but he was a large man, so it worked. He felt the cold metal and strained his gaze.

Then two silhouettes hustled past the mouth of the alleyway.

He couldn't see much, but he didn't need to.

Slater stepped forward and seized the smaller of the pair from behind in a vicious single-arm chokehold. With expert dexterity he looped his bulky forearm around the silhouette's throat and yanked the guy backwards hard, almost taking him off his feet.

The second silhouette took off like a rocket.

One moment he was there, the next he was gone.

King burst off the mark to try and catch him, but it was futile. He'd already vanished. King snatched at thin air anyway, then stumbled to a halt in front of Slater and the man he had in a chokehold.

No, not a man.

A kid.

Probably nineteen or twenty — a pup in comparison to Slater — but even in the lowlight King could see the menace in the kid's eyes. He had long flowing black hair and an evil intensity about him. Veins protruded from his forehead — mostly because Slater was squeezing him half-unconscious — and his teeth were bared in a snarl.

Slater pressed his Glock to the kid's head and dragged him further into the alley, out of harm's way in case the second silhouette decided to take potshots at them from a secluded location.

King followed.

He heard Slater say, 'You just can't leave me the fuck alone, can you, Rico?'

38

Samuel ran for his life, panting, hyperventilating.

He'd never seen something unfold that fast before.

It had sent his adrenaline levels into the stratosphere.

He couldn't believe how quickly it had unfolded. One moment, he and Rico had been sneaking south through Manhattan, hot on the heels of the two men they were pursuing. Then the men were gone, and a few seconds later someone had reared up from the shadows like a pouncing lion and wrenched Rico nearly all the way off his feet. Samuel had his gun in hand, but he'd been spooked. His heart had skipped a beat in his chest, and his first instinct had been to *run.*

So now he was on the opposite sidewalk, maybe a hundred feet from the place Rico had been snatched. He got his wits about him and slowed to a jog, then finally a fast walk. Then he pivoted and worked on bringing his heart rate back down, breathing hard through his mouth.

Gotta go back.

You liked him. He was a friend.

Gotta help him.

But his legs stayed fixed to the ground, like his feet were cast in concrete. He couldn't figure out what had come over him. Nothing had frightened him like that before. It took a few ragged breaths, but eventually he gained some confidence back. He set off before it could dissipate, striding hard, his palm against the Glock slick with sweat. He made it back to the mouth of the alleyway, but Rico was gone, and so was his assailant. There were a few civilian stragglers, wandering aimlessly through the streets, and no one else.

Samuel put his hands on his hips.

He felt so alone.

So abandoned.

So empty.

He thought Rico had been a godsend. Something to keep his mind off the fallout with his family. Now, with the kid gone, Samuel couldn't hope to keep his sanity. He knew it. He shouldn't have done the coke offered to him, but peer pressure had got to him. He had enough of his marbles to know he wasn't all there mentally, which was a paradox, but it made sense to him. Drugs would just make him worse. More unstable. More prone to madness.

A voice whispered in his head.

Just end it.

He looked down at the Glock.

Considered it.

He had nothing left.

Then he heard movement. Quiet, and guarded, so he only caught it at the edge of his hearing, but it was movement all the same. It sounded like five or six people moving in a tight unit. Obviously with some sort of combat training, or Samuel would have heard them coming from a mile away. But now there were tears in his eyes, and his bottom lip had started quivering, and he truly didn't care who they were, or what they were here to do. In that moment he figured if they were going to kill him, then they could go right ahead and do it. He stared up Fifth Avenue and saw them materialise out of the gloom.

There were five of them. Big intimidating men in suits, coated in sweat from moving so fast, but they were still quiet as mice. They reached Samuel and converged around him, staring at him like he was an exhibit in a museum.

They noticed the Glock in his hand, and kept a cautious distance.

But they were armed too.

It didn't take Samuel long to realise there were five handguns pointed his way.

He'd be dead if he lifted a hand.

He briefly considered it. The equivalent of suicide by cop.

Same result either way.

Then he figured he might as well find out who they were, if this really was the end. He kept his voice low and said, 'What's going on?'

One of them said, 'We've been following you all the way from Midtown. Where the hell is he?'

'Who?'

'The guy you were with.'

'Rico?'

A couple of the suits breathed sighs of relief. Like the weight of the world had been lifted off their shoulders. The same guy said, 'Yes. Rico.'

'He was just here...'

'Where'd he go?'

Samuel pointed a shaking finger down the alleyway. 'Down there.'

'Did he run off?'

'No. He was taken.'

'Taken?'

'Someone grabbed him.'

'Where were you?'

'I ran.'

'Why were you with him?' the guy said incredulously. 'Who *are* you?'

'A nobody,' Samuel said. 'A piece of shit. A useless waste of space. That's who I am.'

No one answered that.

One of the suits said, 'Do you know who Rico is?'

'The son of someone important?' Samuel said.

A pause.

'Yeah,' the guy said. 'You could say that.'

'You're his bodyguards?' Samuel said as the veil finally cleared and realisation struck him.

'You could say that,' the guy repeated. 'We're a little more than bodyguards.'

'He ran off on you?'

'He sure did.'

'Where'd you see him?'

'Back there. You two were moving fast.'

'We were chasing someone.'

'Who?'

'Doesn't matter anymore. You going to get him back?'

'We'll try. Can you show us exactly where he went?'

Samuel nodded. Shouldered past them, out of the middle of the pack, and led them down the alleyway.

They followed, guns drawn.

Samuel's pulse rose once more.

He felt alive again.

He smiled.

This is fun.

The men behind him exuded the vibe of a pack of rabid animals. He could sense it below their demeanours, which they were still keeping cool and professional. Something brewed under there. *The cartels,* Samuel remembered. Maybe these were the famed *sicario*s that stabbed and shot and maimed their way through their boss's enemies. Set people alight, skinned them alive...

Maybe.

If so, Samuel was honoured to be in their company.

He led them toward where he thought Rico might be, and basked in their savagery.

39

Slater kept his arm so tight around Rico's throat that the kid wouldn't even try to escape.

If he squirmed, Slater would tighten the pressure. And then the squeeze would become unbearable, and Rico would either pass out from the restricted blood flow to his brain, or the sheer stress alone would get to him and he'd faint.

Slater dragged the kid further away from Fifth Avenue, prioritising secrecy. He noticed King following in stride, but didn't pay too much attention. They operated as one, and King would make sure to cover him in his moment of vulnerability. Slater made it to a narrow alcove between two buildings in the laneway and dragged Rico into it, plunging out of sight of anyone passing by.

King followed.

The alcove was small, barely wide enough to fit the three of them, surrounded on three sides by sheer brick wall. Slater noticed damp gravel underfoot and made a point not to shift his weight around too much.

He muttered, 'Rico, I'm going to release a bit of pressure

on your throat. If you even think about screaming for help, I'll break your nose. It won't feel good. That's going to be your only warning.'

The kid spluttered a frantic affirmation.

Message received.

Slater kept the chokehold in place, but eased off the boa-constrictor pressure. Rico tried his best to quietly gasp for air, but his throat rattled all the same. More for dramatic effect than anything else, King took out his Glock and pressed the barrel to the kid's head.

It might have the side effect of making the kid wet his pants, but it'd sure as hell get him talking.

Slater said, 'Why are you following us?'

'I'm drunk, man. I'm sorry.'

'Not good enough, Rico.'

'I swear. I was just going to shout at you. You know — hurl some obscenities your way. It was a stupid idea.'

'You armed?'

'No, man. Of course not.'

'Check him,' Slater said to King.

King patted the kid's expensive suit down and came away with nothing. He nodded a confirmation.

Slater said, 'Who was your friend?'

'Just a guy from the club.'

'If it was a guy from the club he wouldn't have stayed silent. He would have shit his pants. That guy *knew* to run.'

'I...'

Rico trailed off.

Slater said, 'You were coming after us, weren't you?'

'No, man, I swear—'

Slater didn't tighten his grip. He just leant in closer to Rico and said in his ear, 'I'm going to start hurting you if you don't tell me the truth. Is that what you want?'

Nothing over-the-top. Nothing extreme. A simple statement, with simple truth behind it. Often, it was all that was needed. Slater knew how to ramp up the intensity over time. A slow build instead of trying to induce all-out terror right from the start. But in this case, the steady increase in threats wasn't needed.

Rico broke instantly.

'Yeah, okay, okay,' he panted, on the verge of total panic. 'We were coming after you. It was stupid. I'm so sorry. Don't fucking hurt me, man. Please don't.'

'Who's the other guy?'

'Just some guy. Crazy. Like, he's not all there in the head. Thinks he's responsible for the blackout.'

Slater looked up at King.

Inconclusive, he thought.

But he'd been trained not to treat anything as coincidence.

'Who is he?' Slater demanded.

'His name's Samuel.'

'You got anything else on him?'

'No, man.' Then Rico's eyes lit up. Slater knew what the kid's demeanour meant. The spoiled cartel brat would have said anything to try and keep himself alive, but now he'd remembered something that might be genuinely useful. He was young, and terrible at keeping a poker face. So when he said, 'Actually, this might all be connected,' Slater believed him.

'How?'

'Are you Slater?' Rico said. 'Or King?'

Slater froze. 'What?'

King stared. 'Is that something to worry about?'

Slater looked up. 'He never heard my name from me. Or yours.'

'Oh, shit.'

'Samuel knows you,' Rico said. 'You screwed up his family or something. He's angry at you.'

Slater said, 'You'd better start going into detail or I'm going to—'

Then King cocked his head to one side. Slater almost didn't notice, but he caught it out of the corner of his eye. Like a sixth sense, he honed in on his counterpart with laser focus. 'What?'

King crept toward the edge of the alcove and leant around the corner.

Stared hard for a long beat.

Then he wrenched the olive Glock from his waistband and raised it to shoulder height and fired three shots down the alleyway outside. The gunshots blared, the muzzle flashes bright as day, the noise unrivalled. Rico flinched so hard in Slater's grip that it made Slater himself jolt in surprise.

A cacophony of return fire lit up the alleyway, and King ducked back behind the alcove wall as chunks of old brick shattered off the corner, torn loose by bullets.

King yelled, '*Take the kid and go!*'

'Where?'

'He's valuable! He has info! Get him out of here.'

King leant back out, only a few inches, as soon as he recognised a lapse in the gunfire. He squeezed off another few shots, taking careful aim and firing only when he had a precise target, and an ungodly yell rose up from a few dozen feet away. The yell morphed into a blood-curdling scream — whoever King had hit was mortally wounded, and would soon be dead. Slater had heard the same noises thousands of times before, and he was desensitised to them. But he didn't figure the hostiles would be — even if they were the *sicarios* from the club, as he damn well expected them to be, they wouldn't be used to hearing those sorts of sounds from their colleagues.

So Slater drew his own weapon, kept a tight hold around Rico's throat, and hauled him out of the alcove into open ground.

He took off for the other end of the alley, weaving left and right, as King laid down covering fire.

He made it all the way to the opposite street when air washed past him and—

Thwack.

Searing pain, white hot in intensity, above his left collar bone. The skin burned, and the nerve endings fired.

He'd been hit.

He snarled, lost his grip on Rico, and the kid slipped away.

Slater dove for him as more rounds traced past.

It was dark. It was murky. Pain stabbed at him, clouding his vision and his dexterity. He thought he made out the shape of Rico's silhouette nearby, but he couldn't be sure.

Desperation struck.

He raised his gun and fired.

Missed.

But the muzzle flash lit up the street, like a momentary strobe light, and he saw the kid racing away from him, headed south.

Toward the Bowery.

Slater shrugged.

He had to end up there anyway.

He took off in pursuit of the kid, the skin around his shoulder screaming for relief.

40

Taking fire from four hostiles at once, it took King longer than usual to realise he was still in possession of both duffel bags.

He ducked back behind the alcove as bullets tore past. There was nothing quite like the feeling of being shot at. You never quite adjusted to it. There was an uncanny detachment between the roar of the gunshots and the bone-breaking, flesh-tearing ferocity of the bullets themselves. They came in silent and unseen, and if one of them struck him in the head he knew he'd be dead before he even had the chance to register the report.

Impact.

Lights out.

Nothing.

It terrified him, but he used the fear as fuel. He crouched in the alcove and waited for a pause in the uproar. Seconds passed, and it didn't come. The four remaining hostiles were taking turns with their weapons, firing in a staccato rhythm, laying down suppressive fire of their own.

Suddenly he picked up movement right nearby. He steeled himself for a close-quarters gunfight...

...and found it immediately.

Someone bullrushed his position — from his perspective, all he saw was a big bulky silhouette tear around the corner, gun raised. He caught the slightest glimpse of a brown-skinned face twisted into a desperate grimace, but that was all he saw before he angled his Glock with trained patience and fired two shots through the underside of the guy's chin. The grimace disappeared, replaced by a dark cloud of blood, and the body toppled forward from its own momentum.

King sidestepped it, bounced off the adjacent brick wall, and came back to his original position.

Three to go.

It seemed a whole lot more manageable than five-on-one, but realistically nothing about his circumstances had changed. He was still trapped in the alcove with nowhere to go but out into the alley. He was sure there were three gun barrels trained on the open space a few feet ahead. He tried to listen out for any trace of Slater or Rico, but his hearing was too impaired for that. There was a shrill ringing in his ears — the high-pitched whine of tinnitus. And no wonder — before the gunfight, his surroundings had been as quiet as could be. Now there was war raging on the streets of Manhattan, and he was right in the heart of it.

Then a panicked voice — foreign to King — cried out, 'I saw Rico. He got free. He went right.'

The voice trembled and wavered with each syllable.

'You sure?' a deep voice responded. More measured. More composed.

'Yeah. He—'

Rapid footsteps — a cluster of them, moving fast. King

steeled himself for another Wild West-esque gunfight. *First to the draw.*

But it never came.

The footsteps headed in the other direction.

And he pieced it together, just like that. The wavering voice must be Samuel, Rico's mysterious friend. The *sicarios* weren't affiliated with the kid — they'd simply been using him to get hold of their treasured possession. But with Rico gone, and King a non-factor, they'd hightailed it out of there. Racing back in the other direction, figuring they could intercept Slater or Rico a block or two south.

Suddenly the alley was quiet.

King didn't hurry. Haste had led to the death of many men, so he employed as much patience as he could muster and waited for most of his hearing to return. He didn't even chance a look out. For all he knew, the wavering voice might have been a bluff. The last remaining hostile — Samuel, probably — might be standing two feet away from the alcove, gun trained on King's position.

So for good measure, he reached back and clasped one of the chunks of brick torn free from the wall.

He held it tight, then threw it like a fastball out of the alcove, where it practically exploded against the sturdier brick on the opposite wall.

Half a second later, he materialised in the open space.

Glock up.

Finger on the trigger.

There was a kid standing there. Maybe twenty or twenty-one, drenched in defeat, with a 9mm Glock in his hand and that hand in question pointed firmly at the alley floor. He showed no signs that he intended to use it. His shoulders were slumped and his stare was vacant.

Despite gaining the upper hand, King felt a cold chill work its way down his spine.

The kid was straight up menacing.

He had barely a shred of body fat on his frame, and little muscle either. He was tall and pale and skinny and gaunt, like a skeleton in human form. His eyes were set far back in his head, surrounded by shadow, giving his head a hollow appearance. They were some of the widest eyes King had ever seen. He wasn't blinking, but his eyelids twitched imperceptibly in the lowlight. King noticed every detail.

He kept his own firearm pointed squarely at the kid's head.

He said, 'Are you Samuel?'

'Yeah.'

'Put the gun down.'

Samuel let go of his grip on the Glock. It clattered to the concrete beneath his feet, louder than King anticipated. He almost jumped from the noise, but he controlled himself.

Samuel said, 'I ain't got nothin' left to live for. Shoot me.'

'Not just yet.'

King sensed Samuel studying him.

The kid finally said, 'Do I know you?'

'What's your last name, Samuel?'

'What's that matter?'

'Tell me, or I'll make it painful.'

'I wouldn't mind that.'

'You don't really mean that.'

'Try me.'

'Tell me your name, kid.'

A pause.

A long, drawn-out pause.

Then Samuel told him.

A knot formed in the pit of King's stomach.

The silence was suddenly daunting.

Suddenly cold.

Piece by piece, it started adding up.

'Samuel,' he said. 'My name's Jason King. Is there something you wanted to say to me?'

Samuel's face collapsed, and his eyes went wider.

41

Sometimes, Slater wondered if fate conspired against him.

Truthfully, he should have known what was coming. He and Rico had emerged on Second Avenue, and now they were sprinting through a sea of abandoned vehicles — Rico fleeing, Slater pursuing. He should have considered the fact that Second Avenue cut through the heart of the Bowery, and that the address Violetta had fast-tracked to him and King was positioned along this route. All he knew about it was a rough summary — an old abandoned bank building yet to be refurbished, resting on an ordinarily busy intersection. He figured it'd be a hulking slab of old-school New York architecture, and he figured it'd stand out from its surroundings.

But none of that played on his mind as he ran flat out after Rico Guzmán, his legs burning almost as bad as his collar bone. Blood had soaked through his compression shirt, and the wet material slapped against the wound with each step. All the sensation made him largely oblivious to where he was headed, and he didn't realise what was happening until it was too late.

Rico fled at breakneck speed, his long black hair bouncing up and down as he sprinted. He was covering ground faster than Slater, taking advantage of his youth, his weight, and his desperation. In comparison to the smattering of surrounding civilians, he stood out. He probably had a savage intensity in his eyes, which wouldn't have helped his case. But he threaded through the cars and trucks and vans and burst up onto the sidewalk and pushed himself even faster.

Straight toward a huge looming building across the intersection.

Really, he didn't know what it was. Slater recognised that. The kid had an evil streak, no doubt, but he wasn't wrapped up in a greater conspiracy. He was a hotheaded, volatile little shit with a rich powerful dad and a slew of bodyguards. He had nothing to do with the blackout. The building wasn't even his destination.

But he's sprinting in its direction.

And, if the intel is correct, the residents are prepared to wage war to defend their turf.

Slater opened his mouth to shout a warning.

Before any sound left his mouth, Rico's head exploded.

The long black hair blew apart in all directions and gore showered the sidewalk. A moment later the concussive *boom* of a sniper rifle's report resonated through the Bowery. Impossibly loud. A .50 cal round, without a doubt. Civilians screamed all around Slater, but he barely noticed. As soon as he saw the kid die he hit the deck, lurching forward and diving for cover between two parked sedans. Milliseconds later a round blew past the air he'd been occupying. He knew it was the same calibre, fired from the same long-range sniper rifle, because it felt like a truck had missed him by inches. He knew that amount of displaced air could only emanate from a *huge* goddamn bullet.

And then it impacted a van several dozen feet behind him.

With the force of a bomb going off.

He rolled underneath the nearest sedan, clawing his way to cover. He tore the skin off his hands in his haste, but he barely felt it. He had tunnel vision and unparalleled focus. The cool metal of the sedan's undercarriage pressed hard into his upper back, but he didn't feel a shred of claustrophobia. Being skewered under a stationary vehicle was infinitely more desirable than being out in the open, vulnerable to a .50 cal bullet blowing his bones and muscles and organs apart like they were nothing.

Boom.

The vehicle above him reverberated.

Struck by a round.

Then something flashed beside him. It took him about half a second to recognise it was another bullet, smaller than the first, fired from a different angle. It had sparked off the asphalt and ricocheted into the undercarriage of the sedan.

Oh, fuck.

It had missed him by less than a foot.

Someone could see him from a neighbouring building, and was honing their aim.

He burst into motion, kicking and clawing and scratching for the left-hand side of the car. As he moved he was keenly aware of his lack of recon. He hadn't even managed a decent look at the bank building in question before everything had gone to hell. So he was blind, in the dark literally and metaphorically, focused on sheer survival. He couldn't believe his bad luck.

He made it out from underneath the sedan and leapt into a low crouch. He caught a glimpse of the looming building across the intersection, but all he could make out were multiple rows of dozens of windows framed by granite façades. To make matters worse, King still had both submachine guns. They'd take Slater's head off before he could even attempt to return fire with his Glock, and that didn't even take the second shooter into consideration.

For all he knew, there could be five shooters with their sights trained on him.

Retreat.

His brain spoke the command, and his body answered. He ran flat out through the maze of cars, weaving left and right like an NFL linebacker, anticipating a gunshot at any moment. Spending most of his adult life in combat had helped develop his sixth sense, and he used it now to throw himself down at *just* the right moment. He figured a shot would follow soon after, and—

Two separate rounds impacted the vehicles around him.

One louder than the other.

.50 calibre, versus a standard round.

Dead ahead, resting diagonally across the intersection from the old bank building, was a residential apartment complex. It was a chic establishment, new and stylish, with lots of glass and lots of new brick carefully curated to seem rustic and faded. It was huge, too — he figured there must be at least two hundred apartments within. Not one of them was glowing with artificial light. In his peripheral vision he spotted faint candlelight in some of the windows, but overall the building was just as invisible as the rest of Manhattan.

Most importantly, it had a manual revolving door set beside the electronic doors.

Slater couldn't see a thing inside the lobby.

It was as close to a safe haven as he was going to get.

He made a beeline for it, keeping as low as possible, moving as fast as possible.

Another enormous *bang* sounded across the street, but he didn't feel any displaced air, and all his limbs stayed intact.

So the bullet had gone wide.

Heart in his throat, he sprinted over the sidewalk and leapt into the open partition of the revolving door.

Momentary terror seized him. *What if it's locked in place?*

If the doors didn't move against his resistance, he'd be trapped in a glass box.

A sitting duck to a trained marksman.

He threw his weight into the sturdy glass, hoping, praying, silently pleading.

It rotated instantly.

He pushed it harder until it was spinning faster than it was designed to, which got him to the other side in a couple of seconds maximum.

He dived into the empty lobby and threw himself to the cold tiles on his belly.

The momentum carried him, and he slid a dozen feet into the space. One of the glass panes in the revolving door shattered behind him, accompanied by the distant reverberation of another report. Slater's blood ran cold as he slid, and when the skid petered out he leapt up and ran for his life, toward the abandoned reception desk. He vaulted over it, came down in an ungodly heap on the other side, and lay on his back panting for breath.

Still clutching his Glock 22 in a palm slick with sweat.

Safe.

Just.

42

C*lick.*

She was through.

Violetta sat bolt upright in her chair. She normally maintained a respectable posture in front of the people who worked for her, but fatigue and frustration got to everyone after long enough. She'd been halfway slouched in the seatback, her glassy gaze fixed on the room, her ears prickling in the tense atmosphere. Her men were exhausted, jacked up on copious amounts of caffeine and more obscure stimulants to keep their pulses going long after their bodies were screaming for sleep. They seemed unimportant in comparison to the hard and uncompromising auras of her field operatives like King and Slater, but they were equally as important, if not more so. This was the new world, and most of the new world took place within computers and digital clouds.

But even *they* hadn't managed to make a dent in this chaotic situation.

Now, though, reinvigoration flowed through her as someone finally patched her through.

After endless waiting and countless attempts, she'd managed to get a hold of Detective First Grade Jim Riordan.

Infamous for supposedly being the toughest, meanest son-of-a-bitch in the NYPD.

That's who she needed right now.

She had connected to him via digitally encrypted radio, and she pressed her satellite phone to her ear. 'Do you know who I am?'

'Someone at One Police gave me a vague description,' he said. 'I think I get the idea.'

1 Police Plaza, she thought. NYPD's headquarters on Park Row.

She thought about it.

Figured someone there would be privy to her team's presence in Manhattan.

Shrugged and continued.

She said, 'Do you understand I've been granted full control over any cop I can get a hold of?'

'Yeah,' he said. 'They told me that in the same breath they said who you were.'

She paused. 'You okay with that?'

'I have to do what I'm told, don't I?'

'You understand what's at stake here?'

Riordan grunted an affirmation.

Violetta said, 'You got a problem with someone you don't know telling you what to do, Detective Riordan?'

'No, ma'am,' he said, but his voice betrayed the truth.

She said, 'Is it because I'm a woman?'

He scoffed. 'You think a lot of yourself, lady.'

'How about we cut the shit?' Violetta said. 'Tell me what's really on your mind. I can handle it.'

'I'm on the phone with you when there's people who need help. Does that answer your question?'

'In thirty-six hours there's going to be a million more people who need your help, and that's not an exaggeration. You can't get to everyone. You need to prioritise.'

'And what is it exactly you want me to do?'

'I take it I can rely on your discretion.'

'Stop talking fancy and just tell me what you need. Then I'll see how I feel about it.'

'There's an address in the Bowery. Write it down.' She fed it to him, and faintly heard him scrawling it on a piece of paper. 'That address is the key to cutting all of this short. The intelligence myself and my team gathered has led me to believe there are people in that building who currently have control of the power grid. I'm going to cut right to the chase — I've heard you're the unofficial ballbuster on the force. Your word is law on the street. So right now I need you to round up every cop you can find and get them to that building.'

'What do you want us to do when we get there?'

'Establish a perimeter and await further instruction. I have my own men attempting a breach right now. You and your men are going to be there for backup.'

'Okay.'

'And, Jim,' she said. 'I couldn't care less how you feel about it. You'll do what I tell you because the president's issued an executive order instructing you to do so. Understood?'

'Yes, ma'am,' he said. Then he added, 'But you're lucky I agree with you.'

'Just trying to do the right thing.'

That seemed to lower his guard. He said, 'I'll round up as many men as I can.'

'Thank you.'

'How bad is this?'

She hesitated. Figured she could trust him. If there was anything she'd learned to appreciate in this business, it was people who didn't bullshit. Those who cut right to the chase. She said, 'It could get really bad.'

'What do you know?'

'The power companies have no control over the substations. They've been locked out. What you see now is just the beginning of how badly New York is going to succumb to panic. Right now that building is the key to saving tens of thousands of lives.'

'It's hackers or something?'

'Yes,' Violetta said. 'They're rogue. They're not affiliated with any terrorist organisation — none of them have stepped forward to claim responsibility for this. They're acting independently.'

'And you're sure they're in the building?'

Violetta stared across the room at Alonzo, hunched over his desk, face illuminated by the harsh white glow of the three screens in front of him.

'Yes,' she lied.

'How sure?'

'Very.'

'Then I'll make sure I bring every cop in the city down on it.'

'Thank you, Jim.'

The line went dead.

She hadn't told Detective First Grade Jim Riordan that there was no guarantee the bank building was even populated. She hadn't mentioned how little sense it would make if the rogue organisation's remote HQ was located right in the heart of the grid they'd decimated. How inconvenient that would be for them. How nonsensical. Nothing added up...

...but they had no other leads.

That was the crux of it. If the building was empty, they were in the dark.

So, despite her personal attachment to one of the men she'd put in the line of fire, she hoped like hell both Will Slater and Jason King were in the process of getting shot at. If they weren't, she truly had no idea what might happen.

A situation like this was unheard of in the modern era.

The only sound that permeated the space was the incessant clicking of computer mice and tapping of fingers on keys.

Trying, valiantly, to make progress.

She knew if they didn't, society wouldn't be the same.

43

Slater lay on his back for a few laboured breaths, then eased up into a crouch.

He listened hard.

There was the inevitable outcry of civilians caught too close to the gunfight. Men and women and children unaccustomed to the in-your-face violence of combat. Gunshots sounded a whole lot different in real life than in the movies. Especially those of a .50 cal rifle — probably a Barrett M82. To the untrained ear, the reports would have sounded like bomb detonations. They sure did to Slater, and he'd heard them a thousand times before. He couldn't imagine the terror of inexperience in this realm.

Apart from the faint screams, he heard nothing. No approaching footsteps, no one reloading weapons, no crunch of glass underfoot. The lobby stayed silent, and as his hearing returned he picked up a faint *plip-plip-plip* from outside.

He scrunched up his features and listened harder.

Then it clicked.

Rain.

The skies had opened up.

Cold tension ran through him, constricting his insides. It would have been hard enough breaching the bank building with a clear forecast. Already he could hear the downpour intensifying, transitioning from a faint shower to a genuine storm within minutes. He usually thought he was above getting affected by his surroundings, but something about the mixture of darkness and foul weather churned his guts.

At least he was inside, where he could regroup and then—

What? he thought.

What the fuck can you feasibly do?

He slid his phone out of the back pocket of his jeans and dialled King.

It rang for long seconds, on and on in the quiet of the lobby.

No answer.

He killed the call and put the phone back, then pressed two fingers into his eyes. The echoes of a splitting headache had come to life, deep in his skull. Obviously a side effect of trying to flush out the hangover so fast. Its remnants had finally caught up to him. He recognised that he couldn't take the time to feel sorry for himself, and forced the pain aside.

Then he heard glass crunching underfoot.

A whole lot of it, actually, under multiple feet.

He stiffened.

Didn't move a muscle.

The footsteps spread out, three sets heading in three directions. Slater heard one coming up the middle, another moving diagonally to the left, and the final set diagonally to the right. Surrounding the reception desk from multiple angles.

Shit, Slater thought.

They're trained.

And they know where I am.

Waiting wouldn't achieve anything. The longer he drew it out, the better setup they'd achieve when the gunfight finally kicked off. So he zoned in, narrowing his vision, discarding any point of focus that wasn't completely necessary. It shrank his entire being to a single objective.

Survive.

He moved. Crept forward in the crouch, reaching the left-hand edge of the desk. The Glock stayed fixed to his palm, and he slipped a finger inside the trigger guard. Then he inched out into the open, so slowly it was barely perceptible. He kept the marble wall behind him close, making sure he blended into it. It worked. He was able to get a respectable line of sight on half the lobby.

He saw a hulking figure heading in from the left, its features indiscernible due to the absence of light.

There was only one way to play it.

Slater took a silent breath, raised the Glock, and fired an initial shot at the silhouette.

The muzzle flare lit up the lobby as the bullet struck home, but the figure didn't go down. In the brief flash of illumination Slater soaked in the hostile's features. He was big, and he was clad in serious body armour. Slater spotted a giant vest over his torso and copious amounts of reinforced padding on his arms and legs. His face was obscured by a helmet with a reflective visor, making him appear more like an automaton than a man. There was some sort of assault rifle in his hands — Slater couldn't get a proper look at it, but he figured it might be a carbine.

All in all, the guy was clad in tens of thousands of dollars worth of gear.

A bulletproof tank on legs.

Slater's first shot had accomplished nothing.

So he switched gears and emptied half his magazine in the direction of the throat region. He'd managed a blurry glimpse at the guy's neck and spotted a gap between his vest and helmet. He sent seven more rounds at the guy, his finger pumping faster on the trigger than he could keep track of, and then he threw himself back behind the reception desk.

With an almighty *crash,* the body of the man thundered to the lobby floor.

Slater wasn't done.

There were two more.

He had genetic gifts and an unparalleled work ethic on his side, sure. But there were simple laws of nature you couldn't control. Gunshots in a confined space impair the human ear, ten times out of ten, without fail. No question. The same old whine returned, and everything became muffled, and no matter how many times it had happened to him it never became easier to discern sounds.

So he knew the other two armour-clad men were now charging at him, but he didn't know how fast they were coming in, or what angle they were approaching from.

There simply wasn't enough time to reload a fresh magazine.

Many men might have hesitated.

Overwhelmed by how it had all unfolded.

Hesitation wasn't in Slater's vocabulary.

He stood up and locked his focus on the closest man and emptied the rest of his clip at the guy's face and throat. Eight full rounds. He was fully aware that if he tried to spare ammunition for the third man he was likely to fail to kill the first guy. Better to ensure he turned it into a one-on-one situation.

Out of the corner of his eye he noticed the last man

raising his rifle and starting to squeeze off a shot, but by the time he returned fire Slater was already back behind the desk.

The wonders of inhuman reflexes.

Carbine rounds thudded into the decorative wall behind him, taking entire chunks of marble out of its surface, but none struck Slater.

And the automatic gunfire couldn't mask the sound of the second man smashing into the lobby floor.

Stone dead.

His throat torn apart.

Slater breathed out.

He reached back for a fresh magazine, but he knew it was futile. He understood the timing of life-or-death encounters so well that it was practically second nature, and he knew he'd get halfway through the process of reloading before the final man rounded the reception desk. There was comfort and complacency in knowing it was three-on-one, but now Slater had evened the odds. The last guy would panic. They always did. He'd elect to commit to a full-steam-ahead charge.

And he did.

Slater started slotting the fresh magazine home in the Glock 22's underside, but the footsteps got too close for comfort.

Screw it.

He dropped the gun, timed it perfectly, and burst forward.

He caught the guy around the mid-section, and they flew to the floor in a rabid cloud of testosterone.

44

The body armour covering nearly every inch of the guy's frame was both an advantage and a disadvantage.

It made him cumbersome, slow to manoeuvre his limbs.

It also made him damn near impenetrable to Slater's strikes.

Slater had never been a quitter. He came down on top of the guy and quickly slid to full mount position, throwing one leg over the man's mid-section and pinning him to the ground. Then he reached down and snatched hold of the carbine — an M4A1, just as he suspected — and used brute force to wrench it free from his grip. Maybe, if this had been a blockbuster film, they might have wrestled with the weapon for nigh on thirty seconds, complete with shifts in momentum and the barrel drifting inches from each other's faces in a daring game of chicken. But this was reality, and when someone with Slater's explosiveness gets hold of a weapon it sure as hell isn't staying in one place for long. He probably broke a couple of the man's fingers, still resting in the trigger guard when Slater simply tore the weapon free, and because there wasn't enough room to reverse the carbine around without losing his position, he simply hurled it away like it weighed nothing.

Then the guy truly panicked.

Behind his helmet Slater heard him hyperventilating, his breath likely clouding the reflective visor on the inside. Slater took full advantage of the panic. He reached down and seized the underside of the helmet and yanked it upwards. It didn't come off the guy's head, but it tilted his chin up, exposing more of his neck to the open air. Slater then cocked his other arm at a right-angle and took aim with his elbow and dropped it down with all two hundred pounds of his bodyweight behind it.

Crunch.

Not great for the muscles and tendons in the man's neck, not to mention his throat and windpipe.

Slater heard a spluttering cough behind the helmet.

This was the part where he was supposed to show mercy. He had the upper hand, so clearly he should stand up and help the man to his feet and offer to buy him a beer.

Again, this was real life.

This man had come here to put a bullet in Slater's head and spit on his corpse.

So Slater dropped the same elbow four more times, where it smashed home over and over again in the same spot, as brutal and uncompromising as a steel piston. He gave thanks that it was dark. He felt the guy's throat caving in. He didn't need to see it.

He climbed off the body, panting, and went to fetch the Glock he'd discarded. No one had followed the three armoured mercenaries into the building. The lobby fell quiet, and the sidewalk outside stayed empty. He knew they'd come from the bank building, which meant there were probably many more reinforcements simply waiting for an opportunity to use their considerable arsenal.

He found the Glock, and the fresh fifteen-round magazine lying alongside it, and bent down to pick them up. He stretched his fingers out, and leant forward, and—

Pain seized him, so strong and sudden it made him audibly gasp.

He straightened up and clutched at his shoulder like he'd been shot. At first he thought it was the open wound above his collar bone, but the bleeding had stopped minutes ago. He moved his shoulder an inch, rolling it backward just a touch. The socket *screamed* in agony.

Dislocated, he realised.

Shit.

The extent of his troubles didn't strike home immediately. It was only when he reached up with his left hand to try and poke and prod and shift it back into place that it hit him. Cold sweat beaded on his face, and the headache ballooned into a full-blown migraine, and even the slightest brush of his fingertips against the shoulder sent pain bolting through the limb. He couldn't raise his right arm an inch.

And he couldn't shoot well enough with his left.

Sure, he was respectable at it. An untrained observer might have considered him ambidextrous. But against trained hostiles, he'd fail.

Unnerved, thrown off, he bent down and fetched the Glock with his left hand.

His fingers shook as they clenched it.

Moving slow and tentatively, he chambered the fresh magazine. It took him nearly twenty seconds, and the pain made his vision waver. He kept his right arm pointed straight at the floor, pinned to his side. It was about all he could manage.

The full-strength elbows into the last mercenary had done the trick.

Slater realised that if he'd held back on the last couple of elbows he wouldn't have dislocated his shoulder. And, to make his decision more frustrating, the last man would have still been alive to answer questions in an interrogation. With enough restraint, Slater might have discovered exactly who was behind this, and why.

Now, he had three dead bodies on his hands and a useless right arm.

He figured that was about as bad as it could get.

Wrong.

Movement, on the sidewalk, right outside. He locked his gaze onto the source, and blanched.

No way.

It was three of the *sicarios* from Palantir. Which spelled potential disaster, if they were here and King wasn't. Sure, they were down two men, but they were otherwise untouched. Either they'd seen Slater fleeing with Rico and taken off in pursuit, or they'd overwhelmed King in the alcove and shot him to pieces, then moved on.

Slater's heart skipped a beat.

But he had his own life to preserve, first and foremost.

The *sicarios* were racing for the revolving door, guns in hand. They must have seen Slater entering the building. He furrowed his brow. That didn't add up — that meant they had surely witnessed the three hulking mercenaries following in stride, and he didn't think they'd hurry into a war zone so willingly.

Unless...

There wasn't much, if any, light outside. If they'd seen Slater run into the building, then they might already have been in pursuit as he was chasing Rico. So they might have seen the kid's head explode, and figured he was the one behind it.

In which case, they were dead men walking anyway, as Rico's father would slaughter them when they got back to Mexico for failing to fulfil their sole responsibility of protecting his son.

The cartels didn't mess around with that sort of thing.

They'd be made an example of. Dead no matter what. But maybe if they turned over the body of Rico's killer, they'd be spared a long and torturous demise. That way, the elder Guzmán would make it quick.

And there was nothing more unpredictable than dead men walking.

Slater saw them reach the entrance. They piled into the revolving door, guns up, ready to fire.

Slater had no choice.

The same survival mechanism kicked in, taking into account his mangled shoulder and pounding head and the lack of confidence in using his left hand to shoot with.

So he turned and sprinted for the stairwell.

Retreat.

45

He almost didn't make it in time.

His shoulder screamed for relief with every step. Each footfall on the hard floor of the lobby sent agony spearing through him, making his vision waver and throwing his equilibrium off. He could barely keep his feet underneath him. His brain yelled, *Stop moving! Stop fucking moving!* But he couldn't listen. He heard the *sicario*s piling into the lobby, far behind him. They shouted and hollered in Spanish as they spotted him across the space. No more than an outline in the dark, but that was enough.

A couple of them fired shots. The rounds went wide thanks to copious amounts of adrenaline shaking their hands, but Slater ducked and weaved all the same.

'*¡Pinche gringo!*' one of them shouted.

Slater raced into the stairwell and collapsed on the bottom stair, just out of sight. He tried to suppress a gasp, but couldn't. It came out in a short rattling moan, discharging all the pain he was in. It was indescribable. Like needles behind his eyeballs, impeding his every move. He used every ounce of mental toughness he had to suppress it, and then steeled his grip on the Glock and fired five rounds out the stairwell entrance. They shot through the lobby, almost certainly hitting nothing but air, but his only objective was to use them as a deterrent.

He heard rampant cursing, and the *sicarios* diving for cover.

He turned and leapt into motion, taking the stairs four at a time, making use of flexibility instilled from years and years of Muay Thai. The same agony greeted him with each step upward, but he'd discovered if he simply accepted it, it wouldn't make him pass out. That had been his chief concern, but now he realised it was *just* bearable. Sure, the stairwell had constricted to a black leviathan pulsating and throbbing as it snaked upward into the unknown, but at least he could cover ground without losing consciousness.

He made it up three flights before the first gunshot rang past him, the angle only slightly too extreme to allow the *sicarios* below to squeeze off a decent shot.

Now.

Capitalise.

Clawing his way through the discomfort, he jerked sideways to the railing and pointed the Glock down into the abyss. He thought he made out a silhouette and squeezed a cluster of shots off — three, back-to-back-to-back. The muzzle flare showed the *sicario*'s head snapping backward, spraying blood over the two men behind him. His body bounced and thudded down the first flight of stairs.

Slater didn't bother trying to shoot at the next two assassins. They were already drawing a bead on him, so he threw himself back behind cover and kept ascending.

His vision wavered, a little harder, and fear seized him.

You might actually pass out.

He searched for somewhere to regroup. He figured he

was three storeys up, definitely amongst the residential apartments now, so he scoured the stairwell for the first available exit. He found it two flights up — a plain door reading EMERGENCY EXIT: DO NOT OBSTRUCT. There was dull yellow light emanating behind the glass, and dull white light emanating overhead from an emergency light at the very top of the stairwell.

He pushed down on the handle and put his weight into it and smashed it open, stumbling through into a hallway with hard floors and bordered by decorative pot plants sitting on polished tables. A forward-thinking resident had already lit and placed candles along the length of the corridor, giving the whole space the vibe of a haunted manor.

A quiet, calm, respectable slice of Manhattan real estate.

Not anymore.

Slater made a racket as he powered down the corridor, searching for anything that might constitute an empty apartment. Numbers flashed by: 501, 502, 503, 504...

The door to apartment 505 flew open in his face.

He froze in his tracks, aware that half his clothing was saturated in his own blood, and his face was contorted with pain.

He came face-to-face with a woman in her late twenties, her features lit by the flickering candlelight. She was naturally beautiful — devoid of makeup, with her hair pulled back in a tight bun. She was still dressed in the remnants of smart business attire from a day at the office, with a collared shirt open at the neck under a black vest and a tight-fitting black skirt hugging her hips. She had pale skin and green eyes and long lashes and a face that he imagined would ordinarily be warm and inviting.

Now, it shifted from hopeful to reserved, then to outright fear.

'Oh,' she said, noting the blood all over him and the handgun in his palm. 'I'm so sorry. I thought you were a cop and—'

She was speaking faster and faster with each sentence, terrified of the potential consequences, and now she started swinging the door closed with enough verve to send a message.

Slater heard motion at the top of the stairwell.

The door was halfway shut when he lunged forward, shouldered it back open, and spilled through into her apartment.

46

She opened her mouth to scream and he grabbed her around the mid-section with his good arm.

He used the sole of his boot to gently push the door shut.

Then, just in time, he brought his good arm up and clamped his hand hard over her mouth.

She moaned into his palm, but he didn't budge an inch.

They stayed that way, frozen in the entranceway. He could make out her features better here thanks to the handful of candles lit down the passage, resting on a pair of identical hall tables made of dark polished wood. The floor was thin carpet, cushy under his boots but not thick enough to mask the sound of footfalls entirely. So he didn't dare move. He'd already cut it too close. If the two remaining *sicarios* found him like this, he didn't fancy his chances.

Sometimes, morality spelled disaster. This woman would be caught in the crossfire and he'd hesitate before he shot at anyone if she was between them. The *sicarios* wouldn't. They'd cut through her like she was meat to get to Slater.

If he was halfway coherent, he wouldn't have bothered with secrecy. He would have let her shout for help, and when they busted through the door he'd be waiting there to shoot them in the face. But he could barely see straight. The blood had drained from his head minutes earlier, and if he didn't sit down soon he'd drop like deadweight, passing out from the pain. He'd dislocated a shoulder before. This was nothing like that. He wasn't a doctor, but he knew a whole lot about discomfort. Whatever was happening in the socket had ratcheted his pain levels up to an unbearable height. It was affecting every part of his behaviour, from his choices to his balance.

Two pairs of thudding footsteps came closer and closer, reverberating on the other side of the door.

Practically running.

Zoning in on the door labelled "505"?

Slater tensed up. It took most of his conscious energy to keep the woman silent. She was writhing and struggling against his torso, but he clamped the palm harder over her mouth and the struggling ceased. Then he held his breath.

Closer.

Closer...

Right outside.

He had a choice to make. Take his hand off her mouth, switch hands with the Glock 22, and raise it to the door. Or keep her silent. It all depended on whether the *sicarios* knew he was in here. If they did, the palm over the mouth was futile.

He heard them right there, only feet from the door, and it struck him that the woman was between himself and the door.

No, a voice in his head said. *She didn't ask for this.*

He took a deep, silent breath, and turned her around

with his palm so she could look into his eyes. He stared right back, and he didn't blink. He hoped she could see something in there other than a stone-cold killer. Something to reassure her, convince her everything might be okay. She stared back, and she didn't struggle against his hand. It all unfolded in seconds, but it was the best he could do.

He didn't have time.

He took his hand off her mouth, took the Glock out of his bad hand, pivoted and pointed the barrel right at the door's centre mass.

And there he froze, still as a statue, his back to her.

She could attack him, if she wanted.

Pick up a heavy object and bring it down on the back of his skull. No amount of reflexes would save him there. She probably should do it, too. He'd stormed into her home and practically assaulted her.

All he could hope was that she understood.

He didn't blink.

Didn't move.

Didn't think.

Just listened.

And the footsteps thudded away. They came within a foot of the woman's apartment door and then carried on past, slowing only to maintain a measured pace. They hadn't been running at a destination. They hadn't seen Slater go into the apartment. Seconds after they passed by, they disappeared from the edge of his hearing.

Gone, for good.

Melting away to sweep the rest of the building.

The seconds ticked by, and Slater realised he hadn't been struck from behind. In fact, she hadn't moved. He lowered the gun and turned, slowly.

She was still right there, a few feet away, watching him

with unabashed curiosity.

She kept her voice low and said, 'Who were you running from?'

'Unsavoury people.'

'Did they do that to you?' she said, motioning to his right arm, still pinned to his side, and his bloody collarbone, and his overall state of dishevelment.

He looked himself over. 'Actually, I did most of this to myself.'

'You okay?'

'You should be telling me to leave.'

'But I'm not.'

'I assaulted you.'

'It's been a weird night. You didn't mean it.'

He stood there awkwardly, barely able to think, his shoulder socket drilling sharp bolts through the rest of his body. 'How can you tell?'

'That's why you looked me in the eyes before,' she said. 'To show you were ... vulnerable.'

'Yeah.'

'The type of men who do what you just did don't ever pretend they're vulnerable.'

He nodded toward the door. 'I needed a place to hide. You opened your door. I'm sorry.'

She was still scrutinising him. Then she realised she'd prolonged the silence, and said, 'It's okay.'

'Do you mind if I stay here for a few minutes?' he said. 'I'm—'

Then the needles of pain merged into one giant wave, and it hit him like a tsunami, and he went down on one knee with an uncontrollable grimace.

The next thing he knew, she was helping him to his feet in a daze.

47

'I'm sorry,' he mumbled as she helped him down the hall.

They came out in a loft-style space, like a smaller version of his own penthouse on the Upper East Side. Exposed wooden beams criss-crossed over their heads, adding a rustic vibe to the otherwise modern architecture. The walls were reinforced concrete, and the floor was carpeted in the living area, and the kitchen had tiles the colour of steel. A narrow staircase led up to a second floor loft, where he figured the bedroom lay, overlooking the main space with the help of a thin railing. She hadn't held back on decorations, furnishing the ordinarily cold space with ample throw rugs and a plethora of pot plants and hanging vines draping off the kitchen island lighting.

He liked it a lot, and he wasn't quite sure why he was paying so much attention to it.

Delirium, maybe.

She seemed to notice. She dumped him down on the old-school corduroy sofa and perched herself on the edge of the armchair opposite it, still on edge. She made sure she had a line of sight with the entranceway, and she threw intermittent nervous glances down the length of it to the front door.

She said, 'You like the place?'

It was in jest, considering the circumstances. He was covered in blood, with only half his wits about him, and his right arm rendered useless. Swamped with crippling pain. But he still said, 'Yeah, I do.'

She pursed her lips, as if wondering what the hell to do next.

He said, 'I don't want to bother you—'

'But?' she said, raising an eyebrow.

'I need to get my shoulder back in.'

She winced. 'It's dislocated?'

'Yeah.'

'How'd you do that?'

'Running away from those guys,' he lied.

Didn't consider it prudent to tell her the truth.

I caved a man's throat in.

'Who were they?'

He shrugged. 'Just a couple of gangsters. They saw me on the street and didn't like me.'

'How'd you get in this building?'

'The lobby was open.'

'There are a million better places to run than an unfamiliar apartment building.'

He shrugged. 'Beats me.'

'Did they shoot at you?'

'Yes.'

She nodded. 'There was a god-awful racket a few minutes ago. What sort of firepower did they have?'

'Can we just get my shoulder back into place? Then I'll answer all the questions you have.'

'You'll answer them now or I'll kick you out.'

He paused. Then half-smiled. 'You drive a hard bargain.'

'You're lucky I didn't send you packing straight away.'

'You really should have. That's not usually how I introduce myself to women.'

Now it was her turn to half-smile. The corners of her lips crept upward, despite her best efforts to fight them back down.

Then a commanding voice in his head said, *No.*

She was gorgeous, and her personality was right up his alley. He could banter with her, and nothing would make him happier than speaking to her for the rest of the night. But there were eight million people relying on him, and womanising had to be the last thing on his mind.

He'd confirmed the bank building was occupied by armoured mercenaries. Now, breaching it was priority number one.

He screwed up his face and said, 'I haven't been entirely honest with you.'

'Okay,' she said.

Unperturbed.

'What's your name?' he said.

'Alexis.'

'Alexis, I'm Will.'

'Pleasure to meet you.'

'You too. I work for the government.'

She eyed him. 'In what capacity?'

'That's hard to define. But I'm ... in the middle of something.'

'Okay.'

'So I really, really need you to help me with this shoulder. And then I'll be on my way.'

She shrugged. 'Whatever you say.'

Slid off the arm of the chair, sauntered over to him and took his arm in her hands. Her fingers dug into his bicep, a little harder than necessary. He looked straight ahead. Every part of him wanted to respond to the touch. To look up into her eyes and see what happened from there. He was a man of opportunity, and he didn't usually get opportunities as effortlessly as this, especially after such a harrowing introduction. It showed she had an underlying feistiness. She wasn't easily disturbed. It spoke to him in all the right ways.

But he couldn't speak back.

He said, 'Do you know what you're doing?'

'I'm a paralegal,' she said.

He hesitated. 'What?'

'You heard me.'

'What does that have to do with—?'

'First aid training,' she said. 'Part of the job introduction.'

Then she added a smirk, to let him know she wasn't being serious.

He rolled his eyes. 'Just do it.'

'It's going to hurt.'

'You don't say?'

'Like, a lot.'

'Story of my life.'

'How long have you been working for the government?'

He said, 'Look, I'd love to chat, but—'

Halfway through the sentence, she wrenched his shoulder back into place.

He lost his vision for a split second, plunging into blackness, and when he resurfaced he rode out a wave of agony unlike anything he'd experienced in a long, long time. A breathless gasp exploded from his lips, and he fell back into the corduroy cushions, stunned into silence.

But then the wave crashed on the shores, and subsided, and when it cleared he had full function of his right arm.

He lifted it up, entirely pain-free.

He felt like crying with joy, but he didn't.

He still had a job to do.

She kept standing over him, watching him intently.

He looked up and said, 'What?'

She smiled. 'See? You're fine now.'

'I know.'

She slapped him on his brand-new shoulder. 'There you go. Job done.'

With new life coursing through his veins, he sprung up to his feet. 'Thank you.'

'You're welcome.'

'You got a bathroom?'

She hesitated. 'Uh—'

But the relief that came from crawling out of the pain chamber had blessed him with limitless energy. So instead of waiting for her to respond he spotted a closed door near the kitchen with a handmade wooden sign hanging off a peg reading: RESTROOM.

Cute, he thought.

He levered off the couch, left the Glock on the cushion, and strode for it. His bladder was fit to burst, and he didn't need to put up with that inconvenience in the midst of trying to locate King and storm the fortified bank building.

He thought he heard her say something in protest, but he ignored it.

He also thought he heard something strange coming from behind the restroom door.

He ignored that, too.

Put a hand out and pushed it open.

The strange noise was emanating from two men lying

sideways on the tiled floor of the bathroom. Their hands were duct taped behind their back, and their ankles were bound, and there was thick grey tape over their mouths, too. They were yelling into the tape, but what came out was ineligible muffled nonsense, no louder than murmurs.

Slater froze with his hand still outstretched.

He turned around.

Alexis had his Glock in her hands. She was aiming it at his chest.

From that distance, she couldn't miss.

48

Her voice shook as she said, 'I really need you to leave.'

He soaked in what was happening. Compartmentalised it, then accepted it. He stayed quiet. In a tense situation, less talk was better.

She continued. 'I know you work for the government. So you're going to want to get involved in this. But please, just go. I helped you. I did what you asked.'

He still didn't speak. Just folded his arms over his barrel chest and stared at her.

'Did you hear me?' she said, the barrel lurching up and down as her hands shook.

'How could I not have?' he said.

'Then get out.'

He stayed right where he was.

She said, 'I'm not playing.'

'Put the gun down, Alexis.'

'You're unarmed. I have your weapon. Get out of here.'

'When are you going to work it out?'

'Work what out?'

'I'm not moving,' he said. 'So you're going to have to shoot me if you don't want me to be here.'

Silence.

'I'm not playing,' she repeated.

'You are playing,' he said. 'The fact you had to say it twice shows it's a bluff. If you want to prove me wrong then shoot me in the face. There's nothing I can do to stop you.'

She didn't budge.

Nor did he.

He said, 'So what happens now?'

'I told you to leave.'

'And I politely declined.'

'I've done nothing wrong.'

'Did I say you have?'

'You saw them.'

'Sure.'

'Am I under arrest? Is that what you're saying?'

'I didn't say a word.'

'Don't you have bigger things to worry about?' she said. 'Look what's happening outside. It's going to be chaos soon. You know that. I'm not an idiot. I can work out what'll happen if there's no power for more than a couple of days. You should be working on fixing that.'

'Alexis,' he said, and she went quiet. 'You're doing a whole lot of unnecessary talking.'

'I just want you to leave.'

'I just want you to explain.'

'What does it matter? It's my word against theirs. There's two of them.'

'Says who?'

She rolled her eyes. 'You have to uphold the law, right?'

'No,' he said. 'I don't.'

She paused. 'You don't work for the government, do you? Who are you? Why'd you come in here?'

'Yes, I do.'

'But you don't care about the fact that there's two men tied up in my bathroom?'

'Depends.'

'What exactly do you do?'

'It's complicated. Tell me what happened.'

'They—'

She only got one word into the speech. Then she dropped the Glock on the floor, planted herself down on the couch, and sobbed into her hands.

He crossed the room and fetched the weapon off the carpet. Took it in his fresh right hand as he sat down beside her and put his elbows on his knees. He maintained a respectable distance, just as he'd been taught to do with all victims of trauma. Not too close. Not too far away. He kept his face warm and open.

He said, 'What happened?'

'They're drug addicts,' she said. 'I know they don't look like it, because they've got money. They live down the hall and they work at my firm. I've been a paralegal there for two years. They've been disgusting the whole time. They don't even pretend to hide the fact they stare at me. They're so quiet when they're sober, but when they do coke and ecstasy they get mean. Wall Street drugs, you know. Tonight they did a lot of both. Probably planning a night out on the town. Then the whole city went dark. And they got other ideas...'

'They came here?'

'They knocked on my door, asking if I was okay, after the lights went out. I was nice to them. I could see they were sweating bullets. I knew what was up. I invited them in for a coffee to try and keep things friendly. I was scared, I guess. The darkness spooked me. I wasn't opposed to company.'

'How far did they get?'

'They didn't try it immediately. I could almost see the gears in their heads whirring, you know? Like the common-sense part of their brain was telling them, "*she knows you, you won't get away with this, you'll be held accountable for what happens.*" But I guess when you do enough drugs you can't hear that part of your brain anymore, so it didn't matter to them. The guy with long hair forced me down on the couch and pinned me there. That's when he *really* started sweating. But he was loving it. The other guy started stripping his clothes off. But...'

She reached over Slater's lap and lifted the far couch cushion. He peered into the shadowy space. There was the outline of what appeared to be a taser, resting there against the frame.

He nodded his understanding.

She lowered the cushion.

'How'd it play out?' he said.

'I jabbed the guy holding me and he was done. I guess the drugs had heightened his senses, so it amplified the shock, too. He was foaming at the mouth before he hit the floor. Then the other guy opted to try and wrestle the taser away from me instead of running, so I jabbed him twice and he was out of commission, too. I tied them up pretty fast, and dragged them in there.'

He glanced over his shoulder at the open bathroom door. Saw the two silhouettes squirming there on the tiles.

He said, 'Do you have combat training?'

'No. I just didn't want to get raped.'

'Why didn't you tell me when I walked in here?'

'I tased them pretty bad. Gave them a couple of extra

jolts after I already had them tied up, just to make sure they stayed placid while I worked out what to do. I guess that's why I thought you were a cop through the keyhole. I was desperate for help. Then when you came in here and grabbed me...'

'You thought it was happening again?'

Alexis didn't answer.

She lowered her gaze to the floor, and did her best to stay calm.

49

Slater watched her closely. 'Thank you for trusting me. I can't imagine what was going through your head.'

She looked at him. 'I could tell you were a good man. It's something I can just sense, right away. From the start I knew those two would be trouble, back when I first met them. It's an instinctive thing.'

'Still,' he said. 'I wouldn't have blamed you if you hit me in the head with a steel pipe.'

'I was considering it.'

'Then I'm glad I'm conscious.'

She paused, then said, 'I am, too.'

He looked over his shoulder again and said, 'I can't deal with them right now. I'm sorry.'

'It's okay. They're not going anywhere.'

'You're okay keeping them in here?'

She shrugged. 'I neutralised them and tied them up. It's a whole lot easier to watch over them.'

He said, 'Are you sure you've never been trained in any of this?'

'Is that so surprising?'

'You handle yourself better in horrible situations than any civilian I've ever met.'

'That's what I am?' she said, eyebrow raised. 'A civilian? You sure it's not because I'm a girl?'

He stood up. 'It might be easy to paint all men with the same brush after what happened to you, but that's not me.'

'I know. I'm only playing.'

'One of the most capable government operatives I've ever met was a woman.'

'You two work together?'

Slater bit his lip. 'We used to.'

She seemed to understand all the implications of those three words, and the weight they carried. The aforementioned colleague was more than just a coworker to Slater, and also no longer around, which could only mean one thing in his line of work. Alexis said, 'I'm sorry.'

He made to respond, but his phone barked in his pocket.

He slid it out and read: KING.

Said, 'Would you excuse me one moment?'

'You don't have to excuse yourself to answer the phone.'

He smiled. 'Guess I'm old-fashioned.'

Then he instantly switched demeanours, lifted the smartphone to his ear and said, 'Glad to know you're alive.'

'You, too,' King said.

'Where are you?'

'Closing in on the Bowery.'

Slater dropped into a crouch, moved across the space and peeked over the lip of the big windows running the length of the loft. Sure, the windows were merely one part of a two-hundred-plus apartment complex, but he wasn't about to take unnecessary risks. He observed the streets below from his vantage point.

For the first time he got a decent look at the bank building across the intersection. It was an ancient granite behemoth, eight storeys tall and sporting Renaissance architecture. He saw the entrance portico towering over the rest of the sidewalk, two storeys tall in its own right and bordered by thick unadorned columns. The two visible sides of the building formed the outside of a "V," with the portico resting at the tip of the triangle. The doors were made of heavy wood and seemed damn near impenetrable if there was any sort of reinforcement on the other side, which he knew there would be.

The building loomed over the intersection, and now he saw almost every square inch of asphalt taken up by empty vehicles resting bumper-to-bumper. The traffic had ratcheted up a few notches when all the lights blinked out, and it had caused an overwhelming logjam in the middle of the intersection. With no traffic lights to follow and no way to feasibly escape, it mustn't have taken long for drivers and passengers to give up entirely and leave their cars behind.

That'd be an inconvenient obstacle if he had to make a run at the building.

He said, 'Where are you coming from?'

'Almost at the end of Third,' King said. 'It's about to merge onto the Bowery. I'll cut across to Second.'

'I can meet you there in five minutes,' Slater said. 'But be real careful. I think I turned this place into a war zone.'

'I don't hear any gunshots. I did before.'

'Fighting's over for now.'

'What happened?'

'I chased the kid down Second. It wasn't deliberate, but he sprinted right at the building in question. They blew his head off for it.'

'Shit.'

'They've got armoured mercs. And there's two of Rico's bodyguards left in the building I'm hiding out in. I'll deal with them.'

'They're dangerous,' King said. 'They're not your average security. That's who was shooting at us in the alley.'

'I know.'

'There's something else…'

'Yeah?'

'I've got someone with me.'

'Who?'

'You wouldn't believe me if I told you.'

'Just give me a name—'

'Meet me at the corner of Second and 4th. Hurry.'

Then Slater heard a muffled grunt of protest from King's supposed prisoner, and the pair wrestling — most likely King using his bodyweight to haul the man through the streets.

The call ended on King's side.

50

Slater swore and lowered the phone.

He kept watching the street, but the Bowery was a ghost town. He knew there was an invisible fuse there in the darkness, and that the slightest movement on anyone's end would light it up instantly. There'd be snipers scouring the shadows for signs of resistance, tucked away in vantage points amidst the thousands of windows facing the intersection. There'd be foot soldiers behind the bank building's big wooden doors, clad in body armour, pumped up on Dexedrine, ready to defend its contents with their lives. There'd be reinforcements en route eventually, whether that be the NYPD or the feds or the CIA or the DSS. Violetta would do her job well, and she'd be able to scrounge together some assistance as soon as she got hold of the right people.

But right now there was none of that.

Just constant underlying tension.

The calm before the storm.

Slater turned around to find Alexis watching him like he was a lab experiment.

Which, he guessed, he was.

He said, 'What?'

'What do you do, exactly?'

'Many things.'

'Can't tell me?'

'I'd love to,' he said. 'Now's not the time.'

She nodded. 'I'll let you out.'

He shook his head. 'Those guys I was running from are still in the building. Stay here. I'll let myself out.'

'What if they're out there?'

He slapped his shoulder. 'I don't need to run from them anymore.'

She stared at his shoulder, then looked him in the eyes. She made to say something, but stopped herself short. Then she lowered her head and scoffed in disbelief.

'What?' he said.

'You're... not what I expected a government operative to be.'

'What did you expect?'

'I assume you've killed people.'

'That's an intrusive question,' he said. 'We've only just met.'

'I want an answer.'

He paused. Thought about the two men tied up in the bathroom, and the way she'd handled all this chaos, and the poise she'd shown. He said, 'Yeah. I have.'

She didn't respond.

He said, 'How's that make you feel?'

'That's the strangest part of all,' she said. 'It doesn't change much.'

'Much of what?'

She didn't respond to that, either.

He moved away from the window and came within a few

feet of her, maintaining a respectable distance. 'Are you still basing all of this off your first impression of me?'

'Like I said, I could tell you weren't a bad person.'

'You shouldn't jump to conclusions so quickly. I could be anyone.'

'But you're not.'

'I've killed people. That doesn't deter you?'

'Should it?'

'What are we getting at here?'

She looked at him for a long five count, then seemed to rein herself in. 'You need to go.'

He nodded. 'I do. Thank you for all your help.'

'You're welcome.'

He crossed the loft, refusing to look back in case he let his penchant for the opposite sex distract him even more than it already had. He made it down the hallway and moved quieter, masking his footsteps, listening for any sign of commotion outside. He placed one hand on the knob and turned it and let the door whisper open. A quick glance in either direction down the corridor revealed it to be empty.

He leant back into the apartment and shut the door.

Turned around to find Alexis there, only a few feet away, still watching him.

He said, 'I know you've had bad experiences with guys judging you solely off your looks. I'm guessing, in this city, it's even worse than elsewhere.'

She nodded.

He said, 'I'm no saint. I do the same when I'm out on the town. I can't help myself. I'm superficial when I want to be, I guess.'

Silence.

'But not here,' he said. 'Not now. I want to see you again. Not because of your looks. Because of your actions.'

'What actions?'

'The way you took matters into your own hands,' he said. 'I like that. A lot.'

She seemed to be torn between two options, rocking back and forth on the spot, the common-sense part of her brain listing all sorts of obvious downsides to committing to something so brash with a man she barely knew who'd stormed into her apartment in the midst of a blackout and practically taken her hostage.

He knew the common-sense part of her brain would win.

And for good reason.

So he started to turn away.

Put his hand back on the doorknob.

But suddenly she was close, too close, and he turned back and she pressed his back to the door and cupped his face between her palms and stood up on her tiptoes and kissed him, long and slow.

Only for a few seconds.

Then she pulled away and stepped back and said, 'I'd like that, too. It was nice to meet you.'

He didn't know what to say.

She said, 'Make sure you don't die tonight.'

'I wouldn't dare.'

His head spinning, both with confusion and disbelief, he readied the Glock and slipped out of apartment 505, ruminating on the improbable directions life can take.

51

You could hear a pin drop.

Everyone cooped up in their apartments were keeping quiet, all the way down the hallway. There was no excited murmuring from behind closed doors, no muffled conversation... no noise whatsoever. Slater imagined couples and single city workers sitting on their sofas in the dark, maybe surrounded by faint candlelight, but no more than that. Mulling over what they might do if the power stayed out. Wondering how long it would take until they had to take to the streets, actively searching for resources. This was Manhattan, after all. People were busy. Most ate out, or ordered meal delivery. What little supplies they had in their pantries wouldn't last long.

And then what?

The longer the darkness lasted, the more sobering reality became.

Slater knew he couldn't worry about that. If he did, the pressure would mount. The key to remaining calm was refusing to think about the consequences of failure, but the higher the stakes the harder that became. For now all he could do was move forward.

And reunite with King.

As he set off for the stairwell, he realised how quickly he'd acclimated to working alongside his de facto brother. He'd spent his whole career as a solo operative, but the truth was they functioned better as a duo. Black Force, his old clandestine government unit, should have come to that realisation sooner than they did. The entire division was broken, disbanded and dissolved before the upper echelon put two and two together and invited King and Slater back to work as a team.

Now, he felt strangely exposed on his own.

How quickly the comfort of isolation had worn off…

He reached the stairwell, put a hand out, and pushed the door open.

Stepped into the pitch blackness, one foot at a time, with his Glock raised and ready to fire.

He didn't get the chance.

The darkness morphed, from nothingness to a sudden flurry of movement, and he squeezed the trigger twice and put both rounds through the forehead of the *sicario* lunging at him. The man's own weapon was outstretched, and Slater threw himself sideways as he realised the barrel had lined up with his face. He needn't have bothered — the body sailed on past, splaying forward, but now he was out of position.

He righted himself, and caught the shadows morphing again, and suddenly the final man barrelled out of the darkness in a desperate final-effort lunge. Slater saw both the guy's hands splayed and realised he didn't have a weapon.

He ran out of bullets.

The thought didn't reassure him. Before he could take

advantage of it, the guy had his hands interlocked behind the small of Slater's back. The two of them were roughly the same size and weight, and when that's the case it doesn't really matter how strong either party is. Wrestling technique exists for a reason, and that reason is that it works. So the *sicario* completed the takedown, demonstrating strangely All-American abilities for a Mexican, and drove Slater down to the carpeted floor.

He tried to bring his Glock up between them, but the man's weight on top pinned him in an awkward position.

He threw a slicing vertical elbow into the bridge of the guy's nose, breaking it. The *sicario* grunted, a tight-lipped animalistic noise, but he didn't cry out in pain, and he didn't budge. He got both his hands on Slater's wrist and smashed it against the ground with the strength of adrenaline.

The Glock went off, the gunshot deafening, but it was out of Slater's grip before the bullet had left the chamber. It bounced once, coming down out of reach.

Slater switched to desperation mode. The *sicario* was strong, and capable, and more than aware that he was fighting for his life.

The only thing was, Slater had all three of those attributes in spades, too.

And he knew how to use them a little better.

Instead of wasting time throwing strikes from his back against the pull of gravity, he contorted sideways and reached for the *sicario*'s ankle. He got a tight grip on it, and the man wrenched his leg forward to try and escape the grip.

Slater had been counting on that.

He rolled with the momentum, pushing the guy's leg in the direction he'd tried to escape from. The result was the *sicario* pitching forward, having to tumble over one shoulder to avoid ploughing face-first into the carpet, and when he righted himself Slater had reversed position entirely, winding up with one knee on the guy's chest.

And he didn't need to waste time wrestling for control of a weapon.

He just lined up the perfect target and cocked his left elbow and dropped it on the *sicario*'s forehead, putting all his bodyweight and some extra adrenaline behind it. There was no need for a prolonged exchange of fists. Truth was, in real life, whoever landed the first significant blow usually won the fight. In Slater's case, it happened almost one hundred percent of the time. His elbow bounced off the guy's skull and ricocheted his head off the ground and knocked him unconscious with one brutal *crack*.

Slater stood up, walked over to his Glock, picked it up, came back, and put one round through the centre of the *sicario*'s head.

Right where he'd delivered the elbow.

He checked himself for injuries as the adrenaline wore off, but he was unhurt. Bruised, banged-up, sore, but nothing that would impede his movement for the next couple of hours.

He crossed to the first *sicario*'s body and picked up the weapon the guy hadn't had the chance to fire. It was a Colt M1911, identical to the handgun Rico had wielded at Palantir. A fine gun, with .45 ACP rounds more than capable of tearing through flesh and bone.

He didn't need two handguns.

He went straight back to the door labelled "505" and knocked three times.

It took a long time for the sound of movement to materialise behind it.

'It's me,' Slater said, keeping his voice low.

Alexis opened the door, her face ghost-white, a vein in her neck showing how fast her heart was pounding.

She said, 'I thought you were—'

He handed the Colt over by the grip. 'Take this. If anyone comes through this door with bad intentions, use it. The taser won't cut it.'

'Don't you need—?'

'I've got one.'

'Are you—?'

'I'm fine.'

She reached out and threw her arms around him, burying her head against his chest. He took a giant step over the threshold, backing her into the entranceway of her apartment, separating her from a line of sight with the two bodies outside.

Then he stepped away. 'I still want that date.'

'You've got it.'

He tried to smile, but couldn't. The ice-cold clarity that he'd just narrowly avoided death was still fresh on his mind. He nodded once, and waited for her to close the door.

Then he turned toward the two bodies down the hall.

He set to work moving them into the stairwell, out of sight.

He didn't want her to see what he'd done.

What he was, under it all.

52

With the dead *sicarios* wedged into a dark alcove in the stairwell, Slater descended.

He didn't bother illuminating the way. There was a weak emergency light at the top of the stairwell, supposedly running on a small backup generator. Its glow barely permeated the giant concrete space, but he could make out the outlines of steps ahead, and that was all he really needed. Besides, using his phone as a flashlight would only reveal his location as a beacon if there were more enemies lying in wait.

Nothing would surprise him at this point.

He pulled out his phone and tapped Violetta's contact name. The satellite technology connected to her own customised device, and the call went through immediately, the dial tone slightly different to the default shrilling.

She picked up after three rings. 'Are you okay?'

'Yeah,' he said. 'Don't worry about me.'

'I am.'

'Have you spoken to King?'

'Briefly. Sounds like he's in the middle of something.'

'I got the same impression. Did he tell you anything?'

'No. He's keeping things close to his chest. Which is inconvenient. He was barely on the line for thirty seconds. Are you with him?'

'No. But I'm about to be.'

'You need to pass on critical information.'

'And what might that be?'

He kept the phone pressed to his ear with one hand and used the Glock in the other to sweep the space ahead as he reached the bottom of the stairwell. Uncanny déjà vu swept through him as he reminisced on the exact same sequence playing out in his own building on the Upper East Side hours earlier.

Would the next few seconds be the same, too?

Only one way to find out.

He didn't wait for a response from her end — he simply stepped out of the stairwell, kept his centre mass low and his movements quiet and smooth, and scanned every inch of the lobby that he could see. It was untouched, dormant. There was no one lying in wait.

Then he looked through the huge glass panes and saw something strange.

Empty vehicles still covered the road, obscuring his view of the opposite sidewalk. But amidst the cars there was movement. Coming from multiple places at once. Slater flitted his focus between them, and he thought he made out silhouettes, but they were moving fast and low.

Toward the intersection.

Toward the bank building.

Slater's stomach twisted. 'Your critical information wouldn't pertain to reinforcements you called in, would it?'

'Yes,' she said. 'Have you met them?'

'No,' he said. 'How much did you tell them?'

'I liaised with a Detective First Grade in the NYPD. I heard he was a hard charger. He was our best bet to rally up a bunch of cops in this kind of emergency.'

'How much of a hard charger?'

Silence.

Slater said, 'Violetta, what did you tell him to do?'

She said, 'I'll call you back.'

'It's too late. You won't get hold of him now. What did you tell him?'

'To form a perimeter.'

'Did you stress the gravity of the situation?'

'Yes.'

'So you told a hard-charging no-nonsense detective who's known for street prowess to get together a whole bunch of his colleagues and then hold back at the edge of something incredibly important?'

'I said I had my own specialists handling it.'

'So you undermined him, too.'

'Shit.'

'Yeah, shit.'

'What's he doing?'

'If I'm seeing things correctly,' Slater said, 'he's taking matters into his own hands.'

'Pull them back.'

'If I step out there, it'll kick off regardless. They're too close. There's no way to—'

'Slater, pull them *back*.'

'What part of "*I can't*" don't you understand?'

'Where are you?'

'In a lobby.'

'Where are they?'

'Fifty feet from the kill zone.'

'Can't you—?'

'You think they'd listen to me?' he said. 'They'd probably shoot me before they obeyed me. There's nothing to identify me as an operative. And there's a sniper somewhere out there with a .50 cal trained on the lobby I'm standing in. I'm a sitting duck if I step outside. They saw me go in.'

'Shit,' she repeated. 'Why is Riordan doing this?'

'I assume that's Detective First Grade Riordan, then?'

'Yes.'

'Because he doesn't want to sit back and play the supporting role. Not when there's the opportunity to be a hero.'

'That's not what I instructed.'

'That's life.'

'Use it,' she said suddenly.

'What?'

'If they're walking into a slaughter, use it to get inside the building. As a smokescreen.'

'Is that what you intended this whole time?'

'Christ, *no*. But if it works...'

'I'll see what I can do,' Slater said. 'But it's a tactical nightmare.'

'Just do what you can. That's all I've ever asked of you.'

'What about King?'

'Do you know where he is?'

'A couple of hundred feet in the other direction. Do I use the distraction to get back to his position, or to get inside the building on my own?'

Silence.

A long silence.

She said, 'It's your call.'

'I might not get another shot at a breach.'

'Then do what you spent most of your career doing. Go solo. King will find a way inside.'

'You don't know that.'

'I'm not certain of anything,' she said. 'At least there's *someone* in that building to fight. I'm not even going to start thinking about how little sense that makes.'

'They're defending something. That's for sure.'

'Then there's hope.'

'Why are they here? Why aren't they holed up somewhere remote? Literally anywhere other than the city they've blacked out?'

'I don't know.'

'I think this has something to do with us,' Slater said.

'What?'

'You heard me.'

'You can't be serious.'

'It's just a hunch.'

'You think a lot of yourself.'

'I think there's a reason we're here in the heart of it.'

She didn't respond.

He said, 'I think there are answers in that building.'

'I hope so.'

Outside, the silhouettes trickled closer to the looming bank building. They stood up a little taller. Slater thought he could make out guns in their hands. Tactically, they were doing everything to the letter. There were no flaws in the approach.

Aside from the fact they had no idea what they were up against.

He could almost feel the whole building tensing, the eight-storey slab of granite bristling with anticipation. A silence unfolded, so full and complete that he knew it could only spell one thing.

He said, 'Violetta, I've got to go.'

A moment later, the first .50 cal round seared through the night, and then a cascade of bullets lit up Second Avenue like hellfire.

53

In the lobby, Slater ran straight for the closest armour-clad corpse as the night came alive with muzzle flashes.

He rolled the man over, exposing the M4A1 carbine rifle trapped underneath, snatched the weapon up and checked it had a fresh, full magazine.

Then he ran toward what was left of the revolving door.

Now he had a better look at the carnage. He made use of the constant muzzle flashes and saw NYPD in uniform scattered throughout the street, taking cover behind vehicles and returning fire at the bank building. Six or seven of the building's windows were alive, barrels pulsating like strobe lights within. The skirmish was too widespread and too chaotic to keep track of. Slater would have no idea who was winning until most of the gunfire settled, leaving a bloody, miserable aftermath.

No matter who came out the victor, there'd be casualties on both sides.

It was a lose-lose.

He knew he wouldn't get another opportunity to make a

break for it, so he raced out the revolving door into the night. The cold wind hit him like a wall, but he pushed through it and made it to the closest vehicle in seconds. He threw himself down behind it, his pulse pounding in his ears, unsure how close he'd come to being hit.

Then shots lashed past him, so it was time to move again.

He bolted.

He gave thanks for all the seemingly unnecessary work he'd put into flexibility and dexterity in training. After years of consistent stretching and explosive plyometric work, his hips were as open as a professional gymnast's. It allowed him to practically crab-walk through the maze of cars like some demented contortionist, keeping his centre mass behind the chassis of a vehicle at all times.

He weaved between sedans and hatchbacks and box trucks and snuck up behind a man he'd eyed at the outbreak of the firefight. You could hardly place him as NYPD, but Slater could. He recognised the outfit — leather jacket, black boots, jeans. Not your typical cop getup, but everything Slater had heard — rumours and whispers in the intelligence community — indicated that Detective First Grade Jim Riordan was no typical cop. Which helped if you needed someone to seize the moment and do the hard shit that most people didn't want to do, but in this case it had only led to brazen bull-headedness.

Slater crept up on him, reached around and took the man's service weapon in an iron grip.

Riordan spun, his deeply lined face contorted in horror at the thought of being ambushed. He bunched his free hand into a fist and swung the hard calloused knuckles straight at Slater's head.

Any other man or woman standing there, it would have connected clean.

Right in the centre of the face, probably breaking a nose or shattering an orbital. Riordan swung fast and he swung hard, and you couldn't fluke that sort of power. It took serious practice, if not formal boxing training.

But Slater was Slater, and he had seen the punch coming from a mile away, and he slipped it and wrapped up Riordan's other arm and then shoved him hard into the door of the sedan he was cowering behind.

Not hard enough to draw attention, especially with war raging around them, but hard enough to send a message.

'You don't recognise me,' Slater said, 'but I recognise you.'

Riordan writhed against the car like his life depended on it. He had farmer-like strength — an unimpressive frame, but everything that was in it was hard and wiry and corded.

Slater had that kind of strength, too, and he was thirty pounds heavier.

He slammed Riordan into the car again and stared him in the face. 'Calm down.'

'Get the fuck off—'

'I will,' Slater said. 'But don't shoot me. That's all I'm trying to achieve here.'

'Who are you?'

'You spoke to Violetta LaFleur,' Slater said. 'I work for her.'

Riordan stopped struggling, and Slater released him and moved back a foot.

The cop said, 'How am I supposed to believe you? You got ID?'

'No. I'm not even officially employed. But if I wasn't who

I'm claiming to be, I'd have shot you in the back of the head and you wouldn't be alive to debate this.'

Riordan twitched.

Slater had reasonable faith that he could get his hands on the man's Glock 17 before the detective could bring it up to shoot him, but he suspected he wouldn't need to.

He was right.

Riordan gave up the tough-guy act, too distracted to focus, thrown off by the intensity of the firefight. His eyes were wide as saucers every time Slater caught a glimpse of them. Which wasn't often. Aside from the intermittent muzzle flashes, the light was sparse and the night was full. The initial pandemonium had trickled down to the occasional exchange of gunshots as all parties sought cover and approached the skirmish a little more tactically.

Slater caught the outlines of bodies out of the corner of his eye, either sprawled against vehicles or lying between them. It was too dark to see the blood, but he knew it was there.

Riordan's hard-charging nature had got a sizeable number of his men killed in the Bowery, and that realisation was striking home.

His usual no-bullshit demeanour was replaced with something very close to shell shock.

Slater said, 'You were told to keep a perimeter.'

'I figured the situation was urgent,' Riordan muttered.

'It is. But now it's even more urgent.'

'What's in that building?'

'I know as much as you do. But they're defending it like it's the key to all this.'

'Who are they?'

'I have a colleague who might have a lead on that.'

'Where?'

Slater threw a glance over his shoulder. 'He told me to meet him back there, but that was before World War Three broke out. He won't be there anymore.'

'You two work together?'

'Yeah.'

'You some kind of super-soldier?'

Slater looked at him. 'What makes you say that?'

'No one throws me around like that.'

'I had to make sure you didn't shoot me.'

'I get it.' Riordan bowed his head. 'I fucked up.'

'Yeah, you did. I'm not going to sugarcoat it.'

'What do you need from me?'

Slater thought about it. Thought hard, considering the time constraints. Ran through a dozen different options and arrived at a satisfactory conclusion and said, 'I need to get inside. No matter what.'

'Your colleague...?'

'He could be anywhere.'

Bracing against the constant unsuppressed gunfire, Slater kept low and slipped his phone from his pocket. He angled it against his body to mask the screen glare, instantly lowered the brightness, and then navigated to King's number. He tapped the screen.

It rang, on and on.

Nothing.

No answer.

'Right,' Slater said, his teeth clenched.

He didn't dwell on what that might mean. Now wasn't the time to contemplate the death of his closest friend.

Riordan said, 'That's what we were trying to do before all this happened.'

'What?'

'Get inside the building.'

'You're not me,' Slater said. Then he added, 'No offence.'

'How do you plan on breaching it?'

'There's at least a dozen first-floor windows on both faces. I'd guess they've barricaded the entirety of the ground floor, but you can't reinforce every window. No matter how much manpower they've got. It'd take too much time.'

He didn't really care what Riordan thought of the plan. He wasn't speaking to him. He was vocalising his internal thoughts, testing how they sounded out loud. Speaking to himself. All that mattered was his own conclusions. Years operating solo had taught him to rely on nobody but himself when everything went to hell.

Riordan said something, but Slater didn't hear it.

He snuck a look over the top of the car, taking in what he could of the bank building. He didn't think the first floor windows were reinforced, but he couldn't be sure of anything.

He ducked back down and said, 'I'm doing it. Can you give me a chance?'

'How?'

'Covering fire. I need it. I'm going in.'

54

Riordan grimaced and looked around, still overwhelmed, still in over his head. He said, 'You'll get yourself killed.'

'I don't see how that affects you. You don't know me.'

'Because I'm not an idiot,' Riordan said. 'If you work for the woman I talked to, then you're something else. So if you get yourself killed trying this, then we're fucked. You think I'm stupid? You think I don't realise what's gonna happen if this drags out any longer? Couple of days from now, people are gonna start panicking. I've seen what that's like.'

'You have?'

'Been a cop a long time. Seen some shit. Riots, protests that escalate, you name it. It takes one second of desperation for all this ... civilised shit ... to just vanish.'

Slater pondered that.

'Why the hell were we assigned to this?' Riordan snarled.

The detective's tone was a little heavier, a little shakier. It was sinking home that some of his men were dead. This wasn't a fever dream. This was real life, and the consequences of what happened tonight would last for years.

'Because of the state of the city,' Slater said. 'I thought that'd be pretty obvious. SF crews will get here eventually, but you combine the networks going down with the roads clogging up, and add in a few thousand people who need immediate assistance, and you've got a logistical disaster on your hands.'

Riordan nodded, solemn. He knew that, of course. It *was* obvious, just as Slater had said. But now he was mirroring Slater's earlier actions — speaking to himself instead of the audience. Like, *How did I let this happen? Now I'm going to have to tell wives their husbands are dead. Tell kids their fathers aren't coming home.*

Slater knew it was a downward emotional spiral waiting to happen.

He changed topic.

'The woman I work for,' Slater said. 'The one you mentioned before. You know who she is?'

'I know how much power she has. All the way to the top.'

'Then, by extension, I have the same power, no?'

Riordan shrugged. 'I guess so.'

'I do,' Slater said. 'And I'm ordering you and your men to give me covering fire. All I need is half a minute. Then I'm out of your hair forever. It's not too much to ask for.'

'You don't need to flex your connections,' Riordan said. 'I was gonna help you, regardless.'

'Thank you.'

'Make sure you pull this off. For all our sakes.'

Slater didn't want to tell the guy that it made no difference whether he knew the stakes. If Slater caught a bullet in the brain, that'd be that, and he wouldn't be around to understand what his failure had led to.

Every time he put his life on the line, it encompassed the whole world.

Because the whole world falls away when you die...

He shook himself out of the stupor and said, 'I'm ready. Can you tell your men?'

Riordan nodded and hunched deeper behind cover, pulling his radio scanner close. He mumbled into it, relaying instructions, conveying the importance of the situation. Static crackled and short replies came in fast. It might have taken time for Riordan to amass enough men to help, but when they were together, they worked fluidly.

Slater could admire any facet of law enforcement. He wasn't elitist.

Riordan looked at him. 'On your call.'

Slater nodded. He adjusted his grip on the carbine, then tensed his quadriceps and glutes, one by one, feeling the raw power in them. He'd have to sprint like a madman, and he knew it.

His vision narrowed.

His pulse rose.

The rest of the world fell away.

Then something penetrated the fog of war. Not for long, but a brief flash was enough. It was the face of the woman he'd met thirty minutes earlier, a woman he hardly knew, the result of a chance encounter that didn't mean much in the grand scheme of things.

But that's the funny thing about chance encounters.

Sometimes they mean everything.

He asked himself, *Do you really want to die here?* Sure, it was a long shot, but he might have just met someone — someone to pull him out of the hedonistic, PTSD-riddled cloud he'd been floating along since Ruby Nazarian had died. He didn't know Alexis, he'd hardly interacted with her, but sometimes there was an underlying feeling you couldn't shake.

It was there now.

Slater had slept with more women than he could ever hope to keep track of. But he didn't just want to take Alexis to bed.

He wanted to get to know her.

And he couldn't do that if he was riddled with bullets, sprawled across a sidewalk in the Bowery in a pool of his own arterial blood.

So he froze.

Then Riordan said, '*Now*,' into his radio mike.

And all Slater's thinking fell away.

His instincts took over, and he vaulted over the sedan as gunfire poured at the bank building from multiple locations on the street. It was a whirlwind of unsuppressed shots, fired from semi-automatic pistols and submachine guns and a couple of fully automatic assault rifles that Slater guessed belonged to SWAT. He knew whoever was positioned at the windows, or anywhere along the façades bordering the street, was currently ducking away from the sills, taking temporary cover, to regroup and wait for a lull.

Slater couldn't wait for a lull.

If they came up to return fire, he was a sitting duck.

He worked his way up to a full sprint. His cadence hit maximum, and then he ran like a man possessed across the asphalt, weaving between cars, almost losing his balance in the process. He breathed like he was punching the air out of his body, sucking in oxygen in giant gulps.

Then he ran faster.

He veered up onto the sidewalk, moments away from

plunging into the intersection. There was no cover out there, just a sea of cars spreading in every direction. No walls to cower behind, and no cars large enough to shield his mass. It was simply too close to the building — the men on the top floors could aim down and shoot him through the top of the head if he tried to take cover.

No man's land.

Do or die.

He went for it.

Took three bounding steps and went to leap off the sidewalk and into the middle of the intersection, but before he could commit a looming silhouette came out of the shadows to his right, sprinting just as fast as he was. A large man, who came bounding in to intercept Slater, and before Slater could bring his rifle up to neutralise the target the guy seized Slater in a giant bear hug and wrenched him off his feet and spun him around and threw him into the shadows between two residential façades.

Slater stumbled, and tried to keep his balance, and failed.

He sprawled to the hard ground of an alleyway, gashing his shoulder, crushing half his face against the concrete, nearly breaking his own nose. He rolled with it and came to his feet, ignoring the pain, and spun to put a bullet in the head of whoever had tackled him.

But Jason King was there in his face, wide-eyed, shaking his head.

Slater dropped his guard, and lowered the carbine.

King said, 'Couldn't let you go in alone.'

55

Slater's pulse came down, and something close to calm settled over him.

Close.

But not quite.

Given the circumstances, anything other than total panic was admirable.

The gunfire outside the alleyway suddenly became two-sided, only seconds after King had tackled him. With his blood running cold, Slater realised the man had just saved his life. There wouldn't have been enough time to reach the bank building before its occupants returned fire. They would have shredded him to pieces before he reached the opposite sidewalk, let alone scaled one of the granite faces to reach a first-floor window.

With harrowing clarity, he said, 'Thank you.'

King nodded. 'Saw you making a run for it. Knew you wouldn't make it.'

'You could have got killed yourself.'

'That's the job.'

'I didn't have another choice,' Slater said.

King nodded. 'I know. But you do now.'

'All we've got is a Hail Mary. I don't see another way inside.'

'He does,' King said, jerking his thumb into the shadows only a few feet away.

Slater let his eyes adjust, and made out the shape of a semi-conscious man slumped next to a dumpster. The kid couldn't have been far over twenty, with a lanky frame and a gaunt face made worse by two sizeable black eyes. His nose was swollen and misshapen, and his upper lip was purple.

'Who is he?' Slater said. 'What'd you do to him?'

'I saw you crouched back there, before you made a break for it. I had him at gunpoint, but I knew he'd try to run if I left him alone. I had to make sure he stayed put. All it took was a forearm to the face. He got the message.'

'Who is he?' Slater repeated.

King went quiet.

Slater said, 'What?'

'He's a Whelan,' King said.

Slater froze.

Raised an eyebrow.

King nodded.

Slater said, 'Oh, shit.'

'Yeah.'

'Why's he here?'

'He was with Rico. I think they met by chance. Convenient that the two most soulless individuals in the city came together, but they did. When you got away with Rico, the *sicarios* went after you. Left poor Samuel all on his own. But he hasn't been an easy prisoner. He realised his hopes were vanquished when I got a hold of him, so he lost it. He's barely sane.'

Realisation dawned on Slater. 'Hard to answer the

phone when you're wrestling with an uncooperative hostage.'

King nodded. 'Listen — he can get us inside.'

Slater paused. 'Wait...'

King nodded again. 'Do you understand now?'

'That's why you said I wouldn't believe if you told me.'

'Yeah.'

Slater stood motionless, the gears whirring in his mind. He said, 'I thought we crushed the Whelans.'

'We did. You ruined their reputation by putting most of the family in the hospital with your bare hands, and then I killed Tommy Whelan half a year ago. Without the patriarch, what little power they were clinging to evaporated.'

'But we followed it up,' Slater said. 'After we got back from Nepal, we made sure they were finished. They were scattered across the continental U.S. by then. Most of them fled from Manhattan. It's embarrassing to lose like that. Especially because of who they were before we showed up. They were the largest crime family in New York. And we reduced them to nothing.'

'We reduced them to *something,*' King said. 'Something weaker. But we didn't put out the flame. A handful of them are back, and they fucking hate us with every fibre of their beings, and I've got a gut feeling they chose to do something about it.'

Slater doubled over and put his hands on his knees.

Breathed in and out, slow and controlled.

Trying to calm himself.

Then he stood up and said, 'None of this makes sense.'

'I know.'

'What do they get out of this if we're the ones they wanted to punish? They could have sent an army after us with a tenth of the planning that something like this would have taken. And you really think a few stragglers of the Whelan family — a family that runs drugs and carries out union rackets and executions — has the smarts to take control of the power grid? This is some techno-terrorist shit. This isn't the Whelans.'

'Supposedly, it is.'

Slater didn't respond. They kept looming over Samuel, who by now was mostly awake and alert. Slater figured the kid was concussed — every nearby gunshot made him flinch like crazy. Or perhaps he was just wide-eyed and jumpy in general.

Outside the lip of the alley, the war continued. The NYPD exchanged potshots with the bank building's occupants, and the gunfire adopted a staccato rhythm. King and Slater barely flinched. They'd spent most of their lives in situations like this.

Stress, and panic, and chaos ... to them, it was home.

Slater said, 'What's he told you?'

'Nothing substantial. I wasn't kidding when I said he was barely sane.'

Slater bent down and seized Samuel by the back of the skull and pressed the barrel of his Glock into the kid's forehead. 'I know you understand what this is. Do you want to die here?'

Getting restless, King said through gritted teeth, 'I've tried that.'

Samuel opened his mouth wide and laughed in Slater's face. There was nothing in his eyes — no hope, no optimism. He was resigned to suffer and die, and he damn well wasn't going to give up any secrets in the meantime. Slater's stomach twisted as he realised he was faced with the worst kind of hostage.

The type that didn't care what happened to them.

And, in this case, probably preferred death.

Slater said, 'Give me everything he told you.'

King said, 'He only tells me what he wants me to hear.'

'But you said he can get us into the building? Why would he give that information up?'

King nodded.

Didn't respond.

Slater looked up.

Realisation struck.

He said, 'Because he wants to let us inside.'

'Yeah.'

'He wants us to see what they're up to.'

'Yeah.'

'Which means it's probably too late to stop anything.'

'Yeah.'

Slater put his hands on his hips and stared into the void.

King said, 'All we can do is try.'

56

King could see Slater grappling with the ramifications.

King had been thinking a whole lot as he wrestled Samuel through the Bowery, and nothing good had come from it. They *had* to try, because that was the only option, and because, deep down, they both knew all this had more to do with them than they would have liked.

Wordlessly, King hauled Samuel to his feet, and tossed Slater one of the duffels he'd been carrying. Slater extracted the MP7 submachine gun and readied the weapon for use, putting down his own carbine rifle in the process. A wise move. If they actually made it inside, the compact SMG would prove much more useful than the bulky carbine.

King watched Slater go through the motions, focusing on the task at hand. It put the man in a better headspace by forcing all other thoughts out of his mind.

King gripped his own MP7, the select-fire switched to full auto, and kept a tight grip on Samuel's collar. He said, 'Lead the way.'

Samuel waltzed forward, further into the alley. There was something close to a skip in his step.

He started to whistle under his breath.

King yanked him violently backward by the collar, choking the breath from his lungs, and then thrust him forward again.

Samuel spluttered and retched, but as soon as the discomfort subsided he went straight back to whistling.

King touched the MP7's barrel to the back of Samuel's head.

'Do it,' Samuel said. 'Then you're all out of options.'

He laughed, a high-pitched cackle that the cold night air seized and whisked up and away.

Behind them, Slater said, 'This is reassuring.'

'We just need to get inside,' King said. 'Then we don't need him.'

'That's right,' Samuel said. 'You sure don't. Ain't nobody ever really needed me.'

'You were part of this,' King said.

'Wasn't my idea.'

'You contributed.'

'I did what I was told.'

'Has that always been the case? You ever thought for yourself?'

'Nah,' Samuel said. 'I ain't smart like the rest of you. But I'm good at following orders.'

'What'd they get you to do for them?'

'A whole lot.'

'Care to elaborate?'

'No,' Samuel said. 'I don't think I will.'

King said nothing.

Just kept the barrel pressed against the back of his head.

'What?' Samuel said. 'You going to hurt me? Do it. I'll enjoy it. I *deserve* it.'

'He's a lost cause,' Slater muttered.

Samuel cackled. 'That's me. Lost as you could imagine. Used and discarded by everyone. You two are about to do the same. Won't be anything new.'

'Are you expecting sympathy?' King said. 'You know full well what you've done here.'

Samuel hesitated.

His stride slowed.

He said, 'What do you mean?'

'The blackout.'

The kid burst out laughing. 'You think that's bad?'

'Yeah,' King said. 'I do.'

'I killed over thirty people for them,' Samuel said, his words hollow and devoid of empathy. 'Wrap your head around that.'

King paused. 'For who?'

'I told you my last name. You figure it out.'

'The Whelans aren't around anymore,' King said. 'Either we killed them, or they wised up and ran for it. So there must be somebody else involved.'

Samuel beamed ear to ear, completely manic. 'That's the beauty of the modern world, hey? There aren't "top dogs" anymore. There used to be the head of the family, obviously, but like you said, you killed him. That don't matter much, though. It's all bullshit, in the end. People sucking up to other people to get promotions. The fuckin' hierarchy. Me ... I was never good at that. I ain't exactly ... how would you put it? ... socially intelligent. I ain't get no favours with no one. So they always used me. But nowadays ... prestige means *nothing.* The smarter ones in the family kept a low profile.

The ones who could actually shake things up. That's who stayed behind. That's who you overlooked.'

Samuel let them mull over that as he came to a halt over the lid of a giant storm drain. It was tucked into the shadows in the middle of the alleyway, unassuming, dark metal, a heavy solid thing. There was a thick rusting cylindrical handle on its far side, with a bolt at one end to secure it in place. It was hard to discern much in the dark, but King could see, clear as day, that the bolt had been tampered with. There was nothing securing it to the drain.

Allowing discreet access to the sewers and tunnels underneath.

King fought back apprehension. He gestured at the lid with his MP7.

'Is that where you're taking us?'

Samuel grinned. 'Sure is.'

Slater said, 'You know it's a trap.'

King said, 'Do we have another choice?'

'No,' Samuel said. 'You don't.'

Slater stepped forward. 'Why should we believe you? You talk about being used and discarded. Why do you want to help them by handing us over, when that's what they did to you?'

'Maybe it's not a trap,' Samuel said. 'You ever considered that? Maybe I don't give a shit anymore. Maybe there's no one waiting to ambush you. You won't know until you try.'

King said, 'Is that the truth?'

'I'm tired,' Samuel said, and for the first time a shred of humanity crept into his voice. 'I'm tired of it all.'

'You're *helping* us, then? Is that what this is?'

'I'm not fuckin' helping anybody. They got a lot of reinforcements in that building. They knew they were gonna have to defend it. You'll probably die. But hell, why not let you try?'

'You hate them, don't you?'

'Yeah.'

'But you hate us, too.'

'Yeah.'

'Why not just keep your mouth shut?'

'I'm gonna die tonight,' Samuel said. 'If you two don't kill me, I'll kill myself. Might as well make my last night a fun one, hey?'

King looked at Slater.

And shrugged.

Slater seemed hesitant.

King said, 'What have we got to lose?'

Slater's gaze fell to the drain lid. 'Everything.'

'So it's the same as always, then.'

'Not exactly.'

'How's that?'

'Now's not the time. I'll tell you later.'

King thought he saw something in Slater's eyes. A different attitude. Unusual circumstances. Like the man was holding onto something precious, something he didn't want to lose. They'd shared so many of their most vulnerable moments that it was hard to mask their feelings from one another.

King's instincts told him, *Slater's met someone. Someone who means something. Or* could *mean something.*

But where?

And when?

Slater was right. Now wasn't the time.

King handed Samuel over to Slater, bent down, and heaved on the handle. It took practically all his strength — which, considering he could deadlift north of six hundred pounds on a barbell, was nothing to scoff at. He made sure Slater had his MP7 pressed to Samuel's ear, then put his own submachine gun on the alley floor and switched to a double handed grip.

The lid creaked upward, an inch at a time.

Finally, it passed the point of no return, and dropped with a resonant *clang* to the other side.

A black hole had opened up for them in the ground, with an access ladder just inside the lip.

King picked up the MP7.

Slater said, 'After you.'

57

Slater watched King go first.

King kept the submachine gun pointed below him to intercept anyone who might be waiting for them. He crept down the ladder, one thin rung at a time, until the top of his head vanished from sight.

Slater kept Samuel Whelan in a tight grip. There were a million questions he could ask, but he kept his mouth shut. Samuel was a loose cannon, volatile as hell. The kid had descended into nihilism, and now the world was a sick game to him. Slater had seen it before.

When all hope dies, it's replaced by something close to soullessness.

Samuel could easily feed him misinformation, just for fun.

But a nagging voice told Slater the kid would talk.

At least, to an extent.

And he realised he only needed one answer.

'Which Whelan is behind this?' he said. 'It's just you and me here. I'm only going to ask you one question. Give me the name of the ringleader. It won't make a difference. You know it won't.'

Samuel half-turned, and Slater didn't stop him. The kid looked him square in the eyes with his hollow, unblinking gaze. A skull floating on a skeleton, injected with enough skin and muscle to make the kid appear human.

He said, 'Gavin.'

Slater shivered in the dark.

And he remembered.

Over a year ago, before he'd reunited with Jason King, before the madness of their unification, Slater had been out on his own. A rogue vigilante, a ghost as far as the government was concerned. Here in New York City, he'd first encountered the Whelans, a powerful crime family residing in an impressive townhouse on the Upper East Side. He'd stormed into their home and made a fool out of them and their security measures, beating them down with his bare hands in an attempt to create enough underground chatter to get the attention of an old government contact. He'd used the entire family as a pawn in his overall mission, but he'd especially humiliated one of the sons.

Gavin Whelan.

The man had been making unwanted advances on the daughter of someone Slater knew, and he'd responded by breaking Gavin's ribs and beating him senseless, delivering such a shocking display of violence that it might have taken him half a year to recover. Slater had seen the same situation a hundred times before — a third-generation mobster with feared parents and grandparents, thinking he had all the power and control in the world because he was born into it, pursuing an uninterested woman.

Slater knew how often that power dynamic led to rape.

He'd responded accordingly.

To him, it had been a flash in the pan of his career. That sort of violence was nothing out of the ordinary, and by now his past was a blur of similar encounters. Sometimes, he forgot that actions had consequences.

But ... this?

A near state-wide blackout?

Slater remembered Gavin well. A cocky, useless brat. There was no feasible way he could have pulled off something like this.

Unless Samuel had a point with his earlier spiel.

There aren't really "top dogs" anymore.

A pit formed in his stomach as he formed a hypothetical scenario. A man in his late twenties, the spoiled son of a wealthy and powerful crime family, who kept largely to himself. Because the Whelans were the old world, running guns and drugs and carrying out executions, all things that existed in the *physical* world. Maybe Gavin had other interests.

Maybe he'd figured out early on what you could do with a laptop and some initiative.

What you could accomplish by recruiting the right people.

There was a far-fetched timeline where all this made sense.

But not yet.

Slater shoved Samuel toward the drain and said, 'Down.'

Samuel lingered a moment too long above the lid, the same menacing smile playing across his lips.

'You don't need to tell me what to do,' he laughed. 'I'm the one showing you the way, remember?'

'Just do as I say.'

The kid shrugged. He stepped away from the moonlight, further into the shadows, and his hollow eyes seemed to sink even deeper into his head. He put a foot on the top rung, and a voice from below said, 'Who's coming down?'

King's voice.

Slater said, 'Not me.'

'Got it.'

Samuel clambered down, his arms and legs spindly as he descended. He vanished from sight and Slater shivered, suddenly alone. Behind him the firefight raged on, but the cracking gunshots barely registered. They'd become commonplace by now, and he knew he was well out of the line of fire. Truth was, if Riordan hadn't charged in with reckless abandon, there'd be no distraction to allow him and King to enter the building.

Maybe the deaths of his men weren't pointless after all...

That was if he and King could breach the bank building, neutralise every hostile, and reverse the blackout.

Big *ifs*.

He scrambled down the ladder, eager to get off the street. He felt strangely vulnerable with no light to work with. It would be the same underground, but at least it was an enclosed space.

Either a sewer, or a tunnel.

It turned out to be the latter.

Slater stepped down into a puddle of fetid water, the soles of his boots touching concrete underneath. Harsh white light flared as King fixed an under-barrel flashlight to his MP7 and fired it to life. The beam spilled down a perfectly rectangular, totally filthy concrete tunnel. It was barely wide enough to fit two people shoulder-to-shoulder across, and Slater found his breathing constricted by claustrophobia. But it was only one more temporary discomfort amidst many, so he ignored it.

'What is this place?' he said in a voice barely above a whisper.

'Who knows?' Samuel said. 'We just use it.'

'Why?'

'Gavin is ... meticulous. He had so many ways to avoid suspicion. He didn't want dozens of people to be seen coming and going with supplies, caught on CCTV. He wanted to do it anonymously. He found this tunnel system running only a few dozen feet from the perimeter of the building and just bored his way up into the lobby. Didn't take much effort. Not compared to ... all the rest of it.'

Samuel shivered.

Slater faltered for a moment. Only an instant, but he wondered if the kid had been coerced into doing all of this.

Unlikely.

He had, by his own admission, killed dozens of people for the Whelans. People who were essential roadblocks standing between them and the power grid. That took something far, far worse than brainwashing. It took a psychopath.

Slater shoved him forward, and kept the MP7 trained on his back.

The shadows rose and fell as King trained his own weapon.

The trio advanced into the underbelly of the Bowery.

58

The walls constricted.

Soon enough, King was able to reach out and touch both sides of the tunnel with his elbows. The air turned hot and foul, and the stink amplified, and their breathing started to echo, bouncing off the damp concrete.

Samuel muttered, 'We're close.'

King stifled a grimace. He thought of Violetta, stressed to the eyeballs, locked in her HQ in the tenement building, trying to keep her mind off the fact that her partner might get himself killed tonight. It was a brutal industry to operate in. She was fierce and uncompromising when she needed to be, and most of her coworkers — Slater included — probably thought she was a bitch. He thought she was one of the most respectable people he knew. It took courage you couldn't describe to willingly accept that burden, and try to stay sane in the process.

So he remembered that, and made a promise to make it back to her.

No matter what.

The fog of war settled over him again. They kept moving, using the glare of the flashlight fixed to his MP7 to navigate the tunnel system. Samuel moved fast — almost too fast — and King watched Slater hustle to keep up. The heat became stifling, and sweat beaded across his forehead. A couple of rivulets ran down the back of his neck. He didn't dare wipe them away. All his focus was on Samuel's skeleton physique, practically dancing through the tunnels, manic and unhinged and—

Slater said, '*Stop.*'

Samuel froze.

Behind Slater, King froze too.

Slater said, 'Turn around.'

Samuel turned around. His left shoulder scraped the concrete wall, hard, drawing blood. He didn't even react. He simply stared Slater in the eyes with his soulless gaze.

Pain was nothing to him.

Slater wiped sweat off his forehead and said, 'Where are we going, exactly?'

'I told you...' Samuel said.

'You said this was a passage to cart in supplies. What sort of supplies fit through a tunnel this narrow?'

Samuel smiled, baring his teeth. 'What are you thinking of? Stuff the size of refrigerators?'

'You tell me.'

'All they needed was CPU towers,' he said, a psychotic glint in his eye. 'The type you can fit in a large duffel bag.'

'Who needed them?'

'The people that did this, of course.'

'It wasn't Gavin?'

Samuel laughed, and it reverberated through the tunnel. 'You think *Gavin* wrote malicious code to shut down substations? Are you fucking stupid?'

King said, 'You know more about this than you let on.'

'I know all of it,' Samuel said. 'I don't understand how it works, but I know what it is. They told me that much before they threw me away.'

'Then give it to us. Help us stop it.'

'No.'

'We can make things painful for you.'

'Good. I'd like that. Still ain't tellin' you anything I don't want to.'

King said, 'Who wronged you?'

'Huh?'

'Up there. Who threw you away? "Used and discarded," as you put it.'

'Gavin,' Samuel said.

'I can make things painful for *him.*'

Samuel smiled again, and King found himself dejected by such a simple emotion.

It was a kid with no sanity left, making a mockery of it all.

Samuel said, 'No, thanks. I ain't never got anyone to do my dirty work for me.'

Slater said, 'If you're leading us astray—'

'You'll do *what?*' Samuel said, leering. 'I see you two for who you really are. When you put all the bullshit aside. The reputations, and the ego. You're scary men, yeah? You strike fear into people? They know you can hurt them. But then you run into someone like me. I'd prefer to get hurt. I don't give a shit. What are you gonna do now? How will you make me talk?'

King didn't respond.

Neither did Slater.

'Simple answer,' Samuel said. 'You *won't.* I own you.'

King said, 'Then give us what you want to give us, and let us get on our way.'

Samuel pointed a finger dead between King's eyes, and smiled wider. 'That's it! That's what I was looking for. Humility. You know you can't make me talk. So admit it, instead of going through with your macho crap. Then we can all get along.'

'Can we hurry this up?' Slater said. 'We get the picture. But we're running out of time.'

'Then,' Samuel said, 'it's a good thing we're here.'

He took five steps backward, moving like someone who knew every inch of the tunnels off by heart.

He veered sharply left, into a ragged maw.

Disappeared from sight.

In unison, King and Slater lurched after him. Momentary panic rippled.

What if—?

But when they rounded the corner, he was still there. Patiently waiting for them, like a deranged guardian protecting the doorway to another realm. They were in another tunnel, but this one had been recently formed. The walls were jagged and uneven, dug out in a hurry. Supports held the ceiling up, and damp groundwater had mixed with loose earth to form a slippery paste over the floor.

Samuel lifted a shaking finger toward the sky.

King looked up.

There was a manhole there.

Firmly shut.

Another access ladder spiralled up to it.

Samuel said, 'That will take you to the lobby.'

Silence.

Samuel said, 'You don't need me anymore.'

Silence.

Samuel said, 'Can I go now?'

King said, 'Sure.'

Samuel hesitated. Scrutinised King's features, to discern whether he was telling the truth. Then he took a few tentative steps, rounded Slater's impressive bulk, and made to step past King. And then King saw the façade slip. It was brief, and anyone else would have missed it, Slater included. But King was a keen, almost prescient judge of character, and suddenly he knew everything Samuel told him had been an act.

The kid wasn't really soulless.

Deranged, sure. A psychopath, almost certainly.

But suicidal?

No.

He cared about his life. He didn't want to die. He'd figured that pretending to lose all sanity was the easiest way to escape alive.

King grabbed him by the shirt and threw him back in the direction of the ladder.

Samuel barely kept his feet.

King raised the MP7 and pointed it square between the kid's eyes.

Stared him right in the face.

And suddenly Samuel knew that King knew.

The kid grimaced.

King said, 'You're going up that ladder.'

Beside him, it all clicked for Slater. He said, 'Oh.'

Samuel's eyes turned to ice.

59

Slater put it all together, almost as fast as King had.

Then he stepped forward and grabbed Samuel by the collar and hauled him onto the lowest rung of the ladder. He pressed his own MP7 into the back of the kid's neck and said, 'Climb.'

'No,' Samuel hissed.

He kept an iron grip on the rungs, his knuckles white.

Slater said, 'I've met a couple of people throughout my career who didn't care whether they lived or died. Only a couple. You're not one of them. They're exceedingly rare.'

'Well, you bought it for longer than you should have...'

'Up the ladder,' Slater said.

Samuel went pale. With each passing second, he looked more and more like a real skeleton.

Slater said, 'You don't want to die. Not down here. So you're going up that ladder, or you'll get a bullet through the throat.'

Samuel said nothing.

He stayed frozen, like a deer in headlights.

Slater said, 'If it's a trap up there, then you might survive if they realise it's you. But if they're waiting, they'll be jumpy...'

'Shoot me here,' Samuel muttered. 'I'd prefer it.'

'I will, in five seconds.'

A pause.

'I'm not kidding,' Slater said. 'You're wishing I am, but I'm not. I don't care about you, kid. So make your choice. Die down here, or *maybe* die up there.'

Silence.

'*Five.*'

Samuel didn't move.

'*Four.*'

Samuel didn't move.

'*Three.*'

Samuel lurched up the ladder, scrambling up the rungs in record time, fuelled by desperation. In doing so, he bared his soul. Sure, he had no regard for others, and killing indiscriminately was second nature to him, just as killing for justice was second nature to Slater and King. But at the end of the day, no matter how desensitised you are to violence, everyone wants to live.

Even psychopaths.

'*Two.*'

Samuel ascended the ladder like a spider and put one hand on the bottom of the manhole's lid and heaved with all his might, exposing huge rippling veins in his forearms and biceps to accentuate his rail-thin physique. There wasn't much strength in the kid's frame. He pushed like a man possessed, a man fighting to survive.

'*One.*'

Fight-or-flight adrenaline swamped the kid, and he chose fight, because there was nowhere to flee. It added a little extra strength to his gangly arms, and finally the lid moved. First an inch, then half a foot, then it caught its own momentum and swung all the way up and out.

Samuel burst up and out, his top half above the manhole, screaming, *'No, no, no, it's me!'* at the top of his lungs, but he was too late to prevent the knee-jerk reaction of those lying in wait.

The top of his head came off in a grisly shower of brain matter.

60

King didn't hesitate.

As soon as the first shot was fired above ground, he shouldered past Slater and leapt up the first four rungs of the ladder in a single bound. He kept one hand on his MP7 and used the other to heave himself higher, faster and faster. By the time Samuel's decimated corpse fell off the ladder, losing its grip on the rungs as the brain controlling the hands disintegrated, King was only a couple of feet below him.

Samuel fell on top of him, and King simply shouldered him aside.

The gunfire abruptly ceased, and a deep voice, unsure of itself, said, 'Oh fuck, Rick, that was—'

King almost smiled.

They'd realised they'd killed one of their own.

It would freeze them up, maybe only for a second.

To King, that was all the time in the world.

He reared up out of the manhole, his focus impenetrable, his mind so dedicated to the task at hand that he barely even registered that he was in danger. He took in the recognisable features of a bank lobby, understood where he was, and then tuned it all out.

He spotted two burly silhouettes as the closest to his position, both adopting wide stances, heavy assault rifles in their hands. But both barrels were lowered a few inches. It was an imperceptible, involuntary response to realising you'd just killed one of your own men, no matter how deranged that man in question might be.

There was temporary guilt, and shock, and acceptance.

King had the MP7 on full auto, and he simply squeezed the trigger and worked the barrel in a short horizontal line from left to right. Not quite spraying and praying. More accurate, more surgical. The submachine gun roared and bullets laced the chests of the silhouettes. They jerked and hit the floor.

He calculated his next decision in a split second.

Down, or up?

A quick pivot on the ladder revealed the lobby was a strange combination of traditional Renaissance architecture and a half-completed modern refurbishment. The building must have been in the midst of renovation when it was closed to the public and became a private dwelling. The walls speared up to a dome-shaped ceiling, and they were adorned with pilasters projecting from the marble, giving the space a regal aura. The black-and-white tiled floor spread out in all directions from the manhole, but although the lobby might have previously been one cavernous space, now it was partitioned into separate open-plan sections with the help of a few modern upgrades. King saw glass and wood partitions coloured in warm hues, with thick decorative curtains adding privacy.

If the bank was still open, they might have led through to private consulting rooms and swanky waiting areas.

Now, the lobby was dead and empty.

The only artificial light came from giant floodlights running on backup generators, the only ambient noise. The lights hummed gently between the roaring gunshots, their white beams aimed up toward the dome ceiling, spilling large shadows over the floor and walls.

With the rudimentary analysis of his surroundings complete, King turned to the matter of the hostiles. Gunning down two men in brutal fashion had sent a couple of the stragglers scattering, and he saw them now ducking behind curtains, throwing the heavy material aside in their desperation to retreat and regroup.

But one of them didn't.

A hulking silhouette stood frozen in the corner of the space, draped in the shadow of the modern wall behind him. He was bigger than King, which was impressive in its own right. At least six foot five, with a thicker frame. Basketball-sized hands. A large head, but not brutish. His features were refined, despite his size. It gave him a wholly unique appearance, and something about it scratched at King's memory. He was reminded of an intelligence briefing he'd glossed over months ago, but before he could confirm it, the enormous man raised a semi-automatic pistol and fired twice.

But he'd aimed and fired too fast.

Granted, the shots came close. King felt them whisk past him, and anyone else — besides Will Slater — would have ducked reflexively after nearly having their brains pulverised by tiny pieces of lead. Instead of retreating back down the manhole, King vaulted out of cover, rolled his big frame over the steel lid, and heaved it off the lobby floor. It weighed almost as much as the drain lid back in the alleyway, but this time he had the all-encompassing aid of adrenaline on his side. He lifted it like it weighed nothing and propped it up vertically on its hinges, using it as a circular shield to protect his vitals from follow-up shots.

Just in time.

He tucked his chin to his chest, ruining his situational awareness but saving his life. Three bullets struck the lid dead-centre, each one reverberating against the steel and vibrating through into his bones. He shivered, but then came the inevitable lapse in gunfire as the big guy realised King was safe from harm. King could see a perfect mental image of the guy skirting to the left or right. No way to tell which direction, but easy to estimate how much ground he was covering.

One step. Two steps. Three steps.

King reared up and snapped the MP7 to his shoulder, skewering it hard against his collar bone for support, and then found his target and pulled the trigger.

The guy was smart.

He hadn't stayed in place.

He'd retreated, anticipating what was coming.

He was halfway through the curtains when King's rounds laced his upper back. One of them struck centre mass, that was certain. The others, King couldn't be sure. But there was the meaty *thwack* of a direct hit and then the guy jolted like he'd been electrocuted, and a half-second later disappeared behind the curtains. The thick brown material drifted back into place, obscuring his bulk.

King sent three more rounds through the curtains, hoping for the best, and then turned and bolted for another set of curtains in the opposite direction.

As he took off, he shouted, 'Fifteen!' into the manhole.

He knew Slater would get the message.

He ran flat out, heart pounding, and threw himself

behind the curtains just as a couple of stray bullets tore through the material, right near his skull.

He ducked into a crouch as he burst through them, practically rolling head-first into a half-furnished waiting room complete with oak coffee tables and polished stools arranged around a marble bar.

He barely had his feet under him when he realised there was someone else in the space.

Only a couple of feet in front of him.

The guy was unarmed, and hadn't been anticipating defending the lobby from within, but it didn't seem to deter him. He was a trained combatant — King could tell from his demeanour alone — squat and compact, probably six inches shorter than King but roughly the same weight. A gorilla in human form, with an enlarged jaw and a feverish glint in his eyes. A capable veteran ready to kill for a high price, a price he'd undoubtedly been offered.

King started along the natural trajectory of raising his MP7, but the guy caught it under the barrel and wrenched it upward even faster, using his inhuman strength, sending it arcing toward the ceiling. A trigger pull would achieve nothing, so King abandoned that option, and loaded up to deliver a colossal head butt into the bridge of the guy's nose.

The man jerked sideways, throwing King's aim off, making him hesitate.

Then he wrapped two burly hands around the shoulders of King's bulletproof vest and hurled him off his feet and brought him down on the nearest oak table, crushing and splintering it.

Crushing and splintering King in turn.

61

Perched halfway up the ladder, Slater counted to fifteen, making sure to take it slow.

Anyone in a high-stress environment was naturally inclined to rush. Thankfully, he'd spent most of his life in high-stress environments, and he could calm himself when he needed to. So, with gunshots raging over his head, and the life of his brother-in-arms hanging in the balance, he started ticking away the seconds as accurately as he could manage.

When he made it to thirteen, he heard an almighty *crash.*

It resonated through the lobby, the sound travelling up to the dome ceiling and echoing back down. It sounded eerily like wood splitting, with considerable weight behind the impact, and it had come from the exact direction King had run toward.

Two seconds left.

Indecision plagued him.

Stay, or go?

If he missed his cue, it would be tactical chaos. Together,

he and King formed a cohesive unit, but only if they knew what each other was going to do before they did it. King had instructed him to wait fifteen seconds with full confidence, and Slater knew the man needed the time to set himself up at a vantage point so he could provide covering fire.

But if it was King on the receiving end of that earth-shattering crash, then there'd be no cover fire to speak of.

Slater would raise his head out of the manhole and meet the same fate as Samuel had.

Fourteen.

Fifteen.

He didn't move.

He held his breath, listened to the gunshots ripping through the space, and hoped like hell King was okay.

62

King wasn't okay.

Superficial pain was nothing. In a fight to the death, he could get bruised and cut over every square inch of his skin, and he'd barely notice until he was out of danger. But injuries that impeded his movement ... those couldn't be so easily ignored.

When he pulled himself out of the wreckage of the coffee table and shot to his feet, his ribs lit up like they'd been torched with a flamethrower.

He almost went back down on one knee, but he knew that was as good as suicide.

He barely faltered. Barely wavered. But a half-grimace tickled the corners of his mouth, and the bull-like man across from him noticed. In a fight with stakes like this, it might as well have been the largest display of weakness in human history. The guy's face contorted into a sneer and he broke into an all-out charge, smelling blood in the water, sensing an opportunity to kill.

King readied himself.

There's no feeling quite like being overwhelmed by true

pain. The type of pain that drills deep, that evokes primal fear, that screams at you, *You're really fucking hurt. Don't move! Survive!*

King couldn't listen to it, but it distracted him endlessly. He barely even realised his MP7 was nowhere to be found, and he caught it at the last second in his peripheral vision, buried under the splintered wood of the table. He had no time to reach for it, because the bull in human form had picked up serious momentum, and the next moment he launched himself with barbarism at King, who stood there rigid as if frozen in place.

No, King told the voice. *I have to move.*

His ribs screamed with every slight disturbance, but he didn't pay it a moment's thought. Thousands of hours of practice hardening his mind came together in one collective moment and gave him the strength to side-step, catch the guy under the arm and heave him forward, taking him completely off the ground, using the momentum of his own charge to rotate him half a revolution in the air and dropping him upside down. The top of the man's skull hit the ground so hard that it very nearly split open, but the *thud* told King everything he needed to know. If the guy wasn't dead, he was damn close to it, but King made sure by kicking the MP7 out of the wrecked table, sliding down and lifting it off the ground with three fingers, planting it on the back of the guy's thick squat neck, and sending two bullets ripping through his throat.

Then, with his face contorted into a show of weakness he could finally allow, he ran for the curtains, hoping, praying, that Slater hadn't actually moved after fifteen seconds.

He shouldered through the thick brown sheets, fully aware that he could catch a bullet in the face for his troubles, but also aware that he had no other choice. Slater needed him. He exposed half his frame, but thankfully there was no one paying enough attention to capitalise on it. The enormous guy was nowhere to be seen — maybe wounded, maybe dead.

Two new mercenaries had appeared out of nowhere, but they were focused on the manhole, slinking toward it with Kalashnikov AK-47s aimed dead at the blackness.

The curved magazines, full with lead, seemed to ripple in the lowlight.

Ready to spew forth their rounds into an unsuspecting Will Slater.

King intuitively switched the MP7 to semi-automatic with a flick of his index finger, then shot the first mercenary square between the eyes. Blood geysered out the back of the guy's head, which was sufficient enough to distract his comrade. The second merc wheeled around with his eyes wide, trying to discern where—

King put two rounds into his face, too. He let both corpses drop to the floor, and then trained his vision wide, taking in the entire lobby.

All quiet.

'*Now!*' he roared.

63

Slater had his MP7 trained on the space above the manhole, but his heart rate was through the roof, and he couldn't bring it down.

Fifteen seconds had well and truly passed, and there was no sign of King.

Doubt began gnawing at the back of his mind.

If he's dead, you should regroup.

Of course, there would be the soul-crushing loss to deal with if Jason King had truly met his demise, but all Slater could focus on right now was the eight million who needed power. Compartmentalisation was in full swing, and he started planning a tactical retreat, perhaps a call with Violetta to discuss what sort of reinforcements he had access to...

'*Now!*' King roared from above.

Slater flipped an internal switch.

All thoughts fell away.

He scrambled up the last few rungs, vaulted out into the cavernous space, then spotted King positioned between two brown curtains on the left-hand side of the lobby, his weapon trained to provide covering fire.

Slater recognised that he was covered, and began a beeline for King's position.

Then two rounds hit King full in the chest and sent him sprawling back out of sight.

He vanished behind the curtains.

Slater didn't think. Didn't waste a millisecond. Just jerked hard to the left and ducked low and threw himself forward over one shoulder, rolling wildly to throw off the aim of anyone looking to follow up the initial shots.

And they sure tried.

A chunk of tile exploded in his face as he rolled, and loose shards gashed his cheek and forehead, coming perilously close to removing an eyeball. He realised a bullet had struck the ground directly underneath him, and he lurched to his feet and covered the final dozen feet to another pair of curtains. He realised he'd ended up running in the opposite direction to King's position — he'd shouldered through the curtains to the east, and King was to the west. The shots had come from the north.

He came to a skidding halt in a large bare room with the same tiled floor. There was no furniture, nothing at all besides the beginnings of a modern refurbishment.

But the room wasn't empty.

There was a man standing in front of Slater, five inches taller than him, far wider, far thicker, far denser. Huge hands, huge feet, but sharp, laser-focused eyes and a thin cruel mouth. Handsome features for an otherwise bullish man. He had a hand to his bowling-ball sized shoulder, and his skin was ghost white. Then Slater saw the blood pouring out from between the man's fingers.

He'd been wounded.

Everything happened at once.

Slater raised his MP7 and pumped the trigger.

He got three shots off.

All fired low, because that was literally the only trajectory he could muster in time. If he'd raised the MP7 up to head height, the man would have battered it out of his hands before he could pull the trigger. So all three bullets caught the guy in the stomach and gut, surely tearing his intestines and liver to shreds, so how the hell was the guy still advancing?

It threw Slater off. He couldn't believe someone could defy the laws of physics like that. The survival mechanism was an incredible thing, because suddenly the enormous man was in his face and simply seized hold of the gun and jerked it upward and smashed it into the underside of Slater's chin, knocking a tooth clean out of his mouth, nearly splitting his tongue.

Slater went down like he'd been shot.

It damn well felt like he had.

He fought the urge to vomit, and through the mask of pain he clawed desperately for his weapon. He still had three fingers on it, but a particularly vicious bolt of pain seared through his head and threw off his equilibrium. His whole world swum, and he caught a glimpse of the huge silhouette looming toward him.

He found a grip on the MP7, and scooted backward away from the giant, but he was so dizzy, so faint, so...

The huge man dropped toward him.

Slater rolled. It took all the effort he had.

But the giant hadn't been dropping a blow.

He'd collapsed.

The man came down right next to Slater, rolled over to a seated position, and scooted up against the wall behind them. He opened and closed his mouth, but all that came out was silence. He looked down at his gut, and seemed to notice the three bullet wounds for the first time, and let out a moan. He clasped both hands to the skin, trying to stem the bleeding.

He wasn't dead.

But he was incapacitated.

Slater got to his feet on shaky legs, and now he did spit out a mouthful of blood. He probed the inside of his mouth with a finger and found the gaping hole where a tooth had previously resided. His tongue was lacerated, but he hadn't bitten it off. All in all, he was badly rattled, but it was nothing that would keep him permanently out of the fight.

He loomed over the big man, breathing hard, shocked at how close he'd come to losing.

It wasn't an ordinary occurrence, but this wasn't an ordinary situation. He and King were brutally disadvantaged, forced to fight against near insurmountable odds, but they were still here, and maybe they had a chance to—

Right beside him, the curtains parted, and a gun barrel pointed squarely at his face.

He held his breath.

Jason King slipped inside and regarded the big man at Slater's feet.

'I realised who that is,' King said. 'It's Rick Whelan.'

Slater said, 'Are you hurt?'

'My rib. You?'

'My mouth. And I might be concussed.'

Everything felt distant, detached. He'd experienced it before, but it never made the sensation any less strange. He was depersonalised, a common side effect of a concussion. Waving his hand in front of his face sent a strange response through his brain, like the whole movement was taped on a time delay. Early in his career, it might have thrown him off so drastically that he wouldn't have been able to continue.

Now, he barely thought about it.

He realised Rick Whelan was still breathing, and together he and King exchanged a wordless look.

Time to make him sing.

64

King crouched down first, squatting so his face was lined up with the big man's.

Rick said nothing. Most of his conscious effort was directed toward staying alive. He still had both hands pressed on his bullet wounds, but he seemed to be doing a respectable job of stemming the bleeding. King couldn't help but be impressed by the man's fortitude.

King said, 'Last we checked, you were in Grand Cayman.'

Rick stared straight ahead. Said nothing.

Slater crouched down beside King.

King said, 'You're better off talking to us.'

'And you're better off putting a bullet in my head.'

'That's true,' King said. 'But we've never been the sharpest tools in the shed.'

'You think I'm going to give you anything?'

'You giving us something is the difference between bleeding out here on this cold floor and getting patched up at a hospital.'

'Either way, my life is over.'

'One option gives you at least some semblance of hope for the future, doesn't it?'

Rick stared rigidly forward.

'Come on, Rick,' King said. 'Slater and I aren't stupid. We knew that crushing one of the biggest crime families on the East Coast was going to have consequences. We got back from a job in Nepal a few months ago, and we had some spare time, so we followed it up. Found that most of the major players in the Whelan family, the ones with business smarts and ruthlessness in spades, had fled. Including you. So did you really go to Grand Cayman, or were you here the whole time?'

'Here,' Rick said.

'Because you're intelligent, and you knew we'd be chasing up any remaining leads, so you left a paper trail overseas while you lay low here and licked your wounds and figured out where to go next.'

Rick shrugged. 'Something like that.'

'I know you,' King said. 'Better than you think I do.'

'And you know us,' Slater said. 'We were the motivation for all this, weren't we?'

'Not my motivation. I don't let petty emotions affect me. Never have, never will.'

'For Gavin?'

'Yeah,' Rick said. 'He's a little more impulsive. He fucking despises the both of you.'

'And you don't?'

'I told you how I feel.'

'You did,' King said. 'And I believe you. Every piece of intel we got on the Whelans after we dismantled them indicated that you were the glue holding the entire operation together. Is that accurate?'

Something very close to pride flared in Rick's eyes.

Which had been King's intention the whole time.

But the big man tried to stay guarded. It was hard with mortal pain drilling behind his eyeballs, but he managed to cling onto emotionlessness.

'You could say that,' he said.

King, however, knew what life-threatening pain did to a man. How easily it broke you down. Humbled you. Brought you to the sobering reality that you might be about to blink out of existence. Rick Whelan, a man of incredible ruthlessness, was starting to understand that.

Because, deep down, he knew three bullets in the gut wasn't survivable.

King notched up the pressure to cave. 'You're not insane, Rick. Not like Samuel was. And you're not blind in your hatred for us, like Gavin. You have poise, you have smarts, and you're a master tactician.'

Despite himself, Rick nodded.

King said, 'So what the hell are you doing here?'

Rick's eyes turned glossy. A mixture of crippling agony, acceptance, and resignation. Death awaited. He might as well speak his mind. He wouldn't get the opportunity again.

'To see if it could be done,' he said.

'Why?'

'There's nothing quite like *la pista secreta,*' he said, referring to the Spanish phrase for the path of illegitimacy.

The drug cartels used it to refer to their trade, their business, their "secret track," as it quite literally translated to.

King understood. He'd experienced the same thing when he got out of Black Force for the first time. For ten years, his life had been violent, and relentless, and hard-charging. He'd lived at the very edge of the human experiential spectrum. He'd trained and fought and killed and warred for his country, and when he got out, ordinary life seemed banal in comparison.

Rick Whelan had experienced the same thing.

'I always considered myself smarter than the rest of them,' he said. 'And then you two, a couple of highly motivated vigilantes, tore it all apart with very little effort. All you did was beat the upper echelon into unconsciousness and kill the head of the family. Usually, that's salvageable. There's contingencies in place. Successors. But it ruined our reputation on the street, and in a business like ours, that's the end of the world. So I was out. Directionless. But I had my head screwed on straight, and I understood that the two of you were different beasts entirely. So I didn't bother trying. I was lost, and I needed *something* to make me alive, and then Gavin came to me with a proposition.'

'How much of it was him, and how much of it was you?'

'For a little brat, he's surprisingly visionary,' Rick said. 'He's twenty years younger than me, so he had the ideas I never could have. But, for all his strengths, he's flawed. He drinks, he smokes, he fucks — he spends the money that his father and grandfathers fought tooth and nail to earn. But he knew he needed me. He knew he could never implement the things he wanted to do. He needed someone with razor focus to carry it all out.'

'You're a hacker?'

'No,' Rick said. 'But this is the Internet age, my friend. If you have the assets, you can find people. You can find anyone.'

'That's all it took?'

'That's all it took. That's why I did it. Because I didn't quite believe I could expose the flaws the kid showed me. But they were there, and they were ripe for picking.'

King's stomach twisted.

Rick said, 'If you think about it, I did this country a service, didn't I?'

'Sure,' Slater said. 'You bet. We all learned our lesson. You've shown us the flaws in the system. Now reverse it.'

'I'm dying,' Rick said, smiling through bloodstained teeth. 'Maybe if you'd let me live, I might have had a change of heart. Truth is, I always saw the madness in what Gavin was doing, but I guess I was too awed by the results to stop it. And now...'

He lifted his hands away from his shirt, exposing the crimson stain covering half his torso. Blood overflowed the lip of his shirt and ran down his jeans. It dripped to the floor with finality.

Rick looked King and Slater square in the eyes and said, 'Well, now I don't much care anymore. You killed the one sane man left in this building. Best of luck, boys.'

Then, before either of them could lunge in to try to stem the tide, Rick Whelan bled out.

65

Slater swore out loud, turned and kicked the wall.

Beside him, King swept through the curtains, submachine gun raised, making sure the lobby was still clear. Slater composed himself and followed the man out of the waiting room and, sure enough, it was still a ghost town. They both slotted fresh magazines into their respective MP7s and gave each other the same silent look.

Slater knew what it meant.

Everything was so abhorrently crazy that there was little left to say.

They advanced, clearing the tight corners, one man moving, the other covering him. They repeated the process until they swept up into another broad concrete stairwell. Slater suppressed the odd sensation of déjà vu. Most of his night had been stairwells and lobbies and alleyways and bloodshed.

The cold, alien stink of a city without power.

And the key to its salvation lay within these walls.

He steeled himself as they climbed two flights and came out in the mouth of an entire floor dedicated to office cubicles. The endless space was divided up by waist-high partitions, and it was all dark. There was enough midnight-blue light infiltrating the floor-to-ceiling windows that they could make out the outlines of their surroundings, but apart from that they were blind.

'Ready?' King whispered.

'Go,' Slater said.

King switched on his flashlight.

Gavin Whelan was a dozen feet in front of them, holding an AK-47 at shoulder height, its barrel aimed squarely between Slater's eyes.

Stalemate.

If anyone pulled a trigger, Slater would die, and Gavin would die.

Gavin looked exactly how Slater remembered. Handsome for an Irishman. The last time Slater had seen him, he'd placed him as the son of a powerful mobster and a gorgeous trophy wife. Now, he shared the same sentiment. Gavin had pale skin, and jet black hair falling in locks over his forehead, and full lips, and a strong jaw. He took good care of himself. Despite looking early twenties, he was probably closer to thirty, if not older.

But there were a couple of noticeable differences. A year ago, Gavin had sported the straightened posture and calm confidence of someone used to getting their way. Now, he was slouched, broken, defeated. The confidence was still there, but the foundations had been shattered. He could still get his way, but he'd given up on the fairytale the rest of his life was supposed to have been.

Slater knew why.

'Hey, kid,' he said. 'Haven't seen you in a while.'

His voice ice, Gavin said, 'Glad you're here.'

'I'm sorry about the way things ended last time.'

'That's good to hear,' Gavin said. 'Shame you didn't come to me with your little apology sooner.'

'Must have been the wake-up call of all wake-up calls, right?' Slater said. 'You think you're the man, you think you're unstoppable, and then I break your ribs and slap the shit out of you and leave you in a pool of your own blood. I seem to remember kicking you in the balls, too. Did I rupture one of them? I'd always wondered.'

'Talk,' Gavin said. 'Talk as much as you want. You won't get me angry, and you won't get me to stop this. It's pointless.'

'You can't stop it,' Slater said. 'The people who work for you can. All I need is for you to point us in their direction. You're useless to us otherwise. Always have been.'

That made the kid bristle.

He didn't react, and he brought himself back under control in an instant.

But at least Slater cracked the exterior.

Gavin said, 'We can stand here all night if you'd like.'

'We're not going anywhere. Rick's dead. Everyone downstairs is dead. You don't have much left, kid. It's impressive what you managed to achieve. Let's call it a day.'

Gavin laughed, hollow, empty, drawn-out, until it finally tapered down to silence.

Then he said, 'Oh... you actually thought that speech was going to work? After you killed my grandfather and drove my father and uncle to suicide?'

Slater bristled.

Beside him, so did King.

Slater thought, *Did we know that?*

It was one piece of a psychological puzzle they hadn't even begun to decipher. Rick had given them the barebones explanation, and then he'd died.

'I had everything,' Gavin said. 'I had the whole rest of my life ahead of me. And then you two had to go and kill Tommy.'

'You're a smart kid,' Slater said. 'You could have done anything. Your thug family wasn't the be all and end all.'

'What could I do? Start a small business? Start my own organisation just to see it torn down the moment someone like you caught wind of it?'

So that's it, Slater realised.

That's what had broken Gavin.

The fact that Slater and King had toppled the Whelan empire so *effortlessly.* It hadn't even been their goal, but the law of unintended consequences sometimes fell in their favour. The family had disintegrated, the power had vanished, and depression and suicide had swept through the mafiosos in a wave. And that had ruined Gavin Whelan's confidence, as it probably would for the rest of his life. He'd figured that as soon as he tried to achieve anything for himself, if it was in any way illegitimate, someone with the skillset that Slater or King possessed would storm in and crush him. For a third-generation mobster with a silver spoon in his mouth, that sort of hopelessness was unacceptable.

For Gavin, there would be no point trying to scrape together a normal life.

The failure, and the depression, had driven him to extremes.

Slater looked around, soaking in the darkness.

Sometimes, this was what extremes led to.

66

Gavin said, 'You see? Finally I did something worthwhile. Finally I built something on my own. And now it's going to bring down the city that chewed me up and spat me out.'

King said, 'Where are the rest of your men?'

'You'd *love* to know that.'

'I can hear the elevator moving behind us.'

Gavin went quiet.

King said, 'Which makes me wonder what that guy's doing behind you.'

The oldest goddamn trick in the book.

Gavin didn't look. He wasn't that stupid. But he did tense up involuntarily, anticipating that someone he wasn't familiar with might crack something over his head, or make a lunge for his weapon. That didn't happen, but his aim drifted an inch to the left.

The kid probably didn't even notice.

King did.

He pulled the trigger of his MP7 and sent three rounds into Gavin's thigh, destroying his quadricep, tearing muscle, shattering the femur. The kid collapsed with an ungodly howl and Slater sprinted over and punted the AK47 away, sending it skittering down one of the office hallways. Gavin screamed as he lay there on his side, bleeding profusely, breathing fast, almost hyperventilating. King watched Slater shed his jacket and wrap it tight around the leg. Rudimentary pressure.

Slater stood up, and King raised an eyebrow.

Slater said, 'I need him alive. I need to know how he did it. And why.'

'He told you why.'

'That's not a real explanation. I want to know *exactly* why.'

'You think he'll talk to you?'

'Yes,' Slater said. 'I think he will. But first...'

He hauled Gavin to his feet, pressed the MP7 barrel to his head, and held him out in front as a human shield. King got the message, and jogged over to their position, a couple of dozen feet away from the elevator behind them. Together they turned to face it, and King stepped in behind Slater and rested his own MP7 on Gavin's collar bone, using the man as a gun rest.

Gavin whimpered in pain.

Slater said, 'You haven't felt anything like that before, have you? I hit you and kicked you, but you've never taken a bullet. It's a whole new level of pain.'

Despite everything, Gavin smiled. 'You're fucked now. I was just stalling. You know who's coming?'

'No. I assume you do.'

'Put two and two together,' Gavin said. 'Who was I most afraid of while I was planning this whole ordeal?'

'Us.'

'So where would I go if I wanted to mirror the pair of

you?'

'Nowhere.'

'Oh?'

'You can't mirror us,' King said.

'Oh, but I can. And I did.'

The elevator chimed, and an artificial *ping* echoed through the empty office floor, and a white "down" arrow lit up beside the doors. It was the first thing that made Slater realise some of the building's mechanisms must be operating on a backup generator.

The doors whispered open.

A man stepped out.

Rather, he strolled out.

Lackadaisical, uncaring. Clad neck-to-toe in combat gear — bulletproof vest over a dark khaki shirt and olive green pants. Huge Gore-Tex boots. He was Caucasian, around six feet tall, with a military-style buzzcut and a thick pink scar under his left eye. The lights in the elevator illuminated him from behind, so it was hard to discern his features front-on, but King could have sworn he was chewing gum.

He had a 9mm Glock in his palm, and nothing else.

He took six big steps out of the elevator, practically striding, and came to a standstill with a cubicle on either side of his giant frame.

In a heavy scouser accent straight from the streets of Liverpool, he said, 'Alright then, lads.'

Silence.

Neither King nor Slater were sure whether it was a question, or a demand.

'That's *enough*,' the newcomer said, and his voice boomed like thunder. 'Party's over.'

He spoke with such utter confidence, and was so incredibly sure of himself, that King felt a faint urge to drop his weapon right there.

Instead, he pushed the barrel a little harder into Gavin's skull, and the kid audibly yelped.

'You hear that?' King said. 'That's your paying client. How are you going to collect your fee if he's dead?'

The man said, 'That's assuming there's a fee, mate.'

'You work for free?'

'Who says I'm working for anyone?'

'I am,' King said. 'Because I know your type. What were you?'

'SAS, once upon a time.'

King stiffened. 'That's quite the fall from grace.'

The man shrugged. 'Depends on your perspective. The way I see it, this is the purest form of organised violence there is.'

'Working for anyone who pays the bills?'

The man smirked. 'You take cheques from a government that doesn't give a shit about you. You do their dirty work. You're no better than me. Actually, you're worse, because you pretend you're righteous. I gave up on that performance a long time ago.'

'What's your name?'

'Walker.'

'Walker, I'm—'

'Jason King,' Walker said. 'Yeah. I know. Your friend's Will Slater. You think I'm an idiot?'

'No,' King said. 'I don't think you are. How are we going to solve this little stalemate?'

'You're going to put your guns down.'

'What if we don't want to?'

'That's the only option you have.'

Slater opened his mouth to speak, but before he could

get a word out, Walker said, 'Did I ask for your fucking opinion, mate?'

Slater clammed up.

King said, 'Are we going the Wild West route? First to the draw? I'm not sure you want to try that.'

'Why?' Walker said. 'Because of your reaction speed? You think Black Force has a monopoly on that?'

'Black Force doesn't exist anymore. If you knew as much as you think you do, you'd know that.'

Walker cocked his head to one side. 'I've been out of the loop for a spell. Quite right.'

'And now you're protecting the scum of the earth.'

Walker raised an eyebrow. 'Who might that be?'

'Whoever turned the lights out.'

Walker smirked again. 'That's the extent of your lecture? I killed eight cops with an M82 less than thirty minutes ago, for Christ's sake. Tried to put one in your buddy's head over there, but his reflexes are something special. I'll give him that much.'

Slater said, 'Is this what's going to happen? We're going to stand around talking all day?'

'No,' Walker said, suddenly cold and serious. 'What's going to happen is, I'm going to get fed up with this whole charade. I've got enough in a numbered account to live offshore for a while, which I'm going to need to do after this little disaster. So what I'm going to do is shoot that kid you're holding between the eyes, because he made the timeless mistake of paying me before the job was over. And, if we're being honest, I didn't expect him to actually pull it off. Kid's half-genius, half-dipshit. But I guess you need those qualities, huh?'

'You want to stop this?' King said. 'Then do the right thing.'

Walker said, 'The right thing...'

Silence.

He said, 'Right and wrong don't exist anymore, lads.'

The Glock came up.

King fired.

Slater lunged.

Walker fired.

The world went mad.

67

Slater had never been in a higher state of readiness, and it paid off.

The moment Walker stepped foot out of the elevator, he'd known where the conversation was headed. He'd read the ex-SAS mercenary like a book. There was little light, but in the semi-darkness he'd stared into Walker's soul and seen a man not too dissimilar from Rick Whelan.

A razor-sharp, no-nonsense, get-shit-done enforcer who was only now beginning to realise that Gavin Whelan wasn't as naive as everyone thought he was.

That was when it finally clicked for Slater.

All along, he'd labelled Gavin as a kid. An egotistical little brat with some good ideas and a whole lot of luck. But that was how Gavin disarmed everyone he came into contact with. There was a reputation that came with being a third-generation mobster. People underestimated him. It seemed Rick had gone along with Gavin's grandiose vision just to humour the young man, as had Walker. They'd seen the dollar signs and listened to the spiel about recruiting hackers to drop malicious code into power substations across the East Coast and seize control of the grid. Maybe they'd half-believed it was possible, but not really.

And now the lights were out, and everything Gavin said had come true, and in the darkness their minds were free to run wild, conjuring up all sorts of apocalyptic visions of what might happen if New York stayed dark.

In the elevator Walker had decided that Gavin needed to die, and he himself needed to get as far away from Manhattan as humanly possible, to create as much deniability as he could.

Because even a sociopathic ex-SAS mercenary could see the sheer pointlessness of all this after he was paid for his work.

Walker emptied half the Glock's magazine at Gavin Whelan.

But Gavin wasn't there anymore.

Slater shoved him with both hands, pushing so hard against his shoulder that the kid went toppling into an empty office cubicle head over heels. Then Slater lunged backward, throwing himself off his feet, switching direction, hitting the floor hard enough to exacerbate his concussion. With a spinning head he rolled to one knee, now firmly behind a cubicle divider, out of the line of fire.

He caught a glimpse of King unloading the contents of his MP7 in Walker's direction, and leapt to his feet to add to the barrage.

Walker wasn't there.

King said, 'He went left.'

Slater turned and bolted.

He ran the length of the entire floor at a crouch, staying below the partitions. When he reached one set of windows overlooking the intersection, he veered right and raced toward Walker's last known position. The wall with the elevator at its centre lay dead ahead, and he made it there in seconds, favouring speed and shock over a slow, tactical game plan. He pulled up a half dozen feet from the edge of the aisle, just before they gave way to an open perimeter corridor, and swept the space ahead with his MP7.

Slowly, step by step, he crept toward the edge.

A flash of movement.

Someone rounding the corner.

A shin, flying at his temple.

It came out of the dark with such speed that he only managed a half-second depress of the trigger. The MP7 roared, but Walker had planned accordingly, and kept most of his centre mass exposed. Slater went for the easy target before remembering the bulletproof vest, and Walker's Kevlar absorbed all three shots before the head kick finished its trajectory and slammed home.

It caught Slater above the ear.

In the sweet spot.

His world went dark to match the city.

68

He'd been knocked out before.

Too many times to count.

Slater dreaded what old age might be like, if he made it that far. The long term effects of chronic traumatic encephalopathy — CTE, for short — were widely known. His brain would probably be mush before he turned sixty. But he wouldn't know for sure unless he made it to sixty, which, right now, seemed implausible.

Because when he resurfaced from the shadow realm, Walker had one arm looped around his throat, and Slater's own MP7 pressed to his head.

Walker grunted, 'I think you broke a rib with those shots. Very good.'

Slater didn't answer. He couldn't. He was conscious, but not alert. The same depersonalisation effects of the concussion were back in full force, now even worse. Nothing seemed real. His surroundings were distant, hazy, unfocused. He cursed his ineptitude, cursed the fact that he'd allowed himself to get hit so much. At the same time, he should be dead. He'd survived so far. He could survive a little longer.

'What are you doing?' he mumbled through bloody teeth.

They were in the same position, at the north-west corner of the floor, crouched behind a divider.

Walker whispered, 'You mean — why haven't I killed you?'

Slater nodded.

'If you raise your voice, I will. But your friend over there is rather talented. I need you as bait.'

'He won't bite.'

'Yes, he will,' Walker said. 'You two have been working together for too long, lad. There's personal attachment there, whether you want to admit it or not. It was going to get you killed eventually. I cut all that off early in my SAS days.'

'Maybe that's why you turned out the way you did.'

Walker stewed over that, and then went quiet. Slater could feel his icy anger brimming just below the surface, barely controlled, so close to rage.

And then Slater understood.

'That's it, isn't it?' he said. 'I've met your kind before. You give sanctimonious speeches about the purity of working for the highest bidder, but really you're just a lonely, isolated, pathetic little man who couldn't make friends in the military. Didn't take long when you went out on your own to spiral into what you are now.'

'Shut the fuck up,' Walker said.

'Struck a nerve there?'

'I told you to shut the—'

Footsteps, close by.

Approaching fast.

Walker jerked up, realising his mistake too late. He was impeccably trained to cover all contingencies, but even the best training in the world doesn't factor human emotion into account. He was a lonely man, cut off from personal connection for years, and Slater had exposed that weakness. Of course, any competent SF training teaches you to compartmentalise, to go into a state like ice during times of warfare so that nothing affects you. But all it takes is the right pressure point to crack through that outer shell. Walker hadn't turned irate, hadn't changed his physical state one bit. But he'd lost his situational awareness, and that was all that mattered in this business.

He pulled Slater to his feet, but the MP7 shook loose, away from Slater's skull, the barrel slipping off his skin.

Walker went to bring it back so he could secure his hostage but Slater shouted, 'Clear!' into the dark surroundings.

Jason King needed no further encouragement.

Muzzle flare erupted and a bullet passed by Slater's right ear and Walker jolted in shock and fell away from him, his burly forearm sliding off Slater's neck.

Slater spun, nearly tripped and stumbled, but kept his footing.

Walker had been hit in the collar.

Slater lunged out and found the MP7 with the toe of his boot — it was the best he could manage with his head swimming. If he bent down to pick it up and aim it, he'd waste valuable seconds, and with his equilibrium disrupted he'd probably fumble it anyway. So he eliminated any chances of Walker getting his hands on it by punting it like a pro kicker, just as he'd done to Gavin's AK47. Then he raised the same foot high in the air and brought it down at Walker's unprotected face.

But Walker was sharp.

Sharper than Slater expected.

Even with blood fountaining from his collar bone, he had the wherewithal to throw his head to one side, maybe giving himself whiplash but avoiding a stomp to the face. He rolled with the momentum and came up on his knees and transitioned straight into a rudimentary takedown attempt. He had both arms wrapped around Slater's legs before Slater could move. The disrupted equilibrium didn't help Slater's predicament. He found himself wildly off-balance and tried to lunge out of Walker's grip, but the man held tight, and pressed close up against Slater's frame.

Suddenly Slater was airborne.

Walker lifted him, and took two bounding steps and caught King rounding the corner.

King raised his MP7 to fire but hesitated, because chances were he'd put rounds into Slater's back, with Walker holding him in a rudimentary fireman's carry.

Slater's heart stopped.

Maybe he was right, Slater thought. *Maybe friendship can get you killed.*

Walker maintained the momentum and then planted his feet and heaved.

Slater crashed into King, and the two of them toppled to the floor.

In the movies, combat is smooth and flows from one sequence to the next with beautiful uninterrupted choreography. Real life is a little harsher than that. Both of them went down in a tangle of limbs and Slater came close to striking his head against the ground, which would have put him at three concussive blows within the span of half an hour. He knew his brain was volatile, so he took great care to roll with the landing, even if it meant he ended up out of position.

Bad move.

When he righted himself Walker was there in his face, and the man booted him square in the chest with enough force to throw him through one of the dividers. He crashed to earth again, and this time he stayed down.

He watched King rear up with his MP7 in hand, but Walker was too close.

They brawled.

It would take Slater seconds to disentangle himself from the plasterboard. Seconds he didn't have.

King was on his own.

69

King saw the skirmish unfold in all its chaotic steps, and moved to end it.

He raised his MP7, which he'd somehow managed to keep hold of, but Walker was right there and drilled a left hand into the bridge of his nose.

Crack.

Broken.

Just like that.

His eyes watered involuntarily and he lost sight of his target, which spelled disaster. He brought the barrel around but Walker simply wrestled the submachine gun off him and thundered a boot into his gut. A teep kick, executed beautifully. A symphony of violence. King doubled over and Walker made to deliver the finishing blow but a second wind seized King and he staggered away from the man.

Walker followed.

Slowly.

Patiently.

A vulture circling its prey.

King wasn't sure where the MP7 was. Then he glimpsed

its outline, firm in Walker's hands, and he dove behind the nearest partition even though he knew it would do nothing to protect him.

But it did.

Bullets shredded the plasterboard, tearing straight through, but in a sheer miracle none of them slammed home against his frame. He burrowed deeper into the ruins of the cubicle he'd entered, squirming and writhing away from the gunfire. The crippling sensation of doubt ran through him, weighing him down. He was Jason King. One of the most feared and respected soldiers in government history. And now Walker was running through him, barely breaking a sweat.

Then, through the doubt, he found a morsel of calm.

That was all he needed.

He tapped into the flow state, and the usual icy focus came over him, despite the carnage unfolding all around him.

And then he smiled.

Because he remembered who he was.

He let out a shout of agony as if he'd been mortally wounded, and Walker paused his assault to step forward and rip the plasterboard apart, allowing him a clear line of sight to King's crippled form, but as soon as he tore part of the wall out King reared up and burst back in Walker's direction and tackled him out into the middle of the hallway.

They sprawled, and limbs crashed into torsos, and fists into faces, and foreheads into noses.

A fight to the death.

King didn't know how hurt he was, or how badly he'd hurt Walker. The man was a legitimate phenom — if he hadn't realised it yet, now it struck home. Black Force, in its heyday, would have scooped him up if they had the opportunity. Walker was strong, and fast, and tough, and his reflexes were otherworldly. He would have mopped the floor with anyone sent to subdue him, and it was no wonder he'd found astonishing success as a gun-for-hire.

But all those traits applied to King, too.

And deep down, he had the unshakeable belief that he could *endure* better than anyone else on the planet, no matter how evenly their skills matched up.

So with a broken nose and a bloody mouth and searing pain in his ribs, he fought and clawed for every advantage. He dropped an elbow on Walker's face, stunning the man, and then he rolled off him and snatched up the MP7 and rolled to aim it and—

Shit.

Slater was there, grappling with Walker, misinterpreting the situation and figuring that King needed his life saved. The wrestling match turned ferocious and King held back on pulling the trigger, knowing that one of his shots only had to stray an inch to kill his brother-in-arms.

But Slater was compromised.

From the concussion.

Walker hit him with a perfect right hand to the centre of his chest, sapping his breath away, and when he fell back he landed on King. King lowered him to the ground but it provided just enough of a break in the action for Walker to close the distance and drill the same right hand into King's face, hitting him full in the mouth.

King sat down hard, and Walker took the gun off him like taking candy from a baby.

Game over.

Walker regarded the two defeated, unarmed combatants at his feet.

He wiped blood off his face and said, 'I'll admit, lads, you got further than I thought. What was it, thirty on one? You've done very well. I saw Rick Whelan's body in the lobby before. Now *that's* impressive.'

King said nothing.

Slater said nothing.

Walker seemed hesitant about the anticlimax. He said, 'Well, that's what the power of friendship gets you, doesn't it?'

Silence.

The man said, 'You had so many opportunities to shoot me. But you both wanted to protect your buddy.'

'You're alone,' King said.

'But I won.'

'Against us. But we didn't exactly start at a hundred percent.'

'That's a shame. You still lost.'

Walker levelled the MP7 at King's unprotected face.

'Thought it would be harder than this,' he said.

Slater said, 'It is.'

A gun barrel touched the side of Walker's head.

King didn't recognise the newcomer.

But he realised that Slater did.

70

Detective First Grade Jim Riordan tightened his grip on his service weapon.

Slater had seen him creeping through the shadows from the stairwell, a split second before Walker manhandled him. Slater had run through the odds of success if he tried to keep fighting Walker in his compromised state, compared to admitting defeat for a few vital seconds as Riordan closed the gap.

He'd made the right call.

Now, Riordan said, 'Put that down, my friend.'

'You first,' Walker said, keeping the MP7 pointed straight at King's face.

'You don't want to die here.'

Walker thought about it. Realised resistance was futile. Dropped the submachine gun to the carpeted floor.

'Jim,' Slater said, looking at the detective. 'Listen to me.'

Riordan looked him in the eye, keeping the barrel touched firmly to the side of Walker's neck.

'Shoot him,' Slater said.

'I need to bring him in,' Riordan said. 'To answer for all of this.'

'He's not the man behind it.'

'Who is?'

'We'll get to that.'

'I can't kill him.'

'You've never played by the book,' Slater said. 'Sometimes it landed you in hot water. Most of the time it didn't. This time, it won't. We'll take the blame.'

'I have my line. I won't cross it.'

'If you don't, we will.'

'I'll arrest the both of you if you try that. Killing him is the easy way out.'

Slater said, 'Jim. Listen to me. You don't understand. Shoot him.'

'Or what?'

Walker said, 'Or this.'

Spun, fast as lightning, and smacked the Glock off-course before Riordan could fire a shot. Because there was a world of difference between a genetically gifted phenom and a street cop. Riordan was hotheaded yet principled, steadfast in his vigilante-style morality, but Walker was something else.

So Walker wrenched the Glock free and turned it around and shot Jim Riordan in the forehead before the detective could even flinch.

Thankfully, Slater was genetically gifted, too.

He had Walker's dropped MP7 in his hands before Riordan's corpse had hit the ground and now he angled it upwards and held the trigger and sent five consecutive shots into Walker's groin. Unrivalled pain hit the man in a chilling wave and he collapsed, defenceless, and Slater finished him off by putting a solitary round through his head.

The gunshot reports resonated through the office floor, petering out into nothingness.

Slater stood over the two corpses, panting.

King sat still beside them.

King said, 'Christ.'

Slater put a hand out to steady himself, gripping the top of the nearest cubicle. His head swam, but reassurance sank in that Walker was out of the equation. A truly devastating adversary. Neither of them had realised until he'd overwhelmed them.

'Are we losing a step?' King said.

Slater looked around. 'I don't think so. I think we're just in over our heads.'

'I don't know, Slater...'

Slater looked at him. 'You think anyone else would have managed to do what we just did?'

'You think there's anyone left? My ribs are...'

He trailed off, searching for the right word, then lifted a palm gently to his ribcage and applied a touch of pressure. His face creased in pain.

'My ribs are fucked,' he concluded.

'Your nose, too,' Slater said.

King's septum was broken, and the skin was already ballooning.

Slater listened to the silence.

Complete.

All-encompassing.

The aftermath of war.

Then he looked down at Walker's body.

'I think we're done here.'

'He wasn't Black Force,' King said. 'He was ordinary SAS. And he beat us both.'

'Did he?'

King gave him a questioning look.

'He's dead,' Slater said. 'We aren't.'

King shrugged.

'And he might have been in the SAS, but you and I both know he could have made the cut for Black Force. They just didn't know.'

King nodded.

'There's always going to be people like him,' Slater said. 'We're not the only gifted combatants on the planet. And we're not getting any younger.'

King clambered to his feet.

Slater put a hand on his shoulder, and gripped it tight. 'You okay?'

'Of course,' King said. 'I'm alive, aren't I?'

'That's the way.'

King peered toward the middle of the floor, over the cubicles, searching for one in particular. 'You think he's still there?'

'I think so. He'll be licking his wounds. He's smart, but he's not tough.'

'Then we still have work to do.'

He spat a gob of blood on the carpet between his feet, wiped his mouth, and strode away.

Slater saw the animalistic determination in his eyes.

71

It had been a rough night.

King wasn't in the mood for games. He'd been kicked, punched, very nearly shot dozens of times — the only thing that had come between himself and a lead-soaked death was his reflexes.

Slater's words rang in his ears.

We're not getting any younger.

Maybe so, but he figured he was getting smarter. Experience was a valuable asset, and right now experience was telling him to begin the recovery process. Ribs healed, cuts turned to scars, bruises vanished. Pain receded. Then he could get back to work.

First, he had to get the lights back on.

He barely noticed Slater following in his wake. He hustled down one long carpeted aisle, then veered left, then right. He came to the empty cubicle Slater had thrown Gavin Whelan into, and sure enough the kid was there, lying on his back, his face contorted into a wince.

For the first time King noticed the dark blue light

filtering through the second floor had turned a shade lighter.

The tendrils of dawn creeping into the sky.

King didn't have time to sit around and wait for Gavin to feel better. He stepped through the demolished plaster-board, grabbed the kid by the lapels and hauled him to his feet. Gavin groaned in protest, and King said, 'You ever had a finger broken?'

'What?'

'You heard me.'

'I... can't think straight.'

'Oh,' King said. 'That's too bad.'

He took Gavin's pinky finger in a vice-like grip and wrenched it to the left.

Crack.

Gavin moaned.

King didn't give him a moment to soak in the pain. He seized hold of the ring finger on the same hand.

'Here we go,' he said.

Gavin turned white as a ghost.

'Please,' the kid croaked. 'No. What do you want? I'll give it to you.'

King shot a wry look at Slater. 'See? That's all it takes.'

Slater said, 'What about all your idealism, kid? Where'd that go? I thought you were committed to this.'

'He's not familiar with pain,' King said. 'It always ruins so many grand plans.'

Gavin wheezed, sweat coating his forehead, staining his shirt.

King said, 'The hackers running the show. They're in this building?'

'Yes.'

'Why?'

Gavin didn't answer.

King said, 'You'd better make sure you have a good answer. Otherwise I won't believe you. And then I'll keep breaking your fingers. There's nine left.'

'W-what are you talking about?'

King pulled him close. 'Why, kid, did you set up your base in the middle of the city you were targeting? You got into the grid with malicious code. You could have done that from anywhere.'

Gavin's eyes drooped to the floor, his hope shattered. 'I knew... you would come. I knew you were here. I wanted you to see.'

'I'm sure you figured we might have won.'

'No,' Gavin croaked. 'Mason Walker was...'

He trailed off, consumed by defeat.

'Mason Walker? That's the guy's full name?'

Gavin said, 'He was a prodigy. I got my people to dig up classified intelligence documents. You, your government... they wanted him. They wanted him so bad. They made offers. Staggering offers. Whatever you two got paid... double it, triple it, quadruple it. They knew he was the best on the planet. He turned away from it all. Saw where the ladder led. Didn't want to be a slave. I was so shocked that he accepted my contract that I got hotheaded. Set myself up here because... I thought I had a super soldier on my hands. Because I did all this for you, you see? So you two could see what happens when you push a Whelan too far.'

'Why the power? Why the lights?'

Gavin's solemn expression turned to a half-smile as he tapped into some final vestige of pride. 'Because I could.'

'How did you do it?'

'I'll take you to them,' he said. 'The people who did it. But ... you need to believe me ... it's not up to me. You're going to need to convince them to give up control.'

'You're the ringleader,' King said. 'You tell them what to do, they do it.'

'You want the truth?'

'Yes.'

'It's more cultish than that,' Gavin said. 'That was the key to all this. I'm persuasive. Always have been, but I kept it close to my chest when I was just a spoiled kid with a powerful father, and uncles, and grandfathers. That's how I got Rick on board, and it's how I got Walker. I think they both realised I wasn't an idiot, but they realised it too late. These kids... they're too far gone.'

'What kids?'

'Let me show you. Sixth floor. There's a vault.'

King said, 'If you're leading us to more of your men, I'll break all your fingers, then all your toes, then I'll get started on the rest of you.'

Gavin gulped, genuine terror in his face. He knew the pain of a single shattered pinky finger. King could see his mind struggling to process what sort of agony he'd be in if King truly got going with the punishment.

Gavin said, 'I swear, I'm not.'

'I believe him,' Slater said.

'Me too,' King said.

He shoved Gavin toward the far wall. 'Lead the way.'

Gavin moped away from them, his back turned, his shoulders slumped, not an ounce of resistance in his posture. King had seen it all before. It's easy to inflate your ego in private, convincing yourself that you're unbreakable, unstoppable, indestructible, but it's a very different experience when you're staring down the barrel of more physical pain than your mind can possibly handle.

The kid had caved, as King knew he always would.

Halfway across the floor, King's phone buzzed in his pocket.

72

He pulled it out.

The screen was cracked, but the protective case had done its job, and the phone still worked.

The screen read: VIOLETTA.

He swiped across, touched the smartphone to his ear and said, 'Hey.'

'Oh, thank God,' she said.

'Any news?'

'I need to know how close you are to stopping this.'

'Close.'

'Can you give me a timeframe?'

'Not long,' he said, 'but I can't say for sure. All their forces are down.'

'Great,' she said. 'I'll send in the cavalry to secure the building.'

'No.'

'I'm sorry?'

'Not yet. We have to be alone.'

'Why?'

'Because I'm fairly certain that the guy behind this radicalised a handful of college-aged kids,' King said. 'And Slater and I need to talk them out of it.'

'If we bring them in,' she said, 'we can make them talk.'

'No,' he said. 'I don't think you can. Not with violence. We can't either.'

'But...'

'Trust me,' he said. 'I've been in this field for long enough. If I'm wrong, I'll hand it over to you. But give me thirty minutes.'

'I can't approve that,' she said. 'You know I can't.'

'Then we're going to stay locked out of the grid, and it's all going to hell.'

'It already is,' she said.

He paused. 'What's happening?'

'A few gangs kicked off the looting an hour ago. It's spreading like wildfire. We can barely maintain order.'

Silence.

She said, 'We aren't prepared for this, Jason. Everyone needs help, and we don't have the information they need. All of our infrastructure — *all* of it — is down. Networks, transport, water, sanitation. We have millions of MREs stored in warehouses for this exact scenario, but it's nowhere near enough. The meals will be exhausted in less than a week. We can use the Defence Logistics Agency to bring supplies in, but that's not going to achieve much. Not for eight million people. Do you understand what I'm saying?'

'Yes.'

'If your plan doesn't work...'

'Give us thirty minutes. That's it.'

'Why are you so convinced you'll have any more success than we will?'

'Because the man who organised this is weak,' King said. 'But I don't think the people he recruited are. You and your people might resort to waterboarding them, but you'll just get false information and leads. All they need to do is hold out for twenty-four hours, and they know it.'

'We have trained negotiators...'

'That you'll be using to try and convince them when they're sitting in cells. Not the right environment.'

'Have you met these people?'

'Not yet.'

'Then what the hell are you talking about?'

'Have I failed before?' King said. '*Have I?*'

'No.'

'Thirty minutes.'

'I just need to know what makes you so sure.'

'I think I know exactly who these kids are,' King said. 'I think I understand how we ended up here. If I'm right, we can avoid all the unpleasantries, which wouldn't work anyway. Please.'

'Half an hour,' Violetta said. 'That's it.'

'That's all we need.'

He hung up, and returned the phone to his pocket.

Gavin Whelan and Will Slater watched him intently, very different expressions on their faces.

Gavin had hope, that it was all still possible.

Slater had doubt.

Slater said, 'How are you so sure?'

'That's what she just asked me.'

'Well...?'

King turned to Gavin. 'I know what you did. I might not be the smartest with tech, but I understand people.'

Gavin stared.

King said, 'What makes them tick.'

Gavin kept staring.

King said, 'That cartel kid, Rico. The other kid, Samuel. You. It's all the same, isn't it?'

Gavin's look was blank.

King said, 'You're disenfranchised. You thought you had it all. Then you realised money and power can go away like *that,'* — he snapped his fingers — 'and there was nothing left underneath. Here's the thing you missed, kid.'

King pulled him in close.

'You need to figure yourself out before you go out there and try to own the world. Otherwise you're just an empty shell when you don't get everything you want. And that's when shit like this happens, when you decide to throw it all away and bring everyone down with you.'

King shoved him toward the stairwell.

'For a smart kid,' he said, 'you really don't have anything figured out.'

73

Slater remained in the background, and suddenly it all clicked.

'Oh,' he said.

King turned around.

Slater said, 'I get it now.'

'Yeah.'

'You really think you can talk them out of it?'

'I can try.'

They made their way up four flights of stairs, plunging back into the dark. Dawn had broken, and now the whole building was shrouded in the ethereal pale blue light that comes before the rising sun, but the windowless stairwell was devoid of the light. So it was back to shadow and paranoia and uncertainty. Slater swept every tight corner as King kept a tight grip on Gavin, making sure the kid didn't run off.

But both of them knew he wouldn't.

Just as King had predicted, Gavin Whelan had nothing left. They'd labelled him a kid, but in reality he was a thirty year old man with all the potential in the world, who'd chosen to use it to cause as much destruction as possible when the world hadn't handed him everything. And that was the cardinal sin. In Slater's eyes, that was the weakest act imaginable.

Caving in as soon as the going gets tough.

Giving up on all of it.

Trying to bring it down with you in your misery.

He couldn't relate, and he never would. For over a decade he'd been unshakeable, precisely for this reason. It was a slippery slope. Compromise on your morals once, and you've set the precedent. You've opened the floodgates. Gavin had never had morality to begin with, or mental toughness, or grit. He thought he was tough, thought he could reach out and seize anything he wanted, but when he realised the world hadn't been set up to please him, he'd crumbled.

Slater vowed never to break. Never to fall into that kind of despair.

He'd fight against it until the day he died.

He knew King was the same.

Maybe that's why they were brothers.

Rage against the dying of the light.

74

They reached the sixth floor, and Gavin led them down corridors festering with rot and decay.

It seemed this section of the building hadn't been touched in years, and age had eaten away at most of the decorative features. The aesthetic cedar log walls had termite-ridden holes in them, and the carpet was torn up in places, and the general stink of uncleanliness hung thick and heavy in the air. There were rooms branching off from the corridors with windows facing the Bowery, and a sliver of the dawn light crept in, but not much. Not enough to shed the gloomy atmosphere.

Slater stifled a shiver as they reached the end of the corridor and turned into an antechamber room that led to a giant steel vault. The antechamber was a narrow space with wood-panelled floors and a window to the right — one small piece of the left-hand façade of the bank building. He glanced outside and saw the intersection in the murky blue light, the sea of abandoned cars, the bodies still sprawled in the street, Alexis' building across from them.

Then he turned back to the vault.

It was old, but he imagined it was just as impenetrable as when it had been built.

The old-fashioned cylindrical door was firmly sealed.

Beside it rested a newer keypad.

Gavin thumbed in an eight-digit sequence, and a mechanical *hiss* emanated from the door.

It didn't swing open, but it was unlocked.

'So,' Gavin said, 'what do you think?'

Slater and King froze.

They both read his tone.

There was something in his voice they hadn't anticipated.

The burning desire for approval.

Slater stepped forward and took Gavin away from King, putting the MP7 barrel against his stomach to ensure he stayed put. Then he said, 'Let me tell you something.'

Gavin stiffened.

Slater said, 'I get it. I get why you did it. All your life you've been undermined by your family, but you were always capable. You're smart, you're efficient, you understand persuasion, you understand how to get what you want. But you were never able to use it. Maybe you didn't have the social skills, maybe you just couldn't put it together at the right time, but you were typecast as a spoiled brat and you never shed that reputation. So you were angry. Then you lost what little respect you had in the first place when your family fell apart. So, yes, I can see how that led to this. You thought, "Fuck it, I'll bring the whole world down with me." You saw a flaw in the system and you recruited people who were the same as you. Probably in their early twenties, probably incredibly smart, probably unemployed. Kids with the same ego complex as you. Who thought they were smarter than everyone else but never had anything to show for it. Kids who've sat at their computers for twelve hours a day for their entire childhood, who taught themselves everything about the digital world to compensate for their misery in the real world. Am I right?'

'Yeah,' Gavin mumbled, staring at the floor.

'You used every trick in the book to convert them. I can see how you might have done it. They already hated this country for denying them opportunities. They thought they were brilliant, and they probably were, but not in every way. So, deep down, they despised society, and you tapped into that. You convinced them that it's better off being ripped apart. You made them extremists, and they're too young to know any different. They've spent all their lives inside with computers, and they don't understand people. So you fed them your bullshit until they bought it hook, line, and sinker. They're sitting in that vault now, probably imagining this whole thing is a giant game. They've got no hope for the future, just like you.'

Slater could tell he'd struck a nerve.

Gavin stood there, his psyche laid bare, his closest secrets revealed.

The kid thought he was a manipulative genius.

Really, he was just a piece of shit.

Slater said, 'Maybe you feel bad now that someone else has realised what you're up to. Maybe you're hoping you could take it all back.'

Gavin shrugged, and then gave the faintest hint of a phantom nod.

Maybe hoping Slater and King couldn't see his shame.

But they did.

'Too bad,' Slater said. 'Dozens of people died tonight at the very least. Think about the home care patients who need their machines to survive. And that's just scratching the surface. If the looting gets worse, it'll turn violent. It'll be man on man. And if we didn't come, you would have relished it.'

Gavin said, 'Wait. Let me come in with you. Maybe I can—'

'You crushed your hopes earlier, Gavin,' King said. 'You told us yourself. They won't listen to you.'

Gavin went mute.

He opened his mouth to say something.

Slater realised he didn't care.

He pulled the trigger.

Put two shots into Gavin's gut, and then backed him up to the window and threw him into it with enough force to crack the pane. Instead of cleanly breaking into a million pieces like the movies, the pane splintered and cracked, throwing huge jagged shards everywhere, and Gavin tumbled over the lip and fell six stories to the pavement below.

Slater peered down to confirm the results.

They were as to be expected.

75

Slater leant back inside and stared at the vault door.

Apprehension fell over them both.

King said, 'Now for the hard part.'

'You think they'll be armed?'

'I doubt it,' King said. 'If they are, it won't be much trouble.'

'But we don't want to scare them.'

'No,' King said. 'We don't.'

'How do we play this?'

King thought it over. 'You know how to cut through to the core. But I don't think that's what we need right now.'

'I agree.'

'Let me do the talking.'

'And if you can't convince them?'

'There's always the finger breaking method.'

Slater shook his head. 'You said it yourself. It won't work on them. They're like Samuel, only it's not an act. Samuel was crazy, but he *did* care about his own life. These kids stopped giving a shit about their own wellbeing a long time ago.'

'Then let's hope I'm persuasive,' King said.

'You know what happens if it doesn't work, right?'

'Yeah.'

King shivered, and steeled himself. He wasn't usually nervous in the heat of combat. There were too many variables, too much chaos, to truly be able to pay attention to everything. Now, in the quiet of the antechamber, he could feel his heart thumping, his head pounding, his blood running cold.

If he chose the wrong words, he would fail eight million people, maybe more.

If there was ever a time to be flawless, it was now.

He held his MP7 at waist height, the barrel angled forward, but emptied as much aggression from his posture as he could manage. The gun was a precaution in case one of the kids was sitting in there pointing a pistol at the door, but he didn't think it would be necessary.

He took one step forward, gripped the thick steel handle of the vault door, and eased it open.

76

Slater loitered, opting to go in behind King.

For good reason.

He reminisced on their last two operations and how they'd both ended. Here, he'd broken Gavin Whelan, making the man realise the gravity of his own mistakes, and crushed his soul in the process. If Slater hadn't killed him, Gavin might have killed himself, which is exactly what happened in Nepal. Aidan Parker, an ex-black operations coordinator and future presidential candidate, had gotten his own daughter killed in a ludicrous plot to acquire funding for his campaign. Slater had highlighted, piece by piece, the devastation he'd brought to his own family, and Parker couldn't handle the scathing words. Slater had tossed a gun at his feet, and Parker had done what was necessary. Slater hadn't pressured him into it. The man had simply broken.

Slater knew he had a way with words. He could cut deep. But he recognised his own flaws. He despised the scum of the earth. He was harsh when he spoke to them, and he didn't have a great deal of restraint.

Restraint was needed here.

In spades.

King could do that. He'd always been the purer of the pair, somehow managing to avoid the temptations of drink and drugs to suppress his blood-drenched memories. Here, he could speak to whoever they faced with tact, with level-headedness, with the persuasion that was needed.

Slater wasn't so pure. Slater wasn't so noble.

And he was fine with that.

King stepped inside the vault, and Slater followed. It was a long, wide, tall space with every square inch of the walls taken up by the framework of safe deposit boxes. The boxes had been gouged out long ago, creating a U-shaped skeleton to house a dizzying array of computer towers. There were dozens of them at the minimum, all see-through containers sporting state-of-the-art CPUs within. Fans inside the towers kept all the gear cooled, and for good reason. Slater estimated he was looking at millions of dollars worth of technology. He hadn't seen gear like this since...

Well, since a few hours ago.

It rivalled Violetta's team's setup — in fact, it trumped it. He wouldn't have a clue where to start deciphering the labyrinth puzzle, and he knew that even if Violetta had people who did know, they wouldn't achieve a thing.

He was proven correct with the first words the occupants uttered.

A gangly kid with thinning hair dyed jet black said to King, 'Put that gun down, man. It won't do you any good here.'

King said, 'Won't it?'

'If you take this place by force, you'll stay locked out. We planned for that. You ain't got a hope in hell of cracking the ciphers.'

There were only four of them, the oldest no more than twenty-five. They were practically hunchbacked from spending so much time at their desks.

Three boys, one girl.

The boys rail-thin, the girl soft and flabby. They all shared characteristics — hollow cheekbones, gaunt complexions, glassy eyes. None of them were armed. None of them had even bothered to resist. They sat in swivel chairs with muted, placid demeanours, almost like they barely registered the two enormous soldiers who'd just stepped foot in their lair.

The eyes haunted Slater. There were only a couple of bulbs overhead to illuminate the space, and it seemed to accentuate the deadness of their gazes. There was no hope in them, possibly worse than Samuel, worse than Gavin.

They were disenfranchised, with nothing left to care about, nothing left to strive for.

The living dead.

Slater shivered.

He'd fought terrorists, mercenaries, rogue operatives.

Nothing had put him out of his depth like this.

King looked at the guy who'd spoken — the one with the dyed hair. He said, 'I know.'

He put his MP7 on the floor.

Slater followed suit.

The girl said, 'What happens now?'

'Who do you think we are?' King said.

The guy with the dyed hair said, 'Negotiators, probably.'

'No,' King said. 'If I was a negotiator I'd have a mental checklist ready to go. I'd have bullet points to hit. I'd try to warm you up with some calm talking points, and then I'd slowly transition to what I really wanted. But I'm not going to do any of that, because I've got no plan.'

The boy's gaze lingered on King's physique. 'You going to try and beat us into submission? That's what you people do, isn't it?'

'Sometimes,' King said. 'But I'm not going to do that here.'

'Why not?'

'Because it wouldn't work. You've probably planned for that, too. If we started hurting you, you'd have a series of commands to execute that would make it look like you'd pulled the code out of the control stations. But, really, it'd just be a smokescreen, to make us ease off the pressure. You probably have a dozen different backup plans. Right?'

Slater was impressed that King understood.

The kid slowly nodded. He said, 'You're not going to get us to reverse this. No chance.'

'What do you know about the people who recruited you?'

The girl gave a sadistic smile. 'Whatever you say, mister, it's not going to work. You're staying locked out.'

The boy said, 'In the back of your head, you've got a failsafe, right? You think, if you can't convince us to reverse this, you can bring us in and maybe torture can make us sing.'

King didn't answer.

The boy said, 'We have a failsafe, too. You put one finger on us, and—'

He parted his lips, and bared his teeth, and Slater saw a clear pill with a dark green core.

His heart stopped in his chest.

King said, 'Is that cyanide?'

The other three kids bared their teeth, too, exposing three more pills.

The boy said, 'We're the only ones who know the ciphers. They're in our heads. Not a single other person in this whole operation has them, which I guess doesn't matter, seeing that you probably killed them all to get here. But if we're out of the picture... well, everyone stays locked out for good. You'll have to build a whole new power grid over the old one. How long do you think that'll take? How many people you think'll die?'

Slater thought, *Holy shit.*

77

Outwardly, King gave no reaction.

Inwardly, he panicked harder than he ever had before.

Four bites was all that separated New York from thousands and thousands of deaths.

He said, 'I get it.'

The boy said, 'Good.'

'I still want an answer to my question.'

'What question?'

'What do you know about the people who recruited you?'

'Some crime family, I guess.'

'That's it?'

'Who cares? They were just the bankroll. What's done is done. They gave us what we needed to pull this off. Lined it all up for us and let us knock it out of the park. And it was glorious. I mean, it was nice they hated this country just as much as we do, but in the end that doesn't really matter.'

'The Whelans don't hate America.'

'Yes, they do. They hate the Western propaganda

machine that suppresses the masses and dulls the minds of—'

'Trust me, they don't. They hate *us*.'

Silence.

The boy said, 'You and your friend there?'

'Yeah.'

'Why?'

'We're the reason all this happened.'

'No. We are.'

'You might think that, but the Whelans put you to work. And we infuriated the Whelans.'

'They said something, once,' the boy said. 'I thought it was a joke, but Gavin seemed pretty serious. He said they used to be kings.'

'They did.'

'Here in Manhattan?'

'Yes.'

'What happened?'

'We tore the family apart. They lost their power, and their money, and their resources. Most of them fled the city, and a few fled the country, but a couple of the stragglers came back to do this.'

'Hmm,' the boy said. 'Interesting. Doesn't change a thing, though.'

'It should.'

The boy shrugged. 'Sorry to disappoint.'

'That's all they ever cared about,' King said. 'Their power, and their money, and their resources. Do you four care about that?'

'Of course not. And neither did they.'

'I can see that. You're doing this with no plan. If you don't bite down on those pills, you have no escape up your sleeves. You just wanted to watch New York crumble, right?'

'Right,' the boy said.

The first confirmation.

Deep down in King's core, he felt a spark of hope.

Get him on board.

Get him feeling righteous.

Get him to agree.

'Gavin Whelan had an escape plan. He might have seemed broken, and defeated, and uncaring, but all of this, everything he did... it was because of anger.'

'I doubt that very much.'

'It's the truth,' King said. 'He hated me, and he hated my friend here. Because we took his money and his power away, and he was left with nothing. Look into my eyes. You're a smart kid. You're probably one of the smartest people I've ever met, if I'm looking at what you've managed to do here with a few computers. So look at me. Ask yourself if I'm lying.'

He didn't budge.

He didn't waver.

The kid swept a lock of thin hair away from his eyes and stared hard.

'I don't think you're lying,' the kid said.

'I'm not. Now, ask yourself if what he said to you was legitimate. If he was angry about losing it all, and wanted to lash out and hurt the people who did it, does that line up with the anti-Western storyline he fed to you?'

'It wasn't a storyline.'

'It was. You might have been harbouring resentment — which, believe me, is fucking understandable in this day and age — but he didn't share them. He told you what you wanted to hear. He used you. Keep looking at my eyes — I'm not looking away, I'm not blinking... I'm not lying.'

The boy stayed quiet.

King said, 'You might hate me, because I'm affiliated with the government. That's okay. I'm not going to stand here and try and convince you that this country always does the right thing. When I've had to, I've rebelled against my own employers. Because *I* always try to do what's right. I can't control everything. But when I see pieces of shit leeching off the rest of society like the Whelan family were, I step in and do something about it. The Whelans were partly responsible for the fentanyl epidemic here in New York. I'm sure you have friends, or friends of friends, who've died from overdoses. And you know why they were doing that? For money. They were greedy little pigs, and we stuck them for it, and we're never going to apologise for that. Maybe that's what a negotiator would do. They'd suck up to you. I won't.'

A pause.

King said, 'I just have to hope you understand.'

'I get why you did it,' the kid said. 'But that has nothing to do with—'

'It does. Take Gavin out of the equation. Remove him and all his rage. What's left? Would you have done this if he hadn't been there to talk you into it?'

'Yes.'

'You don't sound like you mean it.'

'I...'

The kid trailed off.

King said, 'Do you know what panic looks like? Have you seen it in-person?'

The boy said nothing.

King said, 'Millions of people are going to panic, and thousands of people are going to die, if you don't reverse this. I know you know that, but have you *really* thought about it?'

Silence.

'Not everyone in this country is a monster. There's bad people in it, but there's bad people everywhere. You're going to kill a whole lot of good ones if you go through with this.'

The boy started breathing faster.

Harder.

Deeper.

King hesitated. Wondered if the kid might start hyperventilating. He eased off, letting the silence drag out, letting them sit there. The other three stayed expressionless, their eyes as dead as the moment he and Slater had stepped into the vault.

But the boy he'd been speaking to wasn't so calm.

King said, 'Do you understand what you've done?'

The boy looked up.

There were tears in his eyes.

He said, 'Yes.'

He bit down.

78

Slater saw King jerk imperceptibly, a visceral internal reaction to what had happened.

His own heart rate spiked, and his hands tingled, and his skin turned cold, and his stomach fell to the floor.

But he didn't let it show, and neither did King. They couldn't. Everything depended on keeping the other three alive.

Which, they both knew, would be no easy feat.

Before the boy had even reacted to breaking through the cyanide pill, Slater spun to face the other three and said, 'Stay calm.'

They stared back at him.

He said, 'Please, stay calm.'

And then it started.

The boy with the dyed hair spasmed in his chair, throwing his head back, the veins in his neck protruding like purple rivers. He let out an ungodly howl, and his whole body tensed in protest. He clenched his teeth so hard that Slater thought he heard one of them crack, and then the trademark foam appeared at the corners of his lips.

'Shit,' he grunted. 'Oh shit, oh my God...'

Then he trailed off, and died in his chair.

Slater didn't look at him directly. He kept his gaze transfixed on the three remaining kids, watching the death play out in his peripheral vision. He remained an island of calm, refusing to react to the violent demise, hoping like hell that it kept the other three subdued.

So they didn't follow suit.

There was nothing Slater could do. There was nothing King could do. If they tried to make a lunge, the other three would bite down on their pills out of reflex. They weren't really kids — they were twenty-somethings — but they were still at risk of contagious behaviour, just like the rest of the world.

The two boys saw the first guy die.

They could have reacted in either direction.

One way, or the other.

They split right down the middle.

One panicked, one didn't.

Slater's stomach fell further.

The boy on the left — pale, sweaty, wide eyes — closed his eyes and bit down.

The boy on the right — caramel-skinned, maybe Latino — saw the violent aftermath of his friend's demise and spat his pill across the room.

The girl let the pill fall from her mouth, too.

Slater said, 'Look at me.'

The pair looked at him.

Slater said, 'Don't look away.'

They didn't.

The pale guy coughed and spluttered and violently succumbed to the cyanide.

Slater kept his eyes on the two remaining hackers.

They kept their eyes on him.

With a final gurgling throat-rattle, the pale guy slid down in his chair and went still.

No one spoke for a long time.

The vault's atmosphere tightened, constricted. There were now two corpses in here with them all, corpses that had once been people. Corpses that had once had personalities, had talked and bantered and maybe sometimes laughed. Now dead, forever.

Slater doubted that the two surviving hackers had ever seen a body before.

With his heart in his throat, he said, 'Please, for the love of God, tell me that one of you knows the ciphers.'

Slowly, one by one, they both nodded.

Slater said, 'Are you going to do it?'

They both stared at him.

King turned around.

Gave Slater a look.

Over to you.

Slater knew what he had to do.

Now was the time to cut deep.

He walked over to the chair containing the kid with the dyed hair and spun it around so the corpse faced the two living, breathing occupants.

They went pale.

Slater said, 'You see this? This is a body. This is a dead man. There's going to be thousands of them out there if you don't fix this. Remember when you were kids, and you saw an old lady crossing the street, or a young couple hand in hand? Remember back then, before you grew up and started to hate the world. Those people still exist. They're the majority. And you're going to kill them, turn them on each other, make them inhuman. Look at this guy right here and ask yourself if that's what you really want.'

Neither of them spoke.

Neither of them budged.

They need more.

Slater took a deep breath and said, 'You want to know something I probably shouldn't tell you?'

The boy stayed mute.

The girl nodded.

Slater said, 'I'm an alcoholic. I drink to forget all the hard shit I've had to do. But I did those hard things because they made the world a slightly better place. I made life brutal for myself so I could stop people getting taken advantage of, and then I dulled all my memories with booze. Which isn't the right response to hard times. Just like this isn't. There's better solutions. Sometimes life isn't fair. But you don't need to do this. Other people recruited you to do it because they were angry, but you're not really angry. You're confused.'

The guy clammed up, reacting harshly to the criticism, to the suggestion that he was naive.

The girl didn't.

She looked Slater in the eyes and tilted her chin downward.

It took him longer than it should have to realise that she'd nodded.

He said, 'Will you fix this?'

She said, 'Yes.'

The guy wheeled around in his chair, venom in his eyes, and lunged at her, a crude switchblade in his hand.

79

But King was there.

He'd seen the resolve in the boy's eyes. He'd seen him double down on his beliefs, refusing to come out of his shell, refusing to admit the fact that he might be wrong.

And then the knife was there, a last-ditch effort to preserve the operation.

He'd seen all that in milliseconds.

And he'd lunged, too.

The boy flew off his chair with his knife hand outstretched and a look of pure terror came over the girl's face, but King darted in and caught him around the waist and threw him like he weighed twenty pounds. The gangly kid rotated an entire revolution in the air and smashed into the safe deposit box framework, probably breaking a couple of bones in the process, and the switchblade fell from his hands.

King picked it up and tucked it away.

The girl watched, horrified.

'You see?' King said. 'We're here to help.'

She nodded, scared, but ultimately glad she was safe.

Slater said, 'Tell us how you did it.'

'I didn't write the code,' she said. 'Dex did.'

'Who's Dex?'

'Long hair.'

'Got it.'

'Then the four of us implemented it.'

'What came first — Gavin, or the code?'

'Gavin,' she said. 'He didn't know how to do it, but he thought it could be done. He showed us some holes in the system. The power grids rely on systems that need to balance supply and demand. If you screw with that balance, the whole thing collapses in on itself. So once we were in, that's all we needed to do. And Dex wrote the code that got us in.'

'How?'

'Do you have all day?'

'Summarise it.'

'It's a worm,' she said. 'It was designed to be invisible, but I'm sure you already know that. It showed the engineers that all was fine, but it gave us control of the regional transmission organisations and the independent system operators. RTOs and ISOs, for short. Once we had those, it was like clockwork. We could change passwords as we pleased. We could shut everyone out. But we didn't do it until we were sure that you'd never be able to get back in unless we wanted you to.'

A chill ran down King's spine.

Then he asked the question both he and Slater desperately needed the answer to.

'How easy was it?'

She looked up at him. 'Easier than Dex thought it would be.'

'Is Dex the only person capable of creating a worm like that?'

'No,' she said.

'Why hasn't it been done before?'

'If I had to guess,' she said, 'it's that no one thought to try.'

Quiet.

The quiet of realisation.

Slater looked over at King. 'Things need to change.'

'That's not our department,' King said. 'We're enforcers. End of story.'

'I know,' Slater said. 'But Violetta needs to hear this. The whole damn government needs to hear this.'

'They will.'

King turned to the girl.

She said, 'What's going to happen to me?'

'If you fix this,' he said, 'I'll do everything in my power to help you.'

'Aren't you just an enforcer?' she reminded him.

'Not exactly.'

Slater said, 'He's dating his boss. He has leverage.'

King half-smiled, and surprisingly so did the girl. Right then and there he understood Slater's usefulness. King knew he had restraint, and tact, and the ability to talk to anyone. But Slater had the no-nonsense approach to almost every situation, and he used it to cut through to the core of the issue. Sometimes, he went too far. Sometimes, it worked brilliantly.

Just like that, he'd dissipated the tension between the three of them.

King said, 'How long will it take you?'

She scooted closer to the desk, still in shock, still horrified by what had unfolded, but with something new in her eyes. They were no longer as dead and soulless as when King had stepped into the room.

He thought, maybe, they might stand a chance.

She said, 'An hour, maybe.'

'That's it?'

She lifted her gaze to him. 'It won't take much to hand back control. The real work came in building the thing. Controlling the worm is simple. Not easy, but simple.'

'If you have the ciphers, you have the key?'

A nod.

He said, 'So you really didn't keep them anywhere physical?'

She shook her head. 'That was our trick. We memorised them and then erased them. If we all died, the system would be impenetrable.'

He was about to say, *Why did you do this?* but he stopped himself short.

Now was not the time to be provocative.

He went quiet, waiting patiently, and the girl hunched closer to her triple-monitor setup and brought up a series of windows. She sunk into the flow state, her eyes wide and unblinking, and her hands started to fly over the keyboard.

King turned to Slater and muttered, 'I'll be back in a moment.'

He stepped out into the antechamber.

It wasn't done yet.

But it might as well have been.

He crossed to the broken window Slater had launched Gavin Whelan out of and rested against the sill. He took a deep breath, ran a hand through his hair, and winced as his ribs lit up with the familiar dull throbbing. His nose had doubled in size since the fight with Walker. He couldn't breathe through it. The septum was mangled.

But in the end pain was nothing.

Victory was everything.

He pulled out his smartphone, touched a familiar contact name, and lifted the device to his ear.

Violetta said, 'For the love of God, give me good news.'

'It's done,' he said. 'Everything will be back to normal within the hour.'

He thought he heard her ordinarily stoic exterior shatter.

She audibly sighed.

She said, 'I don't know how you did it. I don't know what to say.'

'There's nothing to say,' he said. 'I'm just glad it's over.'

'I'll pass the word down the pipeline. The engineers will be ready to get the grid functioning as soon as control is returned.'

'You know what this means, right?' he said.

'What *what* means?'

'It was four kids,' he said. 'Four *kids,* Violetta. That's who did this. Gavin Whelan found them on the deep web and filled them with hate. They wrote the code. They unleashed the worm. They did it all. Because they could.'

'We're going to need an overhaul of the system,' she said. 'Trust me, I know.'

'Literally an overhaul. This can't happen again.'

'That's not for you to worry about,' she said. 'We have entire departments for that. The flaws have been highlighted. Improvements will be made. That's all you need to know.'

'Good,' King said. 'As long as you understand.'

'I understand.'

'Then I'm off the clock?'

'You're done.'

The words released something in him. A permanent tension fell away, and the tendrils of civility crept back in. He came out of "kill mode," and the bank building transformed into an empty dark obelisk instead of a live hostile environment.

She said, 'You did phenomenal. As always.'

'I think my ribs are cracked. My nose is definitely broken. Slater's concussed. He's operating on autopilot.'

'You'll get the best treatment. As always.'

He sighed. 'One more thing.'

'Yes?'

'Keep the ground troops back. This is going to take an hour or so. I don't want her to get spooked.'

'"Her?"'

'One of the coders. Two of them killed themselves with cyanide pills, and I had to throw the third into a wall. But she's complying.'

'Christ,' Violetta whispered. 'The ones that are dead... were they needed?'

'She knows enough to stop it. We're in the clear.'

'Cyanide. How old were they?'

'Couldn't be far over twenty.'

'It's a mad world.'

He stared out the window at the orange glow of the rising sun and said, 'Has been for a long time.'

80

True to her word, Violetta kept the foot soldiers back.

They surrounded the building, a mixture of ordinary NYPD cops and SWAT forces, keeping curious pedestrians at bay, cordoning off the scene, cleaning up the bodies of the fallen. Slater watched them go about their work diligently from the vantage point of the broken window frame.

He was tired. He was in pain. He was hungover. His head swam and spun and throbbed, either from the concussion or the sleeplessness or the overall wear and tear of such vicious combat. The night had been no easier than his last several operations, and, as usual, the stress had threatened to tear his sanity to pieces.

How many times can you come this close?

How many times can you scrape by?

How long until your luck runs out?

Questions that had plagued him since his career had begun.

But he was still here.

Still kicking.

Witnessing another sunrise.

The days ticked ever onward.

King was in the vault with the girl, who'd given them the name Letty. He wasn't sure whether it was real or not, but it was better than nothing. Originally they'd both started in there, supervising, but after tying up and gagging the guy King had thrown into a wall, Slater had almost lost his balance and tumbled off his feet, unprompted.

King had lifted his gaze to meet Slater's and said, 'Why don't you take a break? I'll be here.'

Slater had nodded.

Now, he steadied himself against the windowsill. He wasn't sure whether his equilibrium was still compromised or not — frankly, he didn't have the energy to test it.

One night, he thought.

All this happened in one night.

The surreality dawned on him. Overnight, they'd almost lost the most populated city in America for months. Four kids barely out of their teens had possessed the key to avoiding anarchy in their own heads, and if all four had bitten down on the cyanide pills, the entire New York power grid would have been lost.

He couldn't fathom it.

Couldn't accept it.

It would be a long, rocky road ahead for certain government departments. He couldn't stop thinking about the massive changes that had to be implemented. But as King had reassured him, that wasn't his fight. He and King weren't bureaucrats. They weren't system builders. They built their own bodies, and their own minds, and they went wherever the fight was, and they tried to leave the world a little better than they found it.

And really, that's about all they could manage.

Broken and battered, he focused on his breathing and tried to bring some normalcy back into his existence.

A moment later, King and Letty stepped out of the vault.

Slater looked at them.

Letty stared down at her feet.

Deep in the clutches of shame.

King gave a single nod. 'It's done.'

Slater exhaled.

Letty said, 'I'm so sorry.'

King didn't respond.

Nor did Slater.

She said, 'What happens now?'

'That's not up to us,' King said.

'You said...'

'I said I'd put in a good word,' King said. 'And I will. But we don't run things. We're the ones who get sent in when everything's gone to shit. We're the last resort.'

'I figured that meant you'd just kill me.'

King shook his head. 'Not our style.'

'You probably should kill me. I deserve it. People died tonight, didn't they?'

'They did.'

'Is that why you're not telling me that everything's going to be okay?'

King looked at her. 'Nothing's going to be okay for you, Letty.'

She stifled a sob.

'Don't lose hope,' he said. 'Just do better. Every day of your life. Be a little better than you were yesterday.'

'You make it sound so simple.'

'Because it is.'

She stared at her feet.

'Simple,' he said. 'Not easy. They're two different things.'

She gave a slight nod.

'Can't change what I did,' she muttered. 'All I can be is sorry that I did it.'

King led her to the window, and Slater stepped aside to let them see out. The three of them watched the NYPD officers handling their fallen comrades, maintaining brave faces until they could grieve in private. Letty began to shiver, jackhammering in the morning chill as she realised what her actions had led to.

She said, 'If I didn't do it, he would have got someone else to. I…'

'Everyone makes that excuse,' King said. 'Do me a favour and leave it at that. No one sympathises with it. No one cares. You want my best advice? Accept what you did head-on.'

She nodded, tears in her eyes. Again, she said, 'I'm so sorry.'

'The Department of Defense is flying power trucks in on their own planes,' he said. 'The Federal Emergency Management Agency already has thousands and thousands of people mobilised throughout the city, helping where they can. It wouldn't have been enough, but it was the best we could do.'

She said, 'Why are you telling me this?'

'Because that's most people,' he said. 'I know you were filled with hate, and it probably won't go away with the snap of your fingers. But I want you to see this. I want you to know that most people are good.'

She went deathly quiet.

He said, 'There's always going to be people who try to convince you otherwise. Don't listen to them. They only care about themselves.'

With an audible, all-encompassing *whump,* the naked bulb above their heads came to life.

Slater stared up at it.

Smiled.

Then looked out over a city with power restored, thousands of windows glowing softly under the dawn sky.

King blew out a breath.

So did Slater.

Together, they led Letty downstairs.

The weight of the world lifted off their shoulders.

81

One week later...

Slater couldn't help himself.

He was as nervous as he could ever remember being outside of work. He didn't think that was possible after the stakes of last weekend, but normality had returned to his life faster than he imagined. Sure, there were still the long, hard days of painstaking preparation for the next job, but after a specialist's assessment he'd been given a strict three-week no-contact order. That meant no sparring, no intense exercise, nothing that could aggravate his vulnerable brain as it recuperated from the serious concussion he'd suffered seven days previously. The headaches were gone, as was the disorientation, but given his history he knew following the doctor's orders was prudent.

Hence the ordinary daily routine.

And the nerves of a first date.

He stood on the sidewalk in Koreatown, outside the same speakeasy his night had begun at last weekend. From there, to Palantir, to all-out war. It was a timeline he would never forget for as long as he lived.

He'd never been the superstitious type, so he'd leapt at the chance to return.

Now, someone tapped him on the shoulder.

He wheeled around.

Alexis had dressed in a leather jacket over a figure-hugging skirt. She'd applied a touch of red lipstick, and wore her black hair in bangs that fell gently over her forehead. It was a stunning look. He found himself momentarily taken aback, lost for words. The last time he'd seen her, they'd both looked a little worse for wear.

She noticed, too.

'Damn,' she said. 'You look good when you're not covered in blood.'

He smiled, and stepped in for a short hug.

When he pulled away, he said, 'That was a rough night.'

'For both of us.'

He nodded. 'Have you been here before?'

She glanced at the bar. 'No — can't say I have. Have you?'

'Once.'

'How'd you find it?'

'It's great,' he said. 'Full of interesting people.'

'Like yourself?' she said, and winked, and sauntered past into the warmth of the entrance.

He followed, heart in his throat, praying he didn't screw this up.

He almost froze in his tracks when he realised it was the first time he'd been solely focused on the woman in front of him since Ruby had vanished from his life.

She'd always been there, in the back of his head.

Now, finally, he thought he might manage to let her go.

Which is what she would have wanted all along.

The bar was lively at eight in the evening. They found themselves a small booth in one corner, a comfortable distance away from the nearest patrons, affording them privacy for the discussion he knew they needed to have. It was as inevitable as the sun rising the next day.

He said, 'I have to ask.'

She raised an eyebrow.

'What happened to the guys in your bathroom?'

'The NYPD came through,' she said. 'They took them away. It's going to be a lengthy process, but they're not around to intimidate me. I can't imagine they'll have enough to pay bail with how much of their salaries they put up their noses.'

He said, 'Are you okay?'

'As okay as I can be.'

She looked around, at the couples deep in conversation, at the loud groups laughing and joking with each other, half-finished pints in their hands.

She looked back at him and said, 'Isn't it absolutely crazy?'

'Many things are,' he said. 'What specifically?'

'How... normal everyone is. Because things are going the way they're supposed to. All it took was the lights going off for a few hours for my neighbours to become animals.'

'They were animals before everything went dark,' Slater said. 'The blackout showed who they were under the façade.'

'It showed me who you were, too.'

'That's why you came tonight?'

'Yeah,' she said. 'That's why I came.'

The bartender floated around from behind the countertop and came over to their booth, sensing an opportunity to take an order for drinks during a lull in requests.

'Just the house red, please,' Alexis said.

Slater opened his mouth to order his usual whiskey on the rocks, but cut himself off when he realised he hadn't touched a drink since the previous weekend. He almost hadn't noticed. He'd been busy recuperating, settling into a different routine, in and out of endless rendezvous meetings with King and Violetta and a host of faceless government bureaucrats to discuss after-action reports. There'd been no time for socialising, no time to dip back into his old vices.

And now, he realised, he had an opportunity to change course.

To refuse to give in to the temptations, the dulling of his mind, the separation of his thoughts and memories.

He remembered what he'd said to Letty.

I dulled all my memories with booze. Which isn't the right response to hard times. Just like this isn't.

He took a deep breath and said, 'Water for me.'

He might as well have been speaking Chinese, given his history.

The bartender gave a curt nod and returned to the bar.

Alexis admired him across the table. 'You don't drink?'

He smirked at that. 'If only you knew…'

She smiled. 'New habits, then?'

'Something like that. I made a promise to someone.'

'Oh?'

'Told them that if they changed, I'd change.'

'I figured you were going through changes.'

'Yeah,' he said, thinking of Ruby, or, rather, *not* thinking of her. 'I am.'

'Good or bad?'

'Good, I think.'

'Then I'm glad.'

He said, 'What about you? Are you back at work?'

She nodded. 'I'm about to take some time off, though.'

He waited for her to elaborate.

She said, 'That night made me realise... how quickly it can all end.'

He understood that sentiment.

More than she could have ever known.

She said, 'I want to live a little.'

'Sorry to disappoint with the water, then.'

She laughed. 'It's fine. I admire it. Shows you don't cave to pressure.'

'I used to,' he said. 'Frequently.'

'You don't seem like the type.'

'In all other aspects, I'm not. I guess drinking was my escape.'

'And now what's your escape going to be?'

'Depends how this date goes. Depends if we keep seeing each other.'

Her eyes flashed with curiosity. She said, 'That's forward of you.'

'Sorry. I don't like to waste time.'

'You know... you don't seem like the long-term relationship type.'

'Why's that?'

'Just... something about you.'

'I hope you don't think that's all I'm here for.'

'Depends how this date goes,' she repeated back to him. 'Depends if we keep seeing each other.'

She winked.

He smiled.

A genuine smile.

One of the first he'd had in months.

No drink or drugs to heighten his emotions.

No cheat codes.

Just life.

They talked for hours, and Alexis sipped on shiraz, and Slater sipped on water. All around them old patrons bled out of the bar and new patrons entered, but he and Alexis hardly noticed the ebb and flow of the nightlife. They barely blinked, in their own world, enthralled in each other's stories, and not long into their conversation Slater opened up the floodgates, something he'd never done on a date with a civilian. But there was quite simply nothing else to say about his life if he didn't admit what he really did, and she took it in her stride. She listened to him speak about the people he'd killed, the sacrifices he'd made for his work, the sacrifices he would have to continue to make because of his genetic predisposition and a lifetime of training to be the best in his chosen field. When he finally trailed off, convinced he'd ruined his one shot at finding someone he truly felt a connection to, she said she'd known who he was at his core the moment he'd stepped foot inside her apartment.

A killer, sure, but a righteous one.

One of the rarest things in the universe.

He said, 'If you want to, you can leave.'

She bit her lower lip, and glanced down at her watch face. 'I think I will.'

His heart sank.

'But I'd like you to come with me,' she added.

He stared at her.

Reached over and took her hand.

They didn't talk much after that. There was nothing to say that hadn't already been said. She understood who he was, what he did with his life, what he had become.

And she was still here.

They exchanged small talk for a few minutes, and then Slater said, 'You're sure about this?'

'I'm sure.'

'I'm not... your everyday guy.'

'Exactly,' she whispered, and took him by the hand again, and led him out of the booth.

They paid at the register, and slipped into a waiting cab, and she gave the driver her address.

Slater smiled again.

Maybe a balanced life was possible after all.

A strange sensation gripped his chest. For a moment it was alien, something he couldn't place, couldn't recognise.

Then he put his finger on it.

He was happy.

KING AND SLATER WILL RETURN…

Visit amazon.com/author/mattrogers23 and press "**Follow**" to be automatically notified of my future releases.

If you enjoyed the hard-hitting adventure, make sure to leave a review! Your feedback means everything to me, and encourages me to deliver more books as soon as I can.

And don't forget to follow me on Facebook for regular updates, cover reveals, giveaways, and more!
https://www.facebook.com/mattrogersbooks

Stay tuned.

BOOKS BY MATT ROGERS

THE JASON KING SERIES

Isolated (Book 1)

Imprisoned (Book 2)

Reloaded (Book 3)

Betrayed (Book 4)

Corrupted (Book 5)

Hunted (Book 6)

THE JASON KING FILES

Cartel (Book 1)

Warrior (Book 2)

Savages (Book 3)

THE WILL SLATER SERIES

Wolf (Book 1)

Lion (Book 2)

Bear (Book 3)

Lynx (Book 4)

Bull (Book 5)

Hawk (Book 6)

THE KING & SLATER SERIES

Weapons (Book 1)

Contracts (Book 2)

Ciphers (Book 3)

BLACK FORCE SHORTS

The Victor (Book 1)

The Chimera (Book 2)

The Tribe (Book 3)

The Hidden (Book 4)

The Coast (Book 5)

The Storm (Book 6)

The Wicked (Book 7)

The King (Book 8)

The Joker (Book 9)

The Ruins (Book 10)

Join the Reader's Group and get a free 200-page book by Matt Rogers!

Sign up for a free copy of '**HARD IMPACT**'.

Experience King's most dangerous mission — action-packed insanity in the heart of the Amazon Rainforest.

No spam guaranteed.

Just click here.

ABOUT THE AUTHOR

Matt Rogers grew up in Melbourne, Australia as a voracious reader, relentlessly devouring thrillers and mysteries in his spare time. Now, he writes full-time. His novels are action-packed and fast-paced. Dive into the Jason King Series to get started with his collection.

Visit his website:

www.mattrogersbooks.com

Visit his Amazon page:

amazon.com/author/mattrogers23